ELEMENTS

VOLUME 1

WILLIAM RICHARDS

STALKING P ART

ELEMENTS Volume 1

Copyright © 2021 William Richards

Cover art by: Stalking P

Inner book art by: Stalking P

Edited by: Dylan Garity

For permission requests, contact:
Authorwilliamrichards@gmail.com

ISBN – 978-1-7774734-1-9

https://authorwilliamricha.wixsite.com/williamrichards

https://www.stalkingp.com/

10 9 8 7 6 5 4 3 2

This book is dedicated to all of the people in the world who have ever felt lost or like they didn't measure up, or who wanted to quit. Keep fighting. Great things will come.

CHAPTER 1
WHERE TROUBLE GOES, YOU FOLLOW

HALF A CENTURY AGO, AN EXTRAORDINARY CHILD WAS born, one who could form small flames on the tips of her fingers. Soon after, reports of other children being able to generate and control elements from their bodies started to pop up all around the world. Nobody knew the cause of these strange phenomena, but in time almost half the growing population had been granted such abilities. Society would come to know this newfound race as Elementalists.

While governments attempted to refine laws with this new, stronger race growing, a dangerous rift in the social order started to form—at least until one brave man helped bring peace and unity back to the world. Humans and Elementalists would live with that peace for twenty years, but even as humanity grew more at ease, under the surface lay another threat, one that could change the landscape of the world as people knew it. This is that story.

Sunrays beamed down on the blacktop of Toronto West Junior High. Minisc, a rather plain-looking boy with wavy blond hair, looked on with a mix of frustration and fear as he found himself in the middle of yet another confrontation he had hoped to avoid. He stood between two other boys of the same age, listening to the back-and-forth shouting while doing his best to hold them at arm's length. However, their combined strength overwhelmed him.

"Come on guys, this is dumb," he negotiated, "We don't need to be

fighting over who got into Elemental Academy. It's not a big deal."
However, Minisc's hopes of negotiation proved futile. After all, the
argument had been started by him. Not on purpose, of course—he
would have never voluntarily put himself in such a position—but
more out of unfortunate timing.

The boy on his left had shorter red hair and matching round eyes
with a generally innocent-looking face. That was Jules, his best
friend and overconfident companion. The other boy, dressed in all
black, went by the name Ignis, but most knew him better as the
class bully and a royal pain in Minisc's behind.

The last day of school came to a close, and most students were
moving on to a new high school. A select few would move on to
Elemental Academy, a special school meant for the top upcoming
Elementalists in the city. If one had an element, chances were they
would apply for entry. However, with the growing number of Elementalists year over year, and EA being the only elements-based
school of its kind, getting in proved no simple task. There were a set
number of students allowed each year, and gaining entry required
either a recommendation or an entrance exam showcasing elemental skills in front of a panel of teachers.

What had started this fight, and many in the past, was that Minisc
and Jules had both been granted acceptance based on recommendation, while Ignis had aced the entrance exam—a test he deemed
below his skill set.

"Shut up, you damn wannabe. The only reason you got into EA
was because of Minisc's father. I could wipe the floor with you
damn punks."

"Name the time and place, Ignis. I've been trained by my brother, and he's only one step below the Hero of Light. I'd have you
begging for mercy in seconds." The two were getting so close to
each other that poor Minisc soon found himself squished in the
middle.

"Oh yeah! Try this." Ignis finally broke the war of words, cock-
ing his fist and throwing a punch. Unfortunately, his supposed
target, Jules was not on the receiving end of the errant attack.

Instead, Minisc hit the ground with a thud, his cheek starting to swell soon after.

"What the heck do you kids think you're doing?" A teacher yelled as she stepped out of the nearby door. She started to run across the blacktop with frustration in her eyes.

"This isn't over, punks," Ignis snarled before he stormed off.

Jules reached down and pulled Minisc up, who continued to rub his now-swollen red cheek.

"I hate that guy so much."

"Why'd you have to go and antagonize him? He already hates me enough — don't make him hate you too."

"I had to do something. I wasn't going to just let him talk to my best friend that way."

"Yeah, easy for you to say, I'm still the one who got punched."

"Yeah... that didn't go as planned..."

"But it went exactly as Ignis planned — he pissed you off and still managed to punch me," Minisc sighed, "Now come on, let's just get to the train station. This isn't really how I wanted to start my summer off."

Jules nodded, and the two finally headed on their way.

Over the busy streets of Toronto, the sun arched high in the sky as Jules and Minisc walked to the train station. The streets were quiet for the moment and traffic non-existent, an unusual coincidence considering the time of day. But that didn't matter to Jules, who remained infatuated with the thought of his new school on the horizon.

"So what do you think EA is going to be like next year?" he asked.

"I don't know, probably not much different than class now. You're still gonna have to take math." Minisc laughed, mocking his friend's question.

"Seriously, you have to be even just a little excited. We get to use our elements in school; that's so cool! No other school lets you do that."

"Yeah, I guess so."

"Sometimes I don't get you, Minisc. Your father is the Hero of Light; you of all people should be excited to attend the school he built. It's the next step to joining the Elemental Council. After that, we get to fight crime, be heroes, and make the world a better place. Just like your father."

Minisc mulled over his friend's words. They struck a disappointing chord in him. Not towards Jules—he knew his friend meant no harm, but like most Elementalists, he loved all things elements. For Minisc, however, 'Live up to your father. Your father is a hero. You must want to be just like your father,' were phrases he had heard far too often in his youth. Of course, the fame of his father was not lost on him. Since the time he could talk, and probably before, he'd grown accustomed to being known as the Hero of Light's son, nothing more. Even though his parents tried their best to shield him from the shining light of publicity, as Minisc grew older, he soon realized escaping that notion would be near impossible, though that group failed to get under his skin nearly as much as the other. Those who despised him.

Whether out of spite or jealousy, the vast majority of those who idolized the Hero of Light, deemed him not worthy of such a revered lineage. That group was filled with people who wished to be in Minisc's shoes. They would be the hero the world needed when the time came, not some boy who lacked interest in even honing his element. Minisc tried not to show it, but that group bothered him. And with all that in mind, the topic of living up to his father was a sore one.

Still, the story remained cemented in history, and the Hero of Light would forever be known as the one who ended the war between Luminosa and the rest of the world.

When Elementalists were first integrating into society, an Elementalist known as Dusk rose with the evilest of intentions, and the power to back up his resolve. Infuriated by the heinous treatment of Elementalists at the hands of humans, he soon began to resent the human race and eventually declared his intention to create a world no longer welcoming to such a pitiful species. Soon after, Dusk started recruiting other Elementalists with the same evil in their hearts, and thus created the dastardly group known as Luminosa. Extermination of humans began, and thousands of innocent lives were stolen with no remorse.

That was when the Hero of Light came to be. Don Premier, a budding Elementalist in his own right, would be recruited by the human government, along with hundreds of others, sparking a conflict that would go down in history as the Elemental Wars. For planet Earth, times were dark and uncertainty loomed large, but Don, using a special skill known as Celestial Light, would deal Dusk a finishing blow, saving the world and cementing his legacy.

Minisc knew the tale by heart, as did most, and although he could not have been more thankful for his father's actions, he did not hope to repeat them.

"Honestly Jules, you know I don't really care to live up to my father. Even if I did, he's the Hero of Light. Nobody can live up to that. As long as I can help people in some way, that's more than enough for me. Besides, that was my mother's last wish for me. She always told me to help humans and Elementalists alike, and to make the world a better place in my own way. So that's what I'm going to try and do."

"I guess that is what the EC is all about. Helping people, both human and Elementalist. That's what it's there for, after all."

"Anyways, ignoring school, what do you have planned for the summer?" Minisc asked.

"Actually…" Jules broke into a wide smile, beaming at his friend. "Last night, my brother finally agreed to let me help him at his firm downtown. I'll be helping run a branch that investigates and apprehends the more dangerous Elementalists in the city. It's going to be so cool!" Jules could not contain the excitement as he said it. He admired his brother more than anyone on the planet, even the Hero of Light. Growing up, his dreams were attached to his brother's footsteps, and now after years of asking, his opportunity had arrived. He planned to use that time with his brother and train like never before, returning to EA head and shoulders above his future classmates.

"Doesn't that sound a bit dangerous?" Minisc asked, a hint of genuine concern in his voice.

"We have a standard to uphold. My brother is one of the most well-known Elementalists involved with the Council," Jules boasted.

The Elemental Council was a mix between what one could call the police force and an acting branch of government. Around twenty years before, when Elementalists were becoming more of the norm, the human government decided that the dangers presented to its law enforcement were too great. They were outmatched against a race of superhumans, so they proposed creating a group made up of politicians, emergency service people, and first-generation Elementalists to create a consulting council. More and more people were added until a full branch of government was formed. As the population increasingly filled with Elementalists, naturally some decided they could use their powers for nefarious deeds. That was when the Council started acting as a military force as well.

Minisc looked at Jules, his mouth trying to hide the concern.

"I guess. Just try to stay out of trouble for once."

"Please, I always stay out of trouble," Jules laughed, "Anyway, what are you doing this summer?"

"I haven't really thought about it. Hopefully catching up on some sleep."

Minisc was not being entirely truthful in his words, but to explain the thoughts bouncing through his head would have been impossible. In actuality, he'd spent more time wondering what to do with his two-month vacation than anything else.

Often, Minisc found himself spending summers alone. Unlike most kids his age, that part he had grown accustomed to. His father spent countless hours out of the house, dealing with government officials, endorsement deals, or charity events, not to mention the occasional rescue mission. So Minisc learned to entertain himself from an early age. He would read books, play video games, or explore the forest nearby. Otherwise, Minisc spent most free time with his mother. They would go for walks or do arts and crafts together. Those days were some of the fondest childhood memories he had.

This summer was shaping up to be a little different though. His father would be home more than usual. The Hero of Light was long retired from any full-time work, but now he was breaking away from most public events as well.

Although Minisc had no interest in living up to his father's legacy, that did not mean he disliked the man either. His father was kind and smart, while always trying his best to help others — all traits Minisc shared with him. But for all the ways they were the same, they were equally different. Where Don spent his days pushing himself to be better, Minisc was content with being himself. Don trained twice a day, waking up at 5 a.m., exhausting his element and lifting weights religiously. On the other hand, Minisc rarely ever used his element, had no desire to lift weights, and most importantly hated waking up early. Whether it be by circumstance or by nature, Minisc did not share the same passion or drive that his father had.

Eventually, Minisc and Jules came within a few minutes of the train station, where they started to see a crowd of people on the street ahead. Through the sea of bodies, flashing lights filled the sky with sirens blaring out.

"Did it just get colder?" Minisc muttered with a shiver.

The two paused in their tracks as a flash of white light took hold of the sky. A ways past the crowd, ice started to encase one of the buildings from top to bottom, leaving Jules in awe and Minisc looking for another route home.

"Whoa, what's going on up there? That building's covered in ice!"

"I don't know, but it doesn't seem like we're getting through this way. Come on, we can take another street."

"No way, I want to check this out." Jules saw a path within the sea of people and started to slither his way through.

"Oh come on Jules, not again." Minisc sighed. Despite his trepidation, he followed suit, squeezing and pushed between groups of people. Hearing the groans of those he bumped into along the way, Minisc kept his head down and avoided all incoming angry stares. Not long after, the two managed to force their way to the front of the crowd, but were stopped by barricades and police cars. Officers were holding the crowd back a safe distance away, while on the horizon a far more dangerous event played out.

In the middle of the street stood a man donning a red and white uniform. The gold trim and letters EC stitched into the armband made it clear the man belonged in the ranks of the Council. He remained locked in battle with a shady individual wearing a brown trench coat and a mask over his head. At first glance, the opponent looked to be nothing more than a low-level criminal, but the bank, now covered in a glistening layer of ice, implied anything but. The crook carried a sack of money in his right hand while holding his left hand up like a gun. Only a pale blue frost rose to the sky instead of smoke.

Bang.

He fired an icicle-like bullet toward the EC member, but the man in red matched it with a jagged bolt of lightning exploding out of his left hand.

"No way, this is awesome—we're actually going to see the Elemental Council at work. This robber is toast." Jules stood on the balls of feet, peering around the police, not wanting to miss a moment.

The robber shot off another icicle, which was blocked again, but this time he followed it up by dashing forward before landing a punch into his opponent's midsection. The two continued their standoff, with the police holding everyone dozens of meters away. The officers were so preoccupied with the uproar though, that they failed to notice a little girl no more than the age of three or four squeeze through the barricade. Escaping the vision of everyone around her, she started to freely roam toward the battlefield without a care in the world.

"My baby, where's my baby?" A woman cried from the back of the group. The calls for help quickly caught everyone's attention, and gazes shifted toward the small child, who remained blissfully unaware of the danger. Hearing signs of distress, the EC member turned his head for only a moment, but that would prove to be a crucial mistake. With opportunity staring him in the face, the robber sprung forward, landing a sucker punch into the council-member's stomach. He crumpled to the ground before the robber froze half his body to the asphalt. Gasps spread through the crowd as the robber began walking forward with a confident strut.

Jules glanced behind him at the dozens of people standing stock still. The crowd looked petrified, even the police. They either were terrified at the thought of suffering the same fate as the EC member or were just humans who did not want to get hurt. Either way, Jules knew he had to do something.

In an act disgracing humanity, the robber discharged a blast of ice and watched it sail toward the small, unsuspecting child. Horror painted the crowd, but still, none reacted.

"Minisc, we need to do something," Jules yelled, his voice cutting through the terrified cries of the masses. He wanted to help. He had to help. Allowing an innocent little girl to be the victim of a devastating icicle spear would haunt him till the end of time.

But when he turned to Minisc, hoping for backup on his feelings, he realized his friend had already snapped into action.

Minisc hopped the barricade, running right through the police as if possessed by a spirit.

"Hey kid, get back here. What do you think you're doing?" An officer yelled.

"I don't know, but I'm doing something. Jules, cover me!" Minisc yelled back as he fired a glowing ball of light toward the icicle—a Lum Bomb attack. Nothing more than a small sphere of light energy, it was as basic an attack as any Light Elementalists could use. It also happened to be the one move his father had taught him as a child. Although he had practiced it numerous times as a kid, he could not recall the last time he'd used it.

Cutting through the air, his Lum Bomb intercepted the ice blast, colliding into an explosion that rippled through the streets.

Minisc ran up to the little girl before kneeling on one knee to make sure she was safe. He looked into the child's wide purple eyes, seeing fear abundant. Her eyes were about to water, but Minisc gave her a warm and comforting smile while whispering, "Are you okay?"

The girl nodded, fighting back the tears.

Minisc knew with the EC member frozen to the ground and nobody in the crowd ready to step up, the burden of protecting this innocent girl fell to himself and Jules. Lucky for him, he had a best friend always ready to play the role of hero.

"Look, I don't care about you robbing a bank, or whatever else you've done today, but attacking a little girl in the streets? That's disgusting," Minisc growled, turning back to look at the robber.

In the skills department, Minisc lagged behind most his age, and he had no desire to play hero like his father or Jules, but a force inside him refused to stay quiet in the moment of need.

Hopping the barrier and making his way to Minisc, Jules braced for action. After all, this would be his future career.

Far from intimidated by two teenagers, the robber strutted forward with authority, sights of an easy escape playing in his mind. He smirked, firing two smaller icicles at Minisc and Jules. Ready, Jules began to glow a lime green, expelling a gust of wind from his body. The force halted the ice dead in its tracks before it lifelessly fell to the ground with a crash.

"Hmm, I was hoping for a quick escape, but it looks like you two might have a little more meat on your bones than I thought."

Minisc stood up, putting the kid behind his leg. "Everything is going to be okay," he told her, "I'm here." At that moment, Minisc said all that came to mind—words his mother would say often when he himself was frightened. Except when he used the phrase, he did not believe his own words. The robber had shown great strength in combating an EC member, as well as freezing an entire bank, so surely he would have no issue out-dueling two novices.

"Jules, we need to try and buy some time until other EC members show up, okay? We don't need to fight this guy head-on."

"Right, let's do this." Jules nodded, striking a fighting stance.

"Look, I have no interest in fighting some snot-nose kids, but if you guys are going to try to play hero, then fine, I'll play along. Come and get me!"

Jules obliged, doing his best to trap the man in a vortex of wind.

"Minisc, hit him now."

Following Jules's orders, Minisc fired a couple of Lum Bombs at the man in rapid succession, but after only a few blasts, his muscles tightened up. Unbending them started to feel like his arms were being ripped apart.

That can't be good, Minisc thought, trying to fight through the pain. The grimace did not go unnoticed by the thief.

"Look at this — your friend can't even use his element long enough to help, and you two think you're going to stop me? No chance." The man broke free of his wind-like shackles and dashed forward before landing a punch into Jules's stomach. He tumbled to the ground as the man turned his sights on Minisc.

"Jules, no!" Minisc cried out.

"Say goodnight, kid."

Out of desperation, Minisc's body began to glow a glistening gold, and on instinct, he raised his free hand, blocking the incoming punch.

"First you try to hurt an innocent child, and then you try to hurt my friend. Well, I won't let you," Minisc growled. The light shimmering off his body concentrated into his free hand. Balling it up into a fist, Minisc punched the man square in the chest, sending him skirting backwards. The robber let out a raspy cough, desperately trying to catch his breath. Minisc's bout of rage had stunned the man. Only one problem remained — Minisc's angry strength, much like its arrival, vanished in a flash. His golden aura faded, and his body started to feel frail and weak to the point of not even being able to move. Aches and pains came in waves, leaving Minisc helpless.

What is going on? Why can't I move? Damn it body, move! Minisc continued to struggle, but his muscles refused to respond. Meanwhile, the robber dusted himself off and glared at Minisc.

"Damn kid, that punch actually stung. I'll make sure you pay for that one!" The man snarled. He held his hands out and three icicles sharp as daggers formed. Even seeing the incoming danger, Minisc could not will his body to move. Each second, the pain grew more intense, but it would pale in comparison to being skewered alive.

On top of that, he still had the little girl hiding behind him and a battered Jules on the ground.

"Now you die!" The man yelled sending the icicle hurling at Minisc. On the verge of unrelenting pain, Minisc closed his eyes, waiting for the inevitable, but it never came. Instead, he heard the shattering sounds of ice. Like a bolt of lightning, another man flashed in front of Minisc. He was no ordinary man, nor even an EC member. He had the look of a military sergeant but carried a smile that brought ease and comfort to all those who bore witness to it. Even the intimidating muscles bulging through his shirt could not detract from the aura surrounding him. He was not a man to be feared, but rather praised.

Whispers started to chime through the crowd.

"No way! That's the Hero of Light."

"We're saved!"

"Just in the nick of time, too."

Minisc opened his eyes, looking up at the imposing man.

"Father, what are you doing here?" He asked, more shocked than relieved.

"I should be asking you that very question, but we can talk about this later. For now, allow me to deal with this criminal."

Minisc gulped. A pit in his stomach started to form, and hearing his father's stern voice made him feel as if his actions to protect one girl had been wrong.

"Now go grab Jules, and take the girl back to the police. I'll deal with this on my own," Don said, breaking out his fearless smile.

Minisc obeyed the orders, taking the girl's hand and rushing to Jules.

"You okay, Jules?"

"Yeah, I'm fine. The guy just got a lucky shot in, that's all."

Minisc bent down to be eye height with the little girl. "And what about you, are you okay?"

"I'm okay, thanks to you." The girl smiled and wrapped herself around Minisc's body lovingly.

"Good, now let's get out of here."

He pulled his friend up off the ground wrapping his arm around him before they both sank into the front row of the crowd again.

Meanwhile, Don steadied himself, ready to put the thief behind bars, and they both knew it. The robber took a step back in hesitation. "You — you're... the Hero of Light," he stammered. Don smiled as he walked forward. His heavy steps shook the ground, making it feel like the road would crack under the pressure.

"So my reputation precedes me. Then I suppose you know what happens next?"

"No way, I didn't sign up for this. Screw the money, I'm out of here!" The thief pleaded, dropping the money and bolting the other way down the street. Unfortunately for him, two more EC vans pulled up, with a man and a woman hopping out. The woman stomped the ground, creating an earthquake that tripped up the robber, while the man snapped his fingers, forming a ring of fire around the fallen thief.

Cheers and applause broke out from the crowd, prompting Don to turn and give a heroic wave to his fans. Even if he had done nothing more than look intimidating.

Crisis averted, the robber had been taken away and the commotion from the day had started to die down, but not long after, media vans began to arrive, with cameras and questions at the ready. Minisc did his best to avoid their relentless spotlight, but he could not avoid the parade of flashbulbs that continued to take his picture. Even Don, attempting to shield his son from fielding any questions about his actions, found himself struggling to do so.

From a young age, Minisc had borne the burden of great expectations placed upon him. Not so much from his family, although his father certainly believed Minisc could achieve great heights if he dedicated himself, but more so by the media. That always bothered Minisc, and in some respect turned him away from anything elemental for years. When they started to ask about why he'd pulled the heroic stunt, he answered with what he thought seemed like an obvious reason: "Because it was a little girl in danger." He sounded rather fed up when all the follow-up questions were pointed toward him being like his father. Attempting to avoid showing his frustration Minisc nodded his head and remained cautious in his words. The last thing he needed was to hand out headliner material.

After half an hour and a quick discussion with the EC, everyone went home for the night.

At the end of the long day, the sun had all but hidden away as night began to draw closer and closer. The Premier household was located on the west side of Toronto, just beyond the city outskirts. The family had moved into such a remote home away from the heart of the city so that Don could bring some privacy back to his family. Although it was still common knowledge where the Hero of Light lived, enough time had passed that him living close to the city became commonplace, even if a few super fans would still come looking for an autograph from time to time.

The house itself was a rather nice one-story, three-bedroom place with red bricks and a brown roof, a modest place to live. Nothing about the house stood out. In fact, most could look at the cozy home and never guess that it belonged to Don Premier. The biggest appeal for Minisc, other than having some privacy in his life, was the forest that backed onto his home. As a child, he'd spent almost all of his time in that forest with his mother, but admittedly it had been a few years since he'd returned to his once memory-filled sanctuary.

Exhausted, Minisc sat on the living room couch, not knowing what fate had in store for him. Even in the act of a good deed to save a child, it did not come without consequences. First and foremost, he had risked his own life and could have been hurt, but as if that were not enough, he'd broken the law as well. Unless part of the Elemental Council or granted a license, Elementalists were not allowed to use their element outside of certain restricted zones. The government had enacted such a law in hopes of helping bring ease to humans who were continually worried that Elementalists roaming the streets free to use their powers could be dangerous, especially for kids who lacked control of their abilities yet. Minisc and Jules were both underage and therefore not permitted to use their elements on the streets, let alone unsupervised.

Don walked into the living room and took a seat beside his son.

"Alright, the EC is going to let you and Jules off with a warning this time, because you have a clean record and nobody got hurt. But if you break the law again, I can't promise you'll be so lucky."

Minisc sighed in relief. He'd dodged another bullet for the day.

"Minisc, what were you thinking?" Don continued in a worried voice. "You and Jules could have been seriously hurt."

"I think it's pretty clear I wasn't thinking." Minisc put his hands in his lap and looked down. "I don't know what happened. I just sort of saw the girl in danger, and nobody was doing anything to help. The next thing I knew, I was already running in and fighting."

Don paused for a moment. "Look, Minisc, I don't want to make it seem like you did a bad thing here, because you didn't. You and Jules saved that little girl's life while everyone else stood by petrified. That would be a commendable act by anyone. I just don't want you to get hurt is all. I'm glad everything turned out alright, but you can't be so reckless next time. It's dangerous out there."

"I know. I promise I won't do it again."

"Good. Now, it's getting late—maybe you should try to get some sleep."

Minisc nodded his head before getting up and leaving down the hall to his room.

With his son gone, Don stared on with a faint smile. His son had promised not to be so reckless, but Don knew that to be a lie, even if Minisc had not realized it yet. In no way was he angry or even disappointed by the way his son had acted—quite the opposite, in fact. Most knew Don as a man who would risk his life to save even one person, and although he knew the dangers that followed, he also knew the courage it took. He often would say it was a feeling he could not control, an urge that gripped his body when the time came. A trait passed down to his son, it would seem.

Don looked up at a picture frame on the dusty red walls of the living room. A family portrait with him on the right and his wife holding their giggling baby on the left. She shared the same blonde hair and emerald-green eyes as Minisc. Her perfect smile lit up any room.

"Well Erika, I guess you were right—Minisc is more like me than I thought. I just wish you were here to tell me how right you were."

Off in his room, Minisc lay in his bed, staring up at the ceiling. The room was rather spacious, but that was more so because of how empty it was. Between a desk and computer, along with a few photos in frames, almost nothing popped out. He rolled over to look at the photos beside his bed. One of the pictures was of him and Jules when they were a few years younger, and the second was of him holding a ball of light he had created as a kid. He had a massive grin on his chubby face, and in the background, so did his mother and father. But in the middle of those two sat a picture of Erika holding her son's hand, taken in front of a theme park. Minisc still remembered that day well. He'd refused to go on any of the roller coasters because they moved too fast, so he and his mother rode the choo-choo trains over and over instead. The memory made him smile inside but still sigh on the outside.

The day's events continued to bother Minisc long after they had ended. He still believed he had done the right thing by acting when no one else would, but he understood his father's viewpoint as well. He could have and probably should have been hurt more than he was. He and Jules both.

For the first time in his life, all of the headlines and criticism the media had placed on him felt true. He raised his hand to the ceiling and made a small ball of light, the tingling sensation in his arm returning along with it. The light had a dull gleam before Minisc squeezed his hand shut, extinguishing it altogether. In his action to help protect one little girl, his lack of strength and skill had instead put all their lives in danger, only saved by his father. A real hero.

Minisc remained fixated on the photo of his mother and him.

"I was so weak. If father hadn't shown up... That little girl, Jules, all of us could have been killed."

Minisc closed his eyes for a second, fighting back the frustration before sighing.

"I wish you were here, Mother. You always knew what to say in moments like this."

CHAPTER 2
TRIALS

EARLY-MORNING LIGHT SHIMMERED THROUGH THE SATIN drapes while birds chirped musical tunes through the cracked window. With the arrival of summer break, Minisc planned to take full advantage by catching up on some long-overdue sleep. Those hopes, however, would be forced to wait a little longer as he squirmed around in his bed. Rolling back and forth in frustration, Minisc stretched his hands to the top of his pillow, stroking the soft fur of a heavily worn plush animal. He grabbed the gray-and-blue stuffed donkey, squeezing it under his chicken-like arms. Rolling back over to his left, his eyes flickered open to meet the blurry red numbers beaming off his clock. He rubbed his eyes before letting out a quiet groan.

"Seven a.m." Clutching the navy-blue comforter in his hands, he pulled the blanket back up over his forehead. Minisc had no intention of rising with the sun on his summer vacation. Thanks to the distance he lived from school, travel would often require being up at the crack of dawn to ensure he made his train, something he detested. Yet even with all that practice, he had been born a heavy sleeper, and even over time that refused to change.

Knock, knock, knock.

The soft bangs cut through the peaceful silence, causing Minisc to let out a deeper groan.

The door crept open like in a horror film—although for him, the horrors were only beginning. Since he only lived with his father, that meant the culprit for Minisc's wake-up call had to be the man. As suspected, the macho voice of a hero filled the silence.

"Minisc, are you awake? It's time to get up. We start your training today."

Training? I didn't sign up for training, Minisc thought as he poked his head out from under the covers. Seeing his father in the doorway dressed in workout clothes, he pushed himself up in his bed and rubbed the crusty gunk out of his eyes, his wavy hair disheveled.

"Training? For what?"

"Your elemental training; be in the kitchen in ten minutes sharp." Don closed the door, leaving Minisc bewildered and more than a bit annoyed.

Training was not new to Minisc; he had spent many hours practicing with his father as a child. In fact, at a young age, he'd shown ability far beyond his years, much like his father. However, with the passing of his mother, that interest faded, and Minisc had forgone his training for other non-elemental activities. Preferably activities where he could not be scrutinized by outsiders.

Left pondering the question of why now, Minisc gradually pulled the cozy covers off his body, plopping his feet on the crisp wooden floors. He knew better than to disobey his father.

As he walked down the narrow hallway, a steamy aroma filled Minisc's nostrils. Following the scent, he started to salivate as he noticed the plate of steaming pancakes sitting on the kitchen table, cooked to a light brown perfection.

"Well at least I get breakfast, I guess," Minisc mumbled as he pulled a chair out. Taking a seat at the end of the table, he reached out to pick a few pancakes off the stack, but before he got the chance, the plate slid inches out of reach, leaving him grasping at air.

"This is for after training," Don scolded, moving the food farther out of his son's reach. Don knew his son would need some extra motivation when training, so he had come prepared.

"What? But I can't train on an empty stomach," Minisc said, hearing a small growl from his gut.

"Of course not; for breakfast, you'll be having this."

Don handed his son a glass filled to the brim with a thick green liquid. Minisc shook his head back and forth while plugging his nose, the sweet smell of pancakes becoming a long-lost memory.

"I'm not drinking that."

"It's not as bad as it looks."

"Ohh no... No way, no how."

He pushed the glass away, watching the mossy green liquid fail to move as it slid down the table, firmly glued to the inside of the cup.

"It smells like sewage water."

"Your choice: train on an empty stomach, or drink the shake," Don's voice left no room for debate, and with that, he slid the patio door behind them open. "I'll see you in the forest clearing. Oh, and don't forget to put your training gear on as well." The door slid closed.

On the breakfast counter, folded up, sat a navy-blue tracksuit. It had red trim lacing up and down the sleeves, and underneath were a pair of track pants in matching colors. The red stripe went up the pant leg and around the waistband, giving it a sleek look.

Putting off his breakfast decisions, Minisc first changed into his new gear. It was comfy and form-fitting, but left enough flexibility for him to remain mobile. Despite being unusually picky about his clothes, he liked the look.

Finally ready to leave, he took another look at the green goop on the table.

I really hope this isn't as bad as it looks. Letting out a heavy sigh, he grabbed the glass of sewage. Fighting the overpowering smell, Minisc plugged his nose with one hand while downing the glass as best he could with the other. It tasted like mud and was thick as sludge, and Minisc fought every urge to vomit as he let the cement like shake drip down his throat. Pushed to the breaking point, he let out a raspy cough before slamming the glass back down on the table.

"Who would subject themselves to this?" Minisc coughed as he wiped the rancid taste from his tongue onto his new clothes. He eyed the leftover drink as it slowly dripped down the side of the glass.

"Nope. I'll take my chances."

Without looking back, Minisc walked out the patio door, following his father's path to the forest.

Wide-open, grassy fields stretched back into a beautiful, lush forest more than a mile long. During the summer, all the trees were in full bloom, bringing the portrait-like landscape even more to life.

Looking at the dew on the grass, Minisc saw a series of giant footsteps outlined clear as day. They were heading in the direction of the forest.

Why am I doing this? Minisc thought, still rubbing his eyes. He stepped off the small wooden deck, feeling the damp grass soak into his shoes. Though it was just his father, nervous energy gathered inside him. He was all too aware of his father's rigorous training. They even had an entire room dedicated to the man's workout equipment—heavy dumbbells, a bench press, and all the other essentials to maintaining top-level fitness. It was a room that Minisc never entered of his own free will.

More than just training though, the forest held a lot of memories for the teen. Memories that, although happy, were tough to think of in a positive light.

After a minute, Minisc hit the opening of the forest entrance. He took a deep breath and headed on in.

The forest was eerily silent. No birds, no rustling of branches, only the crunching of leaves and scattered sticks beneath Minisc's feet. He cranked his neck back and forth, taking in the beauty of the blossoming life on his walk. Everything looked just the way his childhood memories had promised. Trees rose thirty feet into the air, filled with red, yellow, and green leaves, and small woodland critters ran across the dangling branches. He looked up at the treetops, admiring the intricate ceiling above his head, rays from the sun seeping through in small pockets along the ground. With each step farther in, Minisc started to forget why he had avoided returning in years. A sense of serenity started to take over.

When young, Minisc would spend hours in the forest, often running around with his mother, or falling asleep peacefully under the base of the trees. The relaxing atmosphere never failed to put him to sleep.

Just as Minisc started feeling a sense of home, a small pit formed in his stomach again. He came to a stop, and his breath caught in his throat. To the left of his pathway stood a well-maintained tombstone covered in flowers. Minisc felt his throat tighten as he looked at it. Kneeling, he read the name out loud. *Erika Premier.*

The grave belonged to his mother. A sense of sadness filled Minisc from head to toe. He missed his mother more than words could describe.

Walking up to the grave, he ran his finger across the top of the tombstone, letting the engraved flowers on the stone guide him. He let out a sigh.

"I wish you were here, Mother. I miss you."

He sighed again, thoughts of the woman free-flowing in his mind. She had taught him so much from a young age. But now, with him growing up, it was his father's turn.

Remembering that he was not on a leisurely walk, Minisc started to hurry along the path again. Keeping his father waiting for too long would not be wise.

After a short time, Minisc entered a vast rectangular opening in the shape of a battlefield. Clearly, the land had been cultivated, covered in dirt but with not a branch in sight. The open land appeared in the heart of the forest, puzzling Minisc. He had no recollection of an arena there as a kid, but it had been years since he explored the area. It seemed fair to assume that his father had taken time to cultivate the land for his own personal training stadium.

Minisc stepped forward, feeling the patted-down dirt below. It had no give, so landing on the surface would no doubt leave a deep bruise.

Next, he turned his attention to his father, who was standing at the far end of the arena. Don was dressed in an all-black tracksuit, matching the style of Minisc's. He stood out like a sore thumb against the backdrop of the lush forest.

Don crossed his arms. "Took you long enough."

"Sorry, I got distracted along the way."

"By your mother's grave?"

Minisc hesitated for a moment, staying silent.

"Minisc, I know it's been hard—I miss her too. But today we shall mark a new chapter, and begin to move forward."

"A new chapter?"

"Correct. Today will be the first day of your new training regimen," Don announced with more positivity than Minisc would have liked.

"Umm, Father, what exactly am I training for?"

"Well, since you will be attending Elemental Academy in a few short months, I figured now would be a good time to give you a head start."

Not being entirely honest with his son on the subject, Don had other reasons on his mind. Increasing crime rates in the city posed more danger to all, but for Minisc, as the Hero of Light's son, Don knew the power he had locked inside. After graduating EA, he would be thrust into action, ready or not. Don wanted to help his son be prepared for that day well in advance. On top of that, with each passing day, he could sense his own strength continuing to fade. Although he never wanted his son to play hero like he once had, he held an unwavering belief that stored inside his son was the power to do so if necessary.

Minisc remained unaware, but Don had seen the burst of energy from his son the day before while facing the crook. That display of ability was rare from an adult, let alone a fifteen-year-old boy with next to no training. However, his body and mind were not ready to draw on such strength. That meant Minisc needed to start training, and after seeing the dangers his son faced the day before, today seemed like the perfect day to begin imparting his wisdom. Even if Minisc seemed less than eager.

When Minisc listened to his father's explanation, he too did not buy into it. Cognizant to the events of yesterday, Minisc believed he was out on a training field at an ungodly hour because of them.

Minisc had displayed how frail and weak he truly was. Because of that, he could negotiate the merits of some light training. Perhaps it would not be as bad as he anticipated. He did want to help people, and realizing how impossible that felt without increasing his strength, he decided to accept some help. Besides, at EA, he would be required to train regardless of whether he wanted to or not.

Now that he was ready to accept his fate, the thought of early mornings and sewage drinks brought into question that readiness. If that was what it took, then perhaps this would be a good time to re-evaluate his life goals. However, none of that would matter, as Don had already made the decision for his son, and Minisc knew he was not getting out of it no matter how much he begged. Either way, he was not going back to bed till his father gave him the okay.

"So… what exactly are we doing to train?" Minisc asked, wondering how he would get stronger by standing in an open dirt patch in a forest.

"Well, I need to run a little evaluation on where you're at, so you and I are going to spar."

"We're going to *what*?"

Minisc's eyes nearly popped out of his round sockets. Ignoring that this was his father, a man who'd trained every day for decades, this was also the Hero of Light, the modern version of a living legend and the most potent Elementalist known to the world. Sparring seemed like a death wish more than a safe or even fair way to train a beginner. It felt like the equivalent of throwing a boy to the wolves and telling him to survive.

Don noticed his son's sudden flinch as the words left his mouth. A small chuckle escaped his lips at the sight.

"Is that fear I sense?" He laughed. "Come on, son. You scared to do a little training with your old man?"

"Why do I get the feeling that saying yes won't get me out of this?"

"Correct. Now show me what you've got — no holding back."

"Oh okay, right into it, no lessons, no advice. Cool. Let's see how badly this goes."

Minisc let out a deep sigh. He knew rushing headlong into the fight would be an exercise in futility. He needed a plan—and quick. Trying to look on the bright side, at least he was not fighting for his life... he hoped.

Tension filled the air as Minisc tried to recall any of the few training sessions he had gone through as a child. His scuffle with the thief had been all on instinct and therefore somewhat useless. He barely even remembered the events as they'd happened.

Still hesitating, Minisc remained fixated on his father, his opponent. The man's confidence was mocking, and so was his tone.

"Any day now, Minisc."

Don stood loose, with no adequate defensive position present, baiting Minisc into attacking. Like an owl hunting a mouse, the man remained motionless until the opportunity presented itself.

"Alright. Here I come."

"Remember, give me everything you've got."

Minisc's body was enveloped in a sparkling gold aura as he drew upon the energy stored deep within. Bright light shimmered through the pockets of the forest. For someone who had not trained in years, his power remained impressive, a fact that did not go undetected by Don.

I always knew you were strong, Minisc, but you might have even more untapped potential than I thought. Except, a strong element rarely ensures victory in battle. One must be equally skilled in combat, as well as being able to adapt to situations on the fly. One without the others will likely lead to a quick defeat.

Energy coursed through Minisc's veins, giving his arms a warm tingle. He decided to open with his patented attack, the Lum Bomb. As he held his hand to the sky, a small ball of energy materialized inches above his palm. It shined bright like a miniature sun. He quickly thrust his hand forward, and the energy blast whipped through the crisp morning air, speeding in Don's direction. But as the attack left his hand, that warm tingle turned into a feeling of compression through his muscles.

It's happening again, He thought.

In a display of cocky confidence, Don stood patiently, waiting for the attack to land. He puffed his chest out, taking the blast as a direct hit. The simplistic move glanced off Don's buff physique, exploding with a whimper and leaving nothing more than a puff of smoke. The man let out a simple antagonizing smirk.

"Surely you can do better than that. I said no holding back," Don jested. Since Minisc was not one for violence, his father knew a little provocation might be needed.

Minisc obliged, channeling a far more significant amount of energy through his body. Holding out both hands, he felt another energy ball form, one much larger than the last.

"That's much better; I might actually feel this one," Don laughed, still standing idle.

"Try this one on for size!" Minisc shouted as he flung his arms forward. The blast spiraled toward his beast of a father, closing the distance quickly. Don continued to remain patient, and just before the blast landed, he raised his right hand. Strings of light wove between the man's fingers, creating a glowing mitt. Minisc's Lum Bomb smashed into his father's hand, sending sparks flying as the ball sputtered to a halt.

Minisc's mouth dropped in awe; he knew his father's power and fighting skills were unmatched, but the man made Minisc's attacks look like those of an infant. Caught up in thought and trying to think of a new strategy, Minisc soon realized his next move would be decided for him.

"I see you still have some power, but let's see how you handle it coming back at you. Brace yourself."

Don reflected the blast toward Minisc, and in no time it gained sprinter's speed, mailed back to its sender. Minisc leaped to his left, his returned attack breezing past him in the blink of an eye. A thunderous roar rang out as the blast crashed into the wall of trees, disrupting the sleeping forest and sending birds scattering from the treetops. Staring back, fixated on the gash in the bark, Minisc felt it was an all-too-real possibility that he could have suffered serious hurt had the attack landed.

"That—that was so fast," Minisc muttered. He turned to his father. "You do realize that could have killed me, right?"

"Nonsense. That attack would have left a bruise at best."

Minisc stared down his father, who had not moved off his perch even an inch. He was being toyed with, and realizing that made him clench his fists tighter. If this was supposed to help him feel less weak, the plan seemed flawed. Growing angry, Minisc began to sparkle the same gold that had taken over his body against the robber. Still, that did not feel like enough—he needed to dig deeper. He needed to draw out all his power. Except, reaching down to the depths of his energy, ready for a ferocious third attack, his body hit its limit.

"Arghh..."

Dagger-like pain ripped through Minisc, dropping him to his knees. The aura around him faded. *It's just like yesterday... I can't move my body.* Pain overwhelmed him, his heart trying to break through his chest with each violent beat. Doing all he could to keep breathing, his vision started to go dark. Any second he would blackout. Thankfully, before Minisc hit that point, he felt a hand fall onto his shoulder. He tried to look back up, recognizing his father's touch.

"Just breathe. Everything is fine. You just overexerted yourself."

Minisc's heavy breaths started to steady. His heart hit the brakes, settling back into his chest, and his anxiety began to dip with the comfort of his father.

"That's enough for today," Don whispered.

Minisc sat at the end of the kitchen table with his feet stretched out on a chair. All over his arms and legs were bags of ice to help numb the pain—a blessing compared to the agony he'd felt minutes earlier. However, that did not detract from being sore, tired, and hungry.

Meanwhile, Don came back from the fridge carrying two more thick bags of ice. He positioned them on his son's chicken legs before taping them in place.

"There we go, leave these on your body for a few hours. It'll clear up any of the bruising. You'll feel fine by tomorrow."

"Tomorrow? The first day of vacation and I have more ice on my body than a snowman."

"See what happens when you exhaust your element?"

"Exhaust my element? You said that earlier; what did you mean by that?"

"Well, as you already know, since we are Elementalists, our physical stamina and bodies' healing capabilities are far more adept than a human's. That's because when we use our elements, it takes a far bigger strain on our muscles than if you were to just throw a punch or a kick. You have to treat your element like an extension of your muscles. It is still a physical ability. You can only use the amount of element your body is capable of handling. Think of it like weightlifting. When you lift too much, you damage the muscles to the point that you can't move your arms without pain. Your element is the same way; the pain you felt was your body's way of telling you that you're outputting more energy than you can handle at one time. I've trained my body and deepened my reserve of energy through years of hard work. That's why I don't stress my body using my element. However, your body is far less adept." Don finished placing the ice on his son's limbs. "After each attack, you could feel some pain in your muscles, correct?"

"Yeah, it was like they were being ripped apart."

"That was your body trying to tell you that you're putting out more energy than it's capable of handling. You have a great wealth of power in you, I can see it, but your body isn't ready to take that toll yet. Putting all that energy into one giant blast will do nothing but destroy your muscles. That's why we need to get your body into a strong enough condition, so that you can make use of that bottled-up energy inside."

Don stood up and walked out of the room, leaving Minisc to mull over his words. This felt like a teaching lesson for the young Elementalist, but did he have to go through such pain to learn it?

Thinking over his father's wisdom, he understood what the man meant. He was in decent shape, but not what one would call fit. *If my body feels like this after one minute of training with Father, how am I supposed to survive four years of elemental school? How would I ever be able to protect people? The only way is to get stronger. But I'm so far behind everyone else already. Most kids have been using their element for years and by now it's second nature. If I'm going to catch them, I need to work non-stop and get as strong as I can – only then, maybe, can I actually be helpful to people... Even if that means sacrificing my sleep.* Minisc shuddered at the thought. No matter the goals he set, and the dedication required, he still hated early mornings.

Opting to look at the positives though, he realized he would not be spending the summer by himself. That would be a new and endearing experience.

In an attempt to distract from his frozen limbs, Minisc looked over at the dusty blue wall on the near side of the kitchen. Three picture frames caught his eye. He had seen all three hundreds of times but never taken the time to examine them. He often found himself shying away from anything Hero of Light related, but for some reason, after training with his father, his interest had been piqued.

Minisc struggled to get to his feet. He reached up to adjust the cold pack on his left shoulder before wincing in pain. Eventually, he stood up, working to keep his balance on the white ceramic tiles. His knees were shaky, though he could not confirm if that was due to the pain in his knees, or the fifty-plus pounds of ice he had strapped to his arms and legs. Like a newborn just learning to walk, he stumbled to the nearby wall of pictures.

The first one on the far left held a tattered newspaper clipping. Atop the piece sat a black-and-white grainy photo with two people in it. The man on the left, whom he recognized as a younger version of his father, dwarfed the man on the right. Minisc wracked his brain about who the other man could be, but since the picture had been ravaged by time, he could not make out any distinctive features. All he could see was that the two were locked in a firm handshake with proud smiles. Underneath was a headline stretched from edge to edge. *HERO OF LIGHT, the savior of humanity.* As with the picture, the print had also faded over the years—despite the headline remaining legible, reading the article in its entirety was near impossible. Minisc knew full well of his father's legacy among Elementalists. Though his reputation had not stopped at Elementalists; in time, it grew to stretch over to the human world, which at one point had seemed impossible.

He shifted his eyes to the second frame, a color photo. The headline along the top read: *Elementalists and humans unite for the betterment of society.* Don stood on the right, bursting out of his luxurious black suit and a bright orange tie strapped around his thick neck. He looked years younger than his current face, and his arm was stretched around the woman standing on his left. Minisc knew clear as day who the woman was. His mother Erika—even with her looking as young as she did, it was hard to mistake her flowing blonde hair and moonlight-bright smile. She stood a full head below her husband and had her hand placed on his broad chest. Underneath was a much clearer paragraph of the article.

Thanks to the combined efforts of Don and Erika Premier, the world has moved forward in Elementalist and Human relations. Along with the couple's efforts to bring Elementalists a safe haven to help learn and develop their powers, they have graciously sponsored the building of a new state-of-the-art school for Elementalists. The school will be for students ages fifteen and up who also show strong elemental powers and would like to one day join the Elemental Council in some capacity.

Minisc had seen this article before; it had always been his mother's wish for humans and Elementalists to be able to live in harmony. Some days, that dream felt like a distant hope, but it had grown substantially more real in the later years of her life. As much as Minisc knew his father as a savior, he often looked at his mother as the true hero. That was why he wanted to help bring her dream to fruition. He wanted to become strong to help keep the peace she so longed for.

Shifting to the third photo, Minisc felt a flood of memories come back. His mother held him in her arms, while his father had his arm wrapped around them both. The two parents wore broad smiles, staring at their newborn, while Minisc tightly snuggled the tiny plush donkey he would keep with him to the present day. Erika and Don both had visible bags occupying the underlids of their eyes, and in no way did they look their best, but neither could have been happier. In thick bold font the headline read: *The Next Hero of Light?*

Minisc mulled the words over. He hated always being compared to the Hero of Light. He was not a hero, nor was he trying to be. He had a patent for helping people, sure, but not for accolades. That philosophy had been instilled by his mother. She had taught him to always help those in need. Not for glory or fame, but simply because they were in need. It was a sentiment that came naturally to Minisc. He hated the spotlight; even the residual spotlight he received by association often drove him nuts. The expectations of the world were always hovering over him, and living up to them was a near-impossible proposition.

"Why would Father even have this article up?" Minisc asked himself.

Not interested in reading the rest, Minisc gingerly turned around, each step of his frozen body sluggish and uncoordinated. He noticed his father, who had re-entered the kitchen carrying bags of ice over his shoulder.

"How're the muscles?" Don asked, pulling the ice off his shoulder and dropping it on the table.

"I don't know; I lost feeling in them a few minutes ago."

"Probably for the best." The man took notice of Minisc staring at the wall. "Looking at old photos?" Don asked. He'd never known his son to read the articles he hung up around the house.

"I was just thinking about school next year. It's going to be quite different than what I'm used to. Using my element in classes, combat training—it still seems strange to me."

Minisc took a seat in the chair while Don began removing the ice bags, sliding them down his son's arm. Condensation started to take the place of ice at the bottom of the bag, making it a simple task.

"Well, I'll admit it might be a bit different. The school is designed for those who want to apply for the Elemental Council after they graduate. It will likely be far more competitive than what you're used to."

"That doesn't sound great, to be honest."

"It won't be that bad. With a bit more training, you'll be top of the class in no time."

Top of the class? Minisc didn't want to say anything, but he had no desire for such accolades.

Finally feeling his body begin to thaw, he let out a small wince. Don attempted to replace the frozen medical packs on his son, but the boy quickly waved him off.

"I'm fine; I'd like to regain some feeling today," Minisc chuckled, rubbing his arm softly. "Is school going to be this painful?"

"No, they would have eased you in much more."

"Gee thanks."

"You will thank me... one day," Don said under his breath.

He walked over to the familiar pictures, examining them for himself. His attention was drawn to the article about the opening of Elemental Academy.

"Why did you decide to fund a school anyway?" Minisc asked. It was a question he had thought of quite often but never bothered to pose.

"It was your mother's idea really. She was the most progressive human I've ever met when it came to Elementalists and humans coexisting. She wanted a safe and productive environment for kids to learn and use their powers. A normal school would never be able to compile the resources for Elementalists as students, so instead of kids experimenting at their own risk, we opened up a school for them. It made the laws about the restricted area much easier to enforce as well, that's for sure." Don turned around to see his son standing, knees still shaking. "Try to take it easy; you'll want to be healed up for day two of training."

"Day two?"

Minisc was smart enough to know training would not be a one-off, but in the darkest depths of his brain, he had hoped for a miracle. Even if the training was to his benefit, that level of pain was borderline unbearable.

"You didn't think it would only be one day, did you? You're going to need a lot of work to catch up to your old man." Don chuck-led, seeing the dread rise on his son's youthful complexion.

Minisc let out a small sigh, and ignoring any pain surging through his battered body, he turned on a heel and began walking down the hallway.

"Where're you going?" Don asked, watching his son limp away.

"I'm going back to sleep."

Closing the door, Minisc walked over to his bed. Falling flat on his back, he started to sink into the mattress like quicksand.

"I can't feel any part of my body," he mumbled to the ceiling before turning to the clock placed on the nightstand.

"8:30 a.m.," he sighed, letting his eyelids droop closed.

A few hours later, Don stood in front of his son's door, giving a simple knock with the side of his knuckle. No response. The door was slightly ajar, so he took a peek through to make sure his son was okay. Instead he saw Minisc passed out awkwardly on his bed, as if he had fallen asleep as his head hit the pillow.

"Maybe I should have started him off a little easier," Don whispered.

Later in the day, Minisc woke up feeling well-rested but still sore. Except now more than anything, he could feel his stomach gurgling up a storm. He made his way to the kitchen, but before he could start looking for food, he found the morning newspaper sitting on the table. Staring back at him on the front page was his own face, and a less-than-flattering photo at that.

The background was blurry, but Minisc could tell the picture had been snapped near the robbery from yesterday. He looked over the article, much to his better judgment. It was, of course, about the bank robbery and Minisc's role. The journalist had decided to take up the position that Minisc had failed where his father had succeed-ed. They did not mention his efforts to save the little girl or even Jules's presence in the fight. No, instead they remained focused on Minisc and highlighting his failures. Normally, such stupidity in the news would put him in a foul mood. He would go to his room and avoid the world of elements all together. Yet this time, he refused that attitude. Instead, he took the paper back to his room and stuffed it in his drawer.

"Never again. Maybe I'm not my father, and I'll never be him, but that doesn't mean I can't help people. Just watch me." He had a fire growing inside, and after the shortcomings in his training, it only added a little bit of motivation to keep him going.

The next two months pushed Minisc well beyond his limits. Every day became more grueling than the last, and more than a few times, Minisc begged his brain to call it quits. But when those days came, he pulled out the article about how he had failed to protect that one little girl; How without his father, he would have been finished. That was more than enough to spur him on and keep him obedient to his father's training regimen, no matter how difficult.

Through the pain he endured each day, he could see and feel visible differences in his physique. He had bulked up significantly, his once-weak body being carved out of stone one day at a time. To many, he would almost be unrecognizable.

Added to that, Minisc could feel his confidence increasing; he had grown leaps and bounds when it came to not only his element but his combat skills as well. The summer had evaporated, and elemental school would soon arrive. That meant before long, he would be starting his new journey.

However, that day would have to wait, as Minisc found himself inhaling the familiar scent of the forest where most of his summer had been spent. Starting with that first sparring session against his father. Two months had passed, and now the forest air was a little crisper and the leaves had all but turned their colors. Autumn crept around the corner, and Minisc was prepared to start school in short order. Before that day would come though, he had one final exam to pass. A one-on-one duel against the Hero of Light — again. Stronger, faster and smarter, Minisc was expecting a far different outcome from his first match.

"Minisc, you have done incredible work this summer. I want to say right now how proud I am of you, but before I consider this a success, you have one last goal to achieve. Land one hit on me. Accomplish that, and we will know just how far you've come."

"One hit? Really? Just one?"

"Correct."

"Well, that seems simple enough."

Don smirked. "It's won't be as easy as you think." He shaped up, not willing to give Minisc anything simple this time around, bracing for far more of a challenge than their first training session.

"On my count. Three... two... one..."

Minisc bolted toward his father, attempting to close the gap. His speed had improved exponentially, even beyond what Don had anticipated. Minisc's hand began to shine as he closed in, strategically opening up with a Lum Bomb mere feet away from his father. Dirt shot up like a geyser spraying high into the sky, forcing Don to raise his arm and shield his eyes. That played right into Minisc's plan. Seeing his chance, the boy burst through the makeshift smoke screen, swinging violently at his father's underbelly, his hands glowing a glimmering gold.

"Gotcha!"

Minisc's fist connected with what felt like a brick wall. The punch echoed out and dirt flew away with the shock waves of such a violent clash. But, once he realized what he had hit his eyes widened to saucers. Don had a tight grip on the boy's fist, snug in the palm of his left hand.

"Clever using the dirt as a smokescreen. But you're going to have to do a lot better than that if you want to land a hit on me."

"I should've figured it wouldn't be that simple."

Don's palm gleamed the familiar yellow glow of energy building. Realizing he was in trouble, Minisc let out an audible gulp. He struggled to free himself as Don thrust his right palm forward to attack. Minisc reacted instinctively, forcing his free hand to meet his father's. The two let off simultaneous blasts, causing an explosive boom throughout the forest. Don slid back from the recoil, tracks visible in the dirt, while Minisc flew backward, somersaulting with composure before landing gracefully a few feet away. Without hesitation, he sprung back into action, punch after punch. Don swiftly blocked the blows, taking notice of his son's improved abilities.

Your speed has increased tremendously, and your fighting sense has grown leaps and bounds. It's almost like you are a different person from my son. You really have come a long way, Minisc, Don thought, while still effortlessly blocking each incoming blow. Minisc's growth was substantial, but it remained mountains apart from where his father's skills were at.

With hand-to-hand combat looking like the least effective option, Minisc hopped back, unleashing a barrage of Lum Bombs. His new plan did little to slow his father down, as Don weaved in out of the blasts, like a choreographed dance. Feeling the tension in his muscles rise, Minisc stopped. He had built substantial muscle and endurance, but prolonged energy usage still took a toll on him. Thankfully Don stayed on the defensive, only attacking as a counter to his son. That gave Minisc a little wiggle room to stop and think.

He's too quick for me to land a hit on — I need another plan.

Minisc's mind began rattling through strategies, rejecting them all. Creativity would be required to pass this test.

Don took notice of the wheels spinning in his son's head. He smirked. Throughout the training, he had learned that Minisc possessed a creative and unpredictable side, and Don knew it was about to be a factor in the match. Conventional thinking was essential but not always the solution in battle. Sometimes, going off script was the key to victory.

A bead of sweat dropped from Minisc's brow as he tried to catch his breath. He was pushing his limits, but for the moment adrenaline kept his ensuing pain at bay.

Only able to devise one idea, Minisc shrugged his shoulders, running full steam at his father.

"Hope this works..."

"Foolish. You know you can't match my speed in close combat," Don warned, bracing himself for the incoming barrage again.

"Not without a little boost!"

Jumping through the air, Minisc spun his body, turning his back to the man. Shining in the sunlight, he fired a ferocious blast in the opposite direction of Don, and like he was shot out of a cannon, Minisc used the momentum from his attack to propel himself at blazing speed. Quickly shifting his weight, Minisc spun and directed a kick straight for his father's head.

Don ducked in the nick of time, feeling the wind graze the top of his hair. Amazed at his son's Hail Mary attempt, he spun around to see Minisc down on one knee.

Then a warm tingle filled the man's chest. He looked down to see a small puff of smoke rising underneath his large nose. Picking his head back up, Don noticed a goofy grin stretching from corner to corner on his son's face.

He actually did it.

"I can't believe that worked," Minisc laughed before falling backward on his butt. He looked even more shocked than his father.

Don could not hold back his growing smile either, as a sense of pride filled him from head to toe. The strides his son had taken in a few months were nothing short of astonishing.

He walked up to the boy, who continued to catch his breath, and stuck his hand out, motioning Minisc to take it. His son obliged and latched on before being lifted to his feet.

"Congratulations, Minisc—you passed."

Later that day, Minisc lay curled up on the soft brown couch in the living room with the TV volume no more than an audible whisper. Don stood in the adjacent kitchen looking at his son, not wanting to wake him. He walked over and gently placed a copper-red blanket on the boy. Then he turned to take one more look at his unconscious son.

"I can't tell you how proud I am of you. I know spending your summer training was probably the last thing you wanted to do. Early mornings, disgusting shakes, bodily torture. But through all of it, you continued to push yourself. You never quit and you never complained. I know it was hard, but I promise, this will serve you well one day."

CHAPTER 3
DAYS OF FUTURES PAST

TORONTO WAS WITHOUT A DOUBT THE LARGEST CITY in the country of Canada. Once, it had been home entirely to the human race, but after the emergence of Elementalists more than forty years earlier, the city's population had slowly become mixed. At first, some Elementalists were annoyed with the limits put on their powers by humans, while others chose to hide their nature altogether. But as crime rates rose and humans realized they could not stop Elementalists who chose to overpower them, the Government enlisted the help of a few Good Samaritans to fight in their ranks. With the population of Elementalists booming around the world, so too did their importance to society. As the Elemental Council gradually formed, ruling over all Elementalist affairs, more crime-fighting firms started to pop up around the city. They would all fall under the Council's jurisdiction, but for the most part they would act independently of each other.

Minisc sat on the edge of his bed after another long day of training. In his left hand, he continued to curl a forty-pound dumbbell, part of his new nightly routine, while his right hand scrolled through his cell phone. He skimmed through an article regarding another Elementalist attack on an EC research facility near the west side of Toronto. Minisc often avoided reading news stories of such ilk, but the headline piqued his interest. *Police, Elementalists battle in a laboratory break-in.* The picture posted at the top of the piece was of a man named Yuri Embroider. Standing tall, he was only a smidge below Minisc's father in height. His frame, however, paled in comparison with a much sleeker body. Short brown hair flowed to the back and bangs parted to the sides, shaping his friendly face. His eyes were a sharp black, piercing with one look. Yuri was considered somewhat of a minor celebrity in the city, someone who had participated in countless rescue missions, apprehendings, and investigations for the Elemental Council. He was no Hero of Light, but most Elementalists would recognize his name. He also happened to be Jules's older brother. That fact was what piqued Minisc's interest more than the story itself.

Minisc had the pleasure of meeting Yuri on a handful of occasions. A kind man who only wanted to help people, he had made a name for himself in short order. At Minisc's age, Yuri had started Elemental Academy, and quickly became known as one of the most gifted Elementalists in his year. He excelled at everything he did.

Shortly after graduating, Yuri joined a branch of the Elemental Council that used Elementalists to help apprehend dangerous criminals. Sailing through the ranks, he soon took over as the lead associate in elemental crime cases before opening up his own branch of the EC, heading off the elite Elementalist criminals in the city.

Jules, much in the way of many younger brothers, looked up to Yuri as an idol. Watching his brother, along with his slight obsession with the Hero of Light, had been what sparked his passion for elements and helping people. Jules dreamed of being like Yuri, using his impressive battle skills and wind element to save the day. That was why Minisc decided to send the article to his friend.

****

"Here you go; this needs to be filled out by the end of the day. It's at the request of your brother."

A tall blonde woman stood over Jules. She wore a white button-up blouse tucked into her knee-high gray skirt, and her hair was pulled into a long ponytail. She looked at Jules before giving him a sad smile through the black-framed glasses that graced her turquoise eyes. Still, regardless of pity, she dropped a tower of papers off on the desk in front of her.

"Come on, more paperwork? I should be out fighting bad guys, saving the day, like Yuri! How am I supposed to do that if I'm stuck in here filing reports all day?"

Jules let out a heavy sigh. Seated in a black leather chair taller than he was, he dropped his head onto the desk. Around the fresh stack of papers to his left laid even more sheets of unfinished reports. Jules could not fight off the boredom anymore. When he'd accepted the offer to work with his brother for the summer, he had visions far grander than this. Fighting bad guys, saving the innocent, being a hero much in the way people viewed his brother. Not for one second had the boy imagined his time would be spent sitting at a desk, filling out paperwork. He had so much more potential.

Jules sat quietly for a moment, listening to the hollowed ticking of the clock. Each passing second felt like minutes, and minutes felt like hours.

"Guess I should get started," he finally uttered in defeat. He collected the papers together, trying to clean up the war zone that he called a desk before grabbing a pen. In defeat, he started to scribble away.

"This is such a waste of time."

After Jules was done for the summer, he would never want to fill out another report in his life.

Continuing to lack concentration and looking for any little distraction, Jules picked his head up when he heard the doorknob jiggle.

"Back for lunch?" he asked as Yuri swung off his long black coat, hanging it on a stand near the door.

"Yeah, I wanted to get a quick bite before the afternoon shift," his brother replied, walking up to Jules's desk.

"How's the paperwork going?"

"Sucks."

"I know it's not the most glamorous job, but the work needs to get done."

"Come on, Yuri; I should be out there with you, on the streets; how can I help people if I'm stuck here filling out this endless pile of paperwork all day?"

"Would it make you feel better if I said I bought you lunch?"

Yuri reached into the pocket of his hung-up coat, pulling out a gleaming silver item. Peeling back the shiny paper, he revealed a thick, juicy hamburger, making sure Jules caught a glimpse. He knew how to negotiate with his brother. Once Jules caught a whiff of the scent, his mind flipped from work to food.

"Well, I mean, it wouldn't hurt," he laughed, fighting back the drool starting to form in the corner of his mouth. Yuri tossed the tightly wrapped delight to his brother while pulling out a second one for himself.

Before Yuri could blink, Jules discarded the paper, sinking his teeth into the sandwich. When it came to food, Jules was a human vacuum.

In a lot of ways, Yuri and his brother were similar; they had a drive to help people, a work ethic to continually improve, and a dream of creating a better world, but when it came to eating etiquette, Yuri far surpassed that of his younger sibling. He reached for a napkin, unfolding the white squares before placing it on top of his brother's copious amounts of paperwork.

"I need to put a hazard sign up when you eat," he joked. Jules paid the comment no mind as he continued to chow down.

"You know, I thought I was going to be your partner this summer, not tied to this desk," Jules sulked, falling back into the chair.

"What you're doing is just as important as actually being on the streets."

"Yeah right. Anybody could be doing this."

Yuri sighed. He knew what his brother's goals were, but at the moment they were too lofty. He had to start small and work his way up through experience. There were no shortcuts when it came to joining the ranks of the EC.

"I'm sorry Jules, it's just too dangerous for you to be out there right now — you have no experience in actual combat."

"What are you talking about? You trained me. How much more experience do I need?"

"Not the same thing, kiddo. Besides, you forget that a minor is not allowed to use their element in the public domain. The Elemental Council would have my head, not to mention my job, if I let you loose on the streets."

Jules slouched further into his seat. Still defeated, his mood perked up when a faint ring chimed out from his brother's chest pocket.

Yuri dropped his meal down on the napkin, pulling out his cell-phone.

"We have an urgent call at the corner of Glenwoods and Kingston, suspect with dark element attacked an EC research lab and is trying to escape on foot. Last seen wearing lengthy black robes, face covered. Considered dangerous, be advised."

The voice was static and choppy, but Yuri got enough of the distress call to understand the urgency. He jammed the phone into his front pocket, springing to his feet.

"Glenwoods and Kingston, that's only a few blocks away; we need to do something!" Jules yelled, vaulting up from his chair.

"You're going nowhere!"

"What, why not? I can help." The excitement washed off Jules's face.

"This could be dangerous. You're staying here, and that's final," Yuri ordered, grabbing his jacket off the coat rack. In a split second, the man bolted out the door.

Jules folded his arms in a pout, realizing his dreams had once again been dashed. "We finally get some action, and I'm relegated to paperwork..." He sunk back into his chair.

Then he paused for a moment. "No way I'm staying here. Besides, if it's dangerous, that means Yuri could use the backup."

Rationalizing his idea, Jules stood up, kicking his chair back into the wall. He hated to disobey his brother's orders, but temptation overwhelmed him. Wasting away in a boring office was driving the boy nuts—he needed some action.

Stealthily peeking his head around the corner of the door, he did a quick check to make sure his brother had disappeared. Once he confirmed the coast was clear, Jules silently shut the door behind him and started tiptoeing his way to the nearby stairwell.

Meanwhile, Yuri stood outside the tall glass building that housed his firm. He looked around, the silence of the street triggering his intuition. The roads were empty, no traffic and no pedestrians for miles. A strange sight for a section of the city that was often bustling with activity. Down the block, however, sirens cried out, calling the man's attention. Not wasting a moment, Yuri sprinted down the empty sidewalk following the flashing lights on the horizon.

"We need backup!" an officer clad in blue yelled, reaching for the walkie talkie strapped to his chest. The man was stationed behind an open car door, trying to keep as low as he could while he continued to call for help.

"This is Officer Marshall we need backup. Unidentified Elementalist resisting arrest. Remains dangerous. I repeat, we need back up." Across from him was a second white and blue police car with the lights on top alternating between a crimson red and sea blue. The driver door had been swung open with a second officer crouched behind it for protection.

Officer Marshall popped his head out to assess the situation again. He held a small handgun at the ready, but his visible shaking made aiming down the sight impossible. They were at the mercy of a figure sheathed in black robes, one who walked down the middle of the hallowed street without fear. Tall and thin, with a red belt wrapped around his pencil-like waist, at first glance he did not pose much of a threat. But that didn't stop him from reeking of intimidation. His walk forward had a certain flair to it, and slung over his left shoulder was a brown briefcase.

"Drop the briefcase and put your hands above your head!" Officer Marshall shouted.

"No thanks, I'll be putting this research to good use." A sense of cheerful mischief followed the cloaked man's words. His voice sounded young, as if he were around his mid-twenties, but showed no lack of confidence. He continued step by step toward the officer's holdout. Each inch closer filled the officers with fear.

"I won't repeat myself—put your hands up and drop the brief-case! Or... Or I'll shoot!" the police officer ordered again.

"Afraid I can't do that, boss; as I said, I need this stuff. Now, you two are blocking my way. So if you'd be so kind as to let me through, that'd be lovely."

The stranger took his free hand and held it out toward the offi-cers, forming a shadowy black ball. The outside was shaded a deep purple, and in the center of the orb sat a midnight-black core with sparks exploding off the element's potent energy.

"My sincerest apologies. Truly," The man laughed, giving a sim-ple flick of the wrist. Taking off like a rocket, the energy ball zipped down the paved roadway like a missile seeking out its intended target.

The cops quickly ducked back behind the improvised barrier, suppressing any last words they had for the world.

"Hold it right there!"

Rushing in headlong, Yuri bolted between the two police cars. He waved his hand forward and a horizontal tornado formed from his palm, absorbing the incoming blast. Evolution Storm—a wind attack that Yuri had made famous. With the speed and force of his element being released, Evolution Storm could make one feel like they were trapped in the middle of a real tornado. Only a handful of people had had the privilege of witnessing such power, let alone surviving it unharmed.

As he threw his hand into the air, the spiraling cyclone soared high through the sky, carrying with it the Shadow Ball. Boom. A sparkling explosion filled the sky like fireworks.

"Hmm... This is an interesting turn of events. Finally, someone with a little meat on their bones," the man muttered, "So who are you, a chipper pedestrian trying to play Hero?" He glared at Yuri, but the mocking words fell on deaf ears. Yuri had already turned his back to check on the cowering officers.

Peeking over the doors, both law enforcement officers breathed a heavy sigh of relief.

"Are you two alright? I got here as fast as I could."

"Yeah, you arrived just in time. Thanks, Yuri. We would have been finished if it weren't for you," the cop on the left said through deep breaths.

"You two have done your duty; leave the rest to me."

The masked man listened to the distant conversation, tapping his foot, patience growing thin.

"Uh, hello," he whistled, "I think you might be forgetting some-one."

Yuri turned around, staring into the abyss of the stranger's dark veil.

"Don't worry, I haven't forgotten about you."

Yuri flamboyantly threw his coat into the air, watching it fall into a heap on the pavement. He donned a blood-red muscle-grabbing shirt that tucked into his black pants. Wrapped around his toned arms were white bands with the words *Serve and Protect* on them.

"Ahh, so you're part of that silly Council. Now things make more sense. As much as I'd like to take down one of the precious coun-cilmembers, I really should be leaving. You know how it is, places to go, things to do."

"You're not going anywhere; now drop the briefcase and we can avoid any unnecessary violence," Yuri spoke firmly, confidently. Bravery and pride were understatements about the man, and he was not about to cower in the face of a criminal. Few embraced the words on his armband more than him. He was there to serve and protect.

The two stood still, like a duel in the Wild West. Each waiting to see what the other would do.

"You guys try to take all the fun out of everything. You and I, we're not all that different. Yet people look at you as a hero, a protector of the people. In the same light, they look at me as a villain, a tormentor who should be put behind bars, or worse. We both use our powers to help people, but because I help Elementalists, and you help these pitiful humans of this cruel world, I'm seen as the villain in this story."

Yuri listened to the man's speech, the words ringing hollow.

"Spare me your lectures; you and I are nothing alike."

"How blind this world has become. But, that's why we'll expose you and everyone else for the frauds you really are."

The man waved his hand to the ground, causing a cloud of thick smoke to appear.

Seeing the mist form, Yuri speared forward in the blink of an eye, fist at the ready. He felt his punch connect, but nothing gave.

"You're quite fast," the hooded criminal mocked.

Yuri unleashed a burst of wind from his body, clearing the smoke field. He tried to pull his arm away but hesitated as the criminal held a vice grip on his left hand. Struggling to break free, Yuri shook his fist furiously, only able to wiggle it an inch or two.

"Who are you?" Yuri whispered to the man. It was becoming apparent he was locked in a battle with no ordinary Elementalist.

"You'll find out soon enough," the criminal chuckled. A surge of dark element sprang from his body, spewing off in all directions like sparks. The shock impacted Yuri's chest, causing him to seize up for a moment. That left an opening for the criminal, who landed a clean kick to Yuri's stomach. He flew back, grabbing at his abs while taking deep breaths. Looking up at the hooded figure, what he saw was a shadowy aura in the shape of a burning flame. The torch-like light enveloped the man's entire body.

A cold chill raced up Yuri's spine as the air filled with a palpable taste, one of distrust and hatred. It was unlike anything Yuri had ever felt before.

Black clouds started to form, wiping away the once-bright afternoon sky. The wind picked up like a storm was coming, and the

glass in surrounding buildings shattered from the raw release of energy surrounding the mystery man.

Yuri braced himself, remaining unaffected by the powerful storm.

"Strange, it was sunny just a minute ago."

Jules exited the side door of the building. Walking toward the deserted street, he saw a blaze of purplish-black fire piercing a hole in the sky. *That cannot be good.* Jules hesitated for a second. *Maybe going is a bad idea. But Yuri might be in trouble. He might need my help!*

Wanting to show no fear like his brother, Jules took off down the street.

Flashing lights and swirling winds tipped Jules off that whatever criminal his brother was chasing had to be a handful. However, knowing if he got in the way — or worse hurt — his brother would scold him, he figured it would be best to keep his distance. Swiftly ducking into an alley nearby, Jules trekked through, rounding the corner into darkness. Between dark skies and buildings that did not subject themselves to light, Jules struggled to see a thing. Luckily for him, he had more than enough experience with the city landscape and could traverse every street by the firm while on autopilot. Before he knew it, he popped out of an alcove right next to the action. Taking caution, he stayed partially hidden by the shadows before poking his head out to see the villain. Out of his peripheral vision, he spotted his brother.

"Yuri..." he murmured. Though he remained a bystander, the darkness ruminating from the strange man gripped Jules. His body started to sweat and his heart began racing faster. Something about this man seemed different. Most criminals were like the one he and Minisc had faced on the last day of school. Strong for sure, but nothing special compared to the EC. Yet this man held a far more treacherous presence.

The villain's cloak fell back down to its elongated form as his energy dropped. He readied for round two, but this time Yuri saw his opening. He dashed forward, landing a hit into the cloaked man's chest and sending him tumbling backward. Yuri followed up with heavy gusts of wind, which blew the man's cloak off, finally revealing the perpetrator's face. He had a face roughly the same age as Yuri's — mid-to-late twenties with long, silver-black hair pulled back, and a trademark cut under the left of his steel-blue eyes. They were cold and filled with hatred.

Yuri stared intently, the feeling that he knew the man occupying his thoughts, but no matter how hard he tried, no names came to mind.

"Still don't recognize me? Unbelievable, some people, I tell ya. The names Bronx — it would serve you well not to forget."

"Bronx?" Trying to jog his memory, Yuri remained clueless to the man.

"Well, this is insulting. You know, you're lucky I don't get my feelings hurt easily."

"Cut the games, Bronx. Now tell me what it is you want with those materials from the EC?"

"I don't think that's any of your business Yuri Embroider. But don't worry, you'll find out in due time. Now once again, it's time for me to take my leave."

Bronx reached down, picking up the stolen briefcase.

"Not so fast."

Yuri unleashed more winds, trapping Bronx in place. Crossing his arms and crouching down, Bronx held his center of balance enough to remain on his feet. Yuri pushed the gusts further. Up against a powerful foe such as this, holding back was no longer an option.

"You're not getting away that easily."

The wind speed picked up, making the force Bronx had unleashed look as if it had come from a child. Yuri started to step forward, concentrating his attack more and more on his opponent. He was taking control, leaving Bronx trapped in the clutches of his swirling vapors.

"I'll admit, you have some power, but let's see if you can keep up with this speed," Bronx mocked before bursting into his scarlet purple aura again. With ease, he began to stand up before evaporating into the air.

"Where'd he go?" Yuri yelled, before feeling a chill breath grace his neck.

"What, am I too fast for you? Bummer, maybe you're not as strong as I remember," Bronx whispered into Yuri's ear. In the blink of an eye, the man cocked his elbow forward, then swung it back into Yuri's gut. Letting out a gasp from the impact, Yuri soared through the air, crumpling to the ground unceremoniously.

"As I said, I'll be taking my leave now." Bronx flung his hand down, creating a shadow that enveloped him. The battle was over.

Jules watched in sheer panic as his brother, his idol, was taken down in one hit. Before his mind could comprehend the defeat, his feet were racing toward the elder sibling.

"Yuri! Yuri, are you alright?" Jules cried out, reaching down to pick his brother up.

"Jules…" Yuri muttered, pushing himself up onto his left knee. He looked no worse for wear, causing a heavy sigh of relief to escape the young boy's lips.

"Thank goodness you're okay," Jules said, throwing his arms around his brother.

For Jules, this would be an important lesson to learn. Amidst all the good things he wanted to do, he was nowhere near prepared physically — and more important, mentally — for the dangers of working with his brother. That day, he saw the real strength of a criminal Elementalist. Not the low-level robber he and Minisc had faced, no, this man was the sort of threat Yuri dealt with most often.

Once the two policemen realized the crisis had been averted, they left their cover to check on their savior.

"Who was that man?" Officer Marshall asked.

"I don't know, but he's not someone to be taken lightly. We're going to have to get more intel on him. Can you two file a report for me?"

"Of course, sir," both policemen replied, saluting simultaneously. "And as for you, Jules..."

Jules gulped, looking toward the ground.

"I told you to stay in the office. You could have been seriously hurt, or worse!" Yuri scolded his younger brother. He was not a yeller by nature, but he could be stern when he felt it appropriate.

"I know, I just couldn't resist getting to see some action," Jules mumbled, avoiding all eye contact.

Yuri stood up, softly patting his brother on the crown of his maroon hair.

"I guess next time I'll just have to lock you in that office."

Jules's head shot up. "Wait, what? That's a bit much, don't you think? I promise I won't disobey you again."

"Good. Now Come on, let's go back to the office—I think that's enough excitement for one day."

Yuri and Jules smiled warmly at each other before Jules nodded in agreement. The charcoal clouds that layered the sky evaporated and the two watched as the sun started to pierce through once more. Feeling exhausted and ready to go back to the office, they began walking into the horizon side by side.

"Besides, you still have paperwork to finish."

"Ughhhh."

****

Minisc lay sprawled out on his bed, the night stars gleaming dully through the window. Another long day of training had left him feeling battered and bruised. Far less than when he started, but enough to make him want to crash early for the night. Sitting on the end table, his phone lit up the dark room, while vibrations along the wooden surface echoed obnoxiously. Minisc jolted awake, sitting straight up. Blinking twice, he came to his senses, turning his attention over to the mesmerizing light beaming off his phone. Two text messages had been left by Jules.

I was there! Read the first. *You wouldn't believe how strong the criminal was, things got pretty crazy.* Underneath it, the second message read, *How's the training going?*

Minisc replied in two words: *Everything hurts.* Which was not far off the truth. It had been a strenuous past two months filled with heavy lifting, intense training sessions, and grueling battles, but he could feel the difference in his body. Since the start of summer, he had developed considerable muscle mass, his athletic endurance had skyrocketed, and his understanding of his powers had grown immensely. Overall the past two months felt like a surprising success. Not once had he felt alone either, despite the absence of his best friend. For the first time in years, he'd had someone to spend his entire summer with, and even through all the pain, Minisc had created fond memories.

Now awake, Minisc walked down the hallway into the living room. He met his father, who was sitting comfortably in front of the television. Don turned as he heard the soft footsteps of his son.

"Oh, you're awake? I thought you might be out cold for the night. Today was pretty intense."

The man stood up, walking to the adjacent room on his right—the kitchen.

"Do you want anything to eat? Something I can make you?"

"No thanks, I'm not very hungry right now."

Minisc instead turned his attention to the television. Plain red text along the bottom of the screen read *Breaking News* over and over again as it scrolled on and off each side of the picture. Then a woman came onto the screen with a small microphone in her hands held up to her pink lips. She was rather young, with a long black ponytail falling in front of her left shoulder. She donned a black suit jacket with a blood-red blouse underneath.

Minisc took a seat on the couch as Don walked back into the living room settling into his previous spot. Minisc turned up the volume, curious as to what all the hoopla was about.

"I'm in front of the Elemental Council's building, where we're patiently awaiting the chief of staff to address the public after today's events. Crime rates have continued to climb over the past year, and with growing concern from the public, the Elemental Council has been called into the spotlight."

Pictures of multiple crime scenes popped up over the woman's voice. Toronto had been known as one of the safer cities in recent years, with the population of Elementalists helping fight crime drastically deterring criminals, but almost overnight it seemed crime rates were beginning to spike. Many humans were becoming more and more frightful that Elementalists were starting to rebel just as they had many years ago.

"We'll be going live now to the Council building, where President Zale Osiris will be speaking," the woman announced, trying to block out the noise around her so she could listen to her earpiece.

The scene shifted to a gallant white building. A dozen wide marble steps stacked their way up to a large, rectangular structure with four towering pillars on each side holding up the triangular awning. Between the posts were white banners with red and gold trim stitching hung to the ground, and perfectly centered on each was a beveled oval with the letters *EC* printed on it. This logo was universally recognized by anyone and everyone as the logo and acronym for the Elemental Council.

Crowds of protesters, reporters, and bystanders piled into a mob of people waiting for the president to address the masses.

Not long into the angry chants, two men walked down the stairs to a parade of camera flashes. The man on the right was tall, finely dressed in a lavish gray suit pulled together with a black and red striped tie. He also had thick, brown hair neatly brushed to the side to match his distinctive features. His face was the kind that seemed to stick in people's minds. Zale Osiris. To his left, lagging a step behind, was a strapping young man, clad in a white dress uniform trimmed with red around the arms, legs, and waist. He wore a round red hat with the brim sticking out the front. On the center of the cap was a matching EC logo. It was a standard uniform.

The two walked down the long set of stairs, making their way to the podium. Zale walked up first, adjusting the mic down to just underneath his chin.

"Hello all, I'd like to take this time with Sgt. Thomas Cooper, to address the growing concern around the recent string of crimes facing our city. We're working tirelessly to apprehend these criminals and bring each and every one of them to justice." Zale's voice cut through the noisy crowd with ease. As he paused to take a breath, questions rang out from the masses.

"How do you plan to stop these criminals?"

"Do you think this spree of crimes is related?"

"Is this believed to be in conjunction with the rise of Luminosa?"

Minisc keyed in on the last question. The rise of Luminosa? Glancing over to his father, Minisc could tell the man was marinating on the same question.

Not having been born yet at the time, Minisc scarcely knew the true atrocities the group known as Luminosa had tried to bring upon the world. History books would call it an attempted extermination of all that the vile group and their followers deemed unworthy, but it was far more. Removing humans from the planet had been only the starting point. The endpoint turned into eliminating any human or Elementalist who opposed their views that Elementalists were a superior race and had been stifled by humans for far too long. Minisc's father, on the other hand, not only had a first-hand account of the horrors but was the reason they'd ended. Such accusations that Luminosa might be reforming could not be taken lightly.

Minisc continued to ponder the thought, but a simple ring of the doorbell called his attention instead.

"It's a little late for people to be coming over, isn't it?" Don asked.

"Don't look at me—who would I've invited over?" Minisc shrugged while standing up and walking down the hall. "Maybe it's someone looking for an autograph."

Don cautiously stood up, watching his son's movements.

Minisc made it to the door but could only see the top half of a looming, shadowy figure through the stained-glass window. He cracked the door open, taking a cautious peek to see who stood on the other side.

"Hello?"

The voice sounded deep but also warm. Figuring the friendly voice showed no threat, Minisc swung the door open more willingly, but when he did, he scrunched his face in confusion. In the doorway stood a giant of a human whom Minisc did not recognize. The man housed big round eyes the color of steel, a large nose, and a bushy goatee. In fact, every feature of the man looked unusually large to match his massive exterior. His clothes were what caught Minisc's eye the most, though. A long white uniform jacket that dropped down to his knees, polished gold buttons climbing up toward the collar, and a flap just under the neck bent back in a V shape. It was lined in red all around, tied together with the EC logo on the left arm. A simple design but elegant nonetheless.

"Hi?" Minisc greeted, more than a bit confused why someone from the Elemental Council stood on their doorstep.

Seeing Minisc's trepidation and the man's uniform, Don decided to intervene in the awkward exchange.

"Is there something we can help you with..." Don paused. "Dwayne? Is that you?" He squinted his eyes, making sure he hadn't mistaken the man.

Minisc stared at his father, wholly lost at what was going on.

"Long time no see," the man replied, a smile tugging at the corners of his lips.

"What are you doing here? I haven't seen you in ages."

"I came to check in on the Hero of Light. It's kind of hard since you've been dodging the spotlight these last few years."

Looking back and forth, Minisc finally blurted out, "Can somebody explain what is going on?"

"Oh, right. Minisc, this is Dwayne. You probably don't remember him — you'd have met him when you were just a baby. Dwayne this is my son, Minisc."

"Boy, you've sure grown, and with those muscles, you'll pass your old man in no time," Dwayne chuckled.

The exchange caught Minisc off guard. He had never heard someone talk to his father so plainly. It was always "sir," or "Hero of Light." Hearing his father be called "old man" was somehow off-putting.

"Please, come in, sit down."

The three took seats around the glass coffee table. Minisc sat in his usual position on the couch while Don sat to the boy's right, and Dwayne took a shine to the leather chair angled to face the sofa.

"So how have you been? It's been way too long," Don asked.

Minisc took notice of his father's unusual jubilance. Not that his father was always stoic, but usually remained more even-keeled. For the moment, though, it appeared Don was quite overjoyed to see Dwayne.

"Well, as I'm sure you can tell from the uniform, I'm still slaving away for the Council."

"You must have your hands full lately with all the rising crime in the city."

"You got that right; everyone's been working tirelessly to put a stop to all this. But things have not been progressing as we had hoped, it seems every time we think we have a lead, the puzzle becomes more complicated. But what about you? The Hero of Light has been gradually turning into a myth," Dwayne joked light-heartedly. He was well aware of the mythical nature that still followed the man.

"I've been keeping busy," Don quipped back.

"You know, Minisc, your father in his heyday was even greater than the stories! He could single-handedly take down an army of Elementalists. It was a sight to see."

This caught Minisc's attention.

"You worked with my father?"

His father never talked about his days of being the Hero of Light, a surprise considering the articles on the wall and pictures around the house. As a kid, Minisc had been quite fascinated with his father, but as he grew up, he lost interest in the lore and stopped asking questions, moving away from elements altogether—especially when the fame started to spill over onto him, leading to strangers bombarding him with questions about his father. That made the boy want to avoid the subject at all costs, but after spending so much time with his father over the summer, his interest had been quietly piqued again. This was a golden opportunity to learn about his father's past a bit.

"Oh yeah, I was saving his tail all the time."

"I remember it slightly differently than that!" Don retorted as they both shared a chuckle.

Before Minisc could dive deeper into the topic, Don slipped in a question.

"So Dwayne, I'm sure you didn't travel all this way in full uniform without a purpose."

"Correct as always. I came because I needed to talk to you." His voice dropped a few decibels, becoming a tinge sterner. "Minisc, this is sort of official business; do you mind if I ask you to leave the room?"

Caught off guard by the question, Minisc nodded. "Oh… yeah, of course." He stood up and headed for his bedroom.

That was strange. I wonder what Dwayne thought was so private that I couldn't be around to hear it. He walked over to his bed and dropped himself onto it, letting out a small yawn.

Back in the living room, Don and Dwayne sat eye-to-eye, the tone of their reunion shifting from light-hearted reacquainting to all business.

"What is this about, Dwayne?"

"The Council has it on good authority that all of these latest crimes are connected. The targets, the men running around in cloaks, it's all starting to add up. Somebody is trying to reform Luminosa," Dwayne spoke in a whisper. His forehead started to glisten with sweat. The magnitude of the topic was not lost on either man.

"I was fearful of that, but how? We eradicated Dusk and his followers years ago. He could not have possibly returned."

"I don't know. We were never able to find his body, but even so, after all these years, we've yet to find a single trace of him anywhere. Someone else may have taken up the mantle, but at this point, we still don't know. We're doing everything we can to get information, but sources have continued to come up empty."

Don's look grew more serious; he knew the damage brought on by another war against Luminosa would be devastating not only to the city, but potentially the world.

"We need to put a stop to this as quickly as possible."

"That's why the Council sent me. We need you, Don; we need the Hero of Light. You're the only one who can help us put an end to this before it starts. Will you join us?"

Don did not react right away; in the back of his mind, when he first saw Dwayne at the door, he knew the reason he had arrived.

"Dwayne, I'd like to help you, I really would, but I just don't possess the level of strength I once did. If Dusk truly is back, I'm not sure I'd be in any condition to stop him." Don's tone was sedated, sounding frustrated and defeated at the same time.

"What do you mean?" Dwayne asked, shocked to hear such a revelation.

"When I first learned the technique Celestial Light, I had been warned that prolonged use of such a powerful skill would eventually drain what strength I had left. When I noticed things were getting worse in the city, I started training Minisc to ensure he could protect himself, but I also wanted to make sure I was at my best should the day come that a new threat arrived. While I was training him, the better he got, the more I tried to draw on my old power, but I couldn't. It was like a fire that I had burned out. I'm simply not prepared or even capable of getting back into the world-saving business. The Council has lots of great young talent coming out of the EA every year — surely they can help."

"Those kids are far too green to get involved in this; they would be overwhelmed in any sort of fight like the ones we used to have. Howland won't even teach them Celestial Light. Says they don't have the strength to use it. Look Don, I don't know how strong or weak you are right now, and you have certainly put in your time to help us in the past, so I'll not begrudge your decision. That being said, think it over a bit — the Hero of Light at fifty percent is still better than ninety-nine percent of the Elementalists on the planet and would be a huge asset for our investigations."

Dwayne stood up slowly. "Just... think about it."

Don waved as he and Dwayne parted ways. He had been left with a lot to think about. The safety of him and his son remained his top priority; that much had not changed. Allowing Luminosa to rise again, however, was not an option Don was willing to entertain. Deciding to play things slow, the man would wait and see how investigations progressed. Even so, one thing became clear: he would need to step up his training.

CHAPTER 4
ELEMENTAL ACADEMY

ELEMENTAL ACADEMY WAS LOCATED IN THE HEART OF Toronto. For Minisc, that meant going back to early mornings and long train rides. By far the most popular form of transportation in the city, it often resulted in the cabins bustling with traffic.

Minisc continued to drown out the murmurs of people stomping up and down the narrow aisle of the train. At the crack of dawn, he pleaded for some peace and quiet. His wish, however, had not been granted. The train remained particularly busy this autumn morning, and every stop prompted a rush of men, women, and kids to exit and enter like cattle.

Nodding off in the middle of each stop, he found himself next to an older lady in a black dress shirt and green knee-high skirt. Also in front of him were two men dressed in iron-gray suits, and all three were working away on small laptops. That allowed Minisc to rest his head against the window and relax his mind. Today was the first day of school. More specifically, Elemental Academy.

A new school year was nothing unusual. It would result in a new teacher and a bump up in schoolwork, but Elemental Academy would be substantially different from his previous schooling. The institution still required students to take regular classes, such as English and math, which helped ease Minisc's stress, but the difference could be found in the elective courses which had been turned into training sessions of sorts. Elemental Academy acted as a prep school for joining the Elemental Council, meaning combat training and elemental training were a must. All of that made

Minisc nervous enough, but the biggest difference, and for him the most concerning, would be the students. Minisc lacked many friends, and that was by design. Being the son of the Hero of Light did not only come with the 'perks' of the media focusing on you, but it also came with a lot of attention from kids who looked up to the hero. For better or worse, Minisc had attended school with the same kids most of his life. That meant students had grown accustomed to being in a class with the Hero of Light's son. He was not bombarded with questions, or with people wanting to be his friend because of his name recognition. At least not anymore. That was the most significant factor in his avoidance of most students. With the exception of Jules, Minisc did not interact with any of his classmates outside of school. Even though Jules was far and away the biggest fan of the Hero of Light, he appreciated that Minisc did not idolize his father.

Along with that, Jules's kind heart and infectious personality were hard to resist. Combine that with his acceptance that Minisc was not interested in talking about his father all day long, it went a long way to creating such a tight bond. Not to say he didn't ask questions, he was simply less intrusive about it.

This year would be an entirely new crop of students. The school had acceptances from all across the province and farther.

Minisc knew for sure of two other people from his school: Jules and another boy named Ignis.

Ignis was known as a hot-headed, short-tempered bully, but he was quite the skilled fire Elementalist. Aside from those two and himself, it would be all new students to deal with.

"Aurora; the next stop is Aurora."

Minisc snapped out of his deep thought, hearing the robotic voice booming over the speakers. He watched as the three people surrounding him stood up, shuffling into line to get off at their stop. Aurora was a stop at the north end of the city that housed many small businesses. Outside of the final stop, Union, Aurora saw the most action daily.

Minisc stretched his legs out, exploring the freedom he had been granted. Only, that freedom would be short-lived, as he heard the soft voice of an adolescent girl.

"Excuse me."

Minisc looked up, his breath catching in his throat. Staring back at him was a pair of soft blue eyes, a tiny nose, and an adorably roundish face. Before Minisc could say anything, she opened up her pillowy pink lips again.

"Is anyone sitting there?" she asked in the sweetest voice Minisc had ever heard.

He stared blankly at the girl, attempting to mouth words. But as hard as he tried, he could not choke out an answer. Resorting to gestures, Minisc shook his head back and forth a couple of times.

The girl tilted her head before smiling awkwardly. Minisc watched in silence as she gracefully spun around, slipping her teal backpack off and holding it against her slender body. She flattened out her sea-blue dress and plopped down in front of the love-struck boy. Minisc continued to awkwardly stare as curls of her chestnut brown hair reached for her shoulders while also admiring the cute blue ribbon tying her long ponytail together. Not knowing what to do, Minisc began looking out the window in embarrassment.

After a few silent minutes, he glanced back over at the girl. She had crossed her legs and pulled out a book reading in silence. Minisc internally debated how to capture her attention.

Should I say something? I should definitely say something... but what do I say? Minisc desperately tried to figure out a conversation starter.

Do I just say hello? No, that's too formal. What about, 'You're cute'? No that's just creepy. Why is this so difficult all of a sudden? Okay... whatever you say, just say it with confidence. Opening his mouth to finally speak, he was mercifully interrupted by the PA system.

"Next stop, Burnaby Lane... Burnaby Lane."

Minisc's mouth snapped shut, stunned that he had spent so much time debating what to say that he had reached his stop. With no other choice but to accept his defeat, he stood up, heading for the cabin aisle. As he rose, he found himself face to face with the same petite nose that had enamored him in the first place. His heart

fluttered as he attempted to choke out a coherent sentence once again.

"You go…"

Two words. That was the best Minisc could spit out, but it would be more than enough to end the awkward encounter.

"Thank you."

The girl smiled graciously at Minisc before heading down the small steps to the cabin door.

Trying to fight off the little tinge of red gracing his cheeks, Minisc quickly followed suit. The last thing he needed was to miss his stop on the first day of class.

As he stepped out onto the tarmac, rays of blistering sun hit Minisc. Shock overtook him as he looked around.

"Am I in the right spot?"

A long alleyway stretched in front of him, while to the east were gray chain-link fences extending as far as he could see. Behind the fences were the backs of damaged buildings where bricks were chipped, doors rusted, and windows shattered. To his west was a small, elongated shelter where people stood while waiting for the train.

Maybe I should get back on the train? This can't be where the school is. Turning around just in time to watch the doors slam shut, Minisc let out a heavy sigh. "Guess there's no turning back now."

Taking a second look at the alleyway, he noticed a few people around his age heading down the path.

I should probably follow them.

Minisc started picking up his pace to a light jog. This looked like the last place he wanted to spend too much time dilly-dallying around.

Chills ran up and down his spine as he caught glimpses of the sketchy buildings surrounding him. At any moment, somebody would pop out and attack, he was certain of it. Luckily, those fears were unfounded.

As the exit came into view, Minisc heard the roar of a nearby engine. Leaving the alley, he turned to his left. Parked on the side of the street was a large yellow school bus, presumably his school bus. Minisc paused for a second; he watched the last person climbing the steps before seeing the doors close. Then the bus gradually pulled off the curb, ready to leave Minisc behind. Although not entirely sure, Minisc felt pretty confident he needed to be on that bus. Besides, he had no interest in staying in his current location.

Minisc dashed down the street, waving his hands frantically, trying to get the driver's attention. Thankfully, his prayers were answered in the form of screeching brakes. He dropped his arms, standing on the curb as the bus pulled up beside him. Two large rectangular doors folded inward, and looking up the steps, Minisc placed eyes on a large, pale man jammed between his seat and the steering wheel. He had thinning snow-white hair and a bushy white mustache covering his upper lip, creating a distinct grandfatherly look.

The driver looked down at Minisc with a jolly smile.

"First day of EA?" The driver reminded Minisc so much of Santa Claus, he couldn't help but smile back.

"Yeah."

"Well grab an open seat and enjoy the ride — we'll be arriving in about twenty minutes."

Minisc nodded his head, walking up two steps which led to the seating. Passing by the driver, he felt a tap on his shoulder. Surprised by the touch, Minisc turned around and found himself eye-to-eye with the man.

"Quick question, friend, are you the son of the Hero—?"

Minisc frantically waved his hands, putting a stop to the man's question.

"Yes, but I'd like to keep that a secret," Minisc whispered, taking careful precaution to make sure nobody overheard their conversation. He could feel the awkward stares of students as he dropped his hands, trying to act normal. Still, those glaring eyes would be nothing compared to the swarm he would endure if he publicly announced his lineage on the bus.

"Oh, okay, no problem, it's our little secret. On one condition... Can I get an autograph? You're going to be famous one day, and driving this bus doesn't quite pay the bills." The driver gave Minisc a sly smile.

"Umm, yeah, sure."

Minisc reached into his bag, pulling out a pen and a scrap piece of paper, then quickly scribbling his name on it. He could feel the inpatient stares burning into the back of his skull. They had to wonder what he was doing.

"Thanks. Now sit back and enjoy the ride."

"Yeah, no problem," Minisc mumbled, taking his leave toward the back of the bus. Walking by each group of two, Minisc could feel eyes on him like he was animal at the zoo. The silent stares of judgment made his heart race in anticipation. Eventually, Minisc spotted a single section in the back-left corner of the bus. Strapping in for the ride, he made himself comfy, placing his backpack on the space beside him. The bus started chugging down the street to its charted course, Elemental Academy.

The ensuing ride felt hours longer than the estimated twenty minutes. Minisc sat in silence, feeling a knot tighten his stomach as he patiently waited for the day to start. It was natural to be nervous on the first day of a new school. He knew that, but the words of the bus driver continued to ping pong back and forth in his head.

You're going to be famous.

He understood it—lots of people had told him similar growing up. His father was a famous icon, so expectations were in many ways, for him, to follow the same path. Only his mother thought differently, continually telling him to be his own person, make his own legacy. She was adamant about him not trying to live up to the lore of his father, and most importantly, not living in the shadow of the man either. That was one of Minisc's anxieties when it came to students and teachers. The expectations for him would no doubt be different than for other students. He would be expected to come out of the gate flying, demonstrating skills and maturity beyond his years. That put a lot of pressure on the teen to deal with. He had trained hard and his confidence had never been higher, but even so, would that be enough to stave off those gunning for him?

Once the bus pulled up to its destination, Minisc stepped off and was once again shocked by where he was.

Unlike the sketchy drop-off area of the train station, now he found himself in a much more luscious setting—freshly cut grass, trees standing tall, and a few picnic benches where students were sitting before class. The real attraction, however, was the school in front of Minisc. He stared up at a towering red-brick building that stretched four floors high. Steel flag poles were protruding from the rooftops with different flags flapping in unison. Eight flags in all, and each had a unique symbol and color stitched into it. They were the symbols of each known element an Elementalists could create in their body. Light, dark, fire, ice, water, lightning, earth, and wind. Large, double-squared windows stacked vertically up each floor of the building, while glistening gold letters were bolted into the bricks between the third and fourth floors. They read *Elemental Academy* with each word on its own row. Minisc was in awe of the sheer scope of the place. He could not believe this would be his new school.

"This place is massive," he gawked.

Pulling out his phone, he looked at the clock that flashed on the screen.

"Eight forty-five... crap, class starts at nine. If I'm late on the first day I'll be so dead."

Knowing he needed to get a move on, Minisc headed up a set of broad stairs with a metal rail that filtered students who were coming and going, like two sides of an escalator.

Walking into the luxurious building, Minisc laid eyes on the chaotic cafeteria. There were two levels to the room. The bottom section hosted between twenty and thirty round wooden tables, which could fit three to four people around each with ease. Behind that, four long, rectangular tables stretched across the room, and on the east side, a cozy marketplace so students could buy lunch. Despite its size, from the glimpse Minisc caught, it looked like a fine dining restaurant. Highly efficient, yet chaotic to the untrained eye. Following the vibrant red walls up, he saw that a balcony surrounded the entire lower floor, and staircases to the right of the entrance led people up to the second level.

"Jeez, Father... how much of my inheritance did you spend on this place?"

Loud chatter rang out through the café, making it hard for Minisc to hear his thoughts. He remained enamored with his new surroundings but had no time to explore further. He needed to get to his classroom, and quick.

Minisc's first class took place on the third floor. Lightly jogging up a few flights of stairs, he peered out into an elongated and wide hallway. Small gray signs hung high over every door lined down both sides of the hall. They were indicators of each room's assigned number. Even numbers were on the left side and odd numbers along the right. Minisc checked his phone again. "Two minutes... better hurry."

As he walked past each door, nervous energy welled up inside Minisc. A new chapter of his life was about to begin. He had spent so much of his summer preparing for what was to come, but how could he be sure if he had done enough? He knew the only way to find out would be face it head-on.

Halfway down the hall, Minisc looked up. Room 312. Bringing his eyes back down, he saw a plain white door blocking his path. The only thing left between him and a whole new world. On the other side was nothing but silence, much to his surprise. Minisc expected to hear chatter, lectures, some level of interaction. Instead, nothing.

Steeling his nerves, he reached out with his left hand and twisted the metallic doorknob. As soon as the door creaked open, he heard a harsh, intimidating voice.

"You're late! Class starts at nine a.m. sharp!"

Minisc was taken aback as the voice pierced his ears. Still gripping his phone in his right hand, he tapped the bottom to see the time.

9:01...

"What's your name?" the woman demanded. Her eyes were cross and her weathered face scrunched up. The wrinkles on her forehead gave a strong indication of her mature age. She was at eye-level with Minisc but only thanks to a pair of arched black heeled shoes, which provided her with a good three inches of height. Wearing a knee-high black skirt and a white blouse, she had a professional look about her.

Minisc hesitated to answer. His attempt to draw less attention had backfired. Answering the question would shine the brightest spotlight imaginable on him one minute into his first class. But he had no choice.

"Minisc," he sputtered out.

"Last name?" the woman grunted.

Minisc gulped, trying to swallow the apple-sized lump forming in his throat.

I guess they were going to find out at some point, might as well get it over with now.

"Minisc… Premier."

A buzz filled the room, students turning in all directions to say something to the person beside them. Minisc could pick out some of the lines being thrown around.

"His father is the Hero of Light."

"We share a class with greatness."

"Who is the Hero of Light?"

The last comment caught Minisc off guard. He scanned the classroom, trying to decipher the mouth which those words had left, but had no luck. He did however notice one full-faced grin in the group. Jules sat in the back of the classroom, smiling at his best friend. Finally seeing a friendly face, Minisc let out a content sigh. Even so, he was not out of the spotlight yet, he turned his attention back to his teacher. She continued to give him a glare that could kill.

"Minisc Premier, hmmm… I was warned you'd be in my class. Tardy on the first day. Don't think just because your father helped build this school that I'll let you get away with whatever you want. Do not let this happen again. Now take a seat."

"Yes ma'am, thank you."

Nodding his head in a short bow, Minisc peeled out of the spotlight and headed toward the back of the classroom. There were ten wooden desks split into two rows going back five deep. Two students could fit at each desk.

Minisc walked up the middle of the room, taking his place next to Jules.

"Couldn't help making an entrance, could you?"

"You know me, always looking for the spotlight," Minisc muttered sarcastically.

With the embarrassment momentarily passed, Minisc looked back up at his new teacher, who proceeded to address her students.

"Hello class, my name is Ms. Wright. I'll be your teacher for the next four years while you attend Elemental Academy. You may refer to me as Ms. Wright." The woman held an intimidating presence that spread through the room. Her long-curled copper hair whipped through the air as she turned on a heel to face the classroom again. She grabbed a list off the podium in front of her.

"Please say present when I announce your name. Coro Normanday... Jules Embroider..." She read the names off, with each person raising their hand to signal their presence.

"Lily Martel?" the woman called out.

"Present."

One row in front of Minisc sat a young adolescent girl, her voice soft, sweet, and joyful. It sounded familiar, but he could not place his finger on it. Then he noticed the bright blue ribbon fixed into the girl's hair.

"Is that her?" Minisc whispered under his breath before hearing the call of his name.

"Minisc Premier... Well, we know you're here." Sarcasm dripped off the woman's lips.

Minisc slumped back into his chair.

"Great, she already hates me," he muttered. Feeling a small bump on his shoulder, he turned to see Jules's infectious smile.

"Cheer up, we're in the same class, it's just like old times. This is going to be great."

Minisc let a smile slip as he pulled himself back up to a more proper posture. The upbeat Jules was right; maybe things would be alright.

"Now, you've all been accepted to EA because in one way or another, you have shown some ability that surpasses a normal Elementalist's. Also, I assume most of you want to potentially work for the EC one day as well. As new students we have a few rules to go over, though. First, just because you're in school and learning how to best master your element doesn't mean you have free will to use it all over campus. As first-year students, you'll be restricted to certain classes and designated training times. If I'm informed that you have disobeyed these commands, then I'll be the one deciding the punishment for you. Here at EA, we take the job of preparing the next lineup of students for the EC very seriously. Thousands want to be where you sit right now, which means that you must be prepared to work harder than anyone else to be the best you can be. Once you have done that, you will have to push even further. Only a select few will ever actually make it into the ranks of the EC, but the good news is that will be decided by you, not us. The amount of effort you put in, the level of training and commitment you give in these next four years will make all the difference in your futures."

The room remained silent. A commanding presence was one thing, but this woman instilled fear into each student with just a look.

Ms. Wright proceeded to run down her list of rules, before continuing with her introductory lesson. Time flew by, and soon lunchtime had arrived.

"That's all for this morning. After lunch, I'll be evaluating each student regarding the effectiveness of their element. I need to know where each of you stands; that way, I know where to start. So be prepared. Class dismissed."

Everyone shot up, bolting for the door as if it were a jailbreak.

All except for a few students who directed their attention to Minisc.

"Hey Minisc, why don't you come and have lunch with us?" a tall, black-haired boy asked.

Minisc hesitated before answering.

"Thanks, but I'm going to pass."

"Oh, so what... you think you're too good for us, is that it?" The boy's attitude shifted on a dime. Was everyone going to be as angry when he denied their requests? If so, Minisc would be in for a world of annoyance like he had never seen.

Before Minisc could defend his choice, the group walked out the door, leaving him and Jules as the only two left. It was probably for the best. Minisc had recognized the boy's gleeful, yet devious eyes when Ms. Wright had announced his name. An off-putting look, to say the least. He felt he was being asked because of his father's name, instead of somebody wanting to be actual friends. Typical, but not something Minisc cared for.

"Why did you turn them down?" Jules asked.

Minisc grazed over the question, paying it no mind.

"Come on, let's go."

Reaching down for his black-and-blue backpack, Minisc swung it over his shoulder before heading for the door.

"We finally get to use our element — it's so exciting."

"Yeah, it should be fun." Minisc shrugged nonchalantly. In truth, he was more excited than he let on. Despite his nature to deflect the spotlight, he wanted to show off the hard work he had put in with his father during the summer.

The two cut through the waves of people, finding their way to the third-floor balcony. Jules leaned over the rail taking in the sights and sounds of the café below.

"This place is amazing! Your father did such a good job."

Minisc couldn't help but grin. The enthusiasm his friend was showing filled him with similar excitement.

"Come on, we should grab a table before it gets too busy."

The two made their way down the spiral staircase bringing them to the marketplace.

"Over there, I see an empty table." Jules pointed to the corner of the room, where a freshly cleaned-off table remained barren. The two took seats at opposite ends.

"So what did you think of the other students? Did you see that one with the gray hair? He looked pretty powerful." Jules babbled on, the excitement flowing with each word. He had been studying each of his classmates carefully, sizing them up to see who the competition would be. The school was turning out to be just as competitive as they'd anticipated, and Jules would not be beat. He had a legacy of his own to live up to, and he wanted to be just like his brother, another top student.

"Minisc?"

"Huh? Honestly, I was busy trying to pay attention to what Ms. Wright was saying; she's the most terrifying teacher I think we've ever had."

"Yeah right, you were too busy staring at the girl in front of us."

"What? No I wasn't," Minisc defended while refusing to look his friend in the eyes.

Jules chuckled at the response; he knew he was right.

"I overheard a kid in the front row talking about him — Coro was his name, I think?"

"He was the one that looked stoic the entire time, correct?"

"Yeah him. I heard one of the kids say that Coro's a special exemption student. He's a year younger than what the school allows, but he's incredibly skilled, apparently."

"Really, him? He looked no different than the rest of us."

Minisc tried to picture the boy as an imposing figure with immeasurable power, but he could not see it. To his eye, Coro was nothing more than an average, everyday-looking teenager.

Before long, the two had finished their lunches and were heading off to their next class. The evaluation test.

A brisk autumn breeze swayed the freshly cut grass back and forth. Ms. Wright's class stood lined up in two separate rows like a military squad. They were all donning brand new red and white T-shirts and shorts, the customary training outfit for the school.

The class looked around, checking out each other's new threads. Red trim traced along the cuffs of the neck and armholes of the apparel, and two parallel red stripes lined the sides of each pant leg.

Jules twisted around, stretching his body out.

"These clothes are really comfy, and they look like the EC uniforms."

"Yeah, I kind of like them," Minisc agreed, lifting his arms to the sky, wanting to see how far he could stretch the material. The clothing was lightweight and made of spandex, gripping the boy's muscular arms.

Minisc stood along with Jules in the middle of the front row. Like everyone else, they were fixated on their teacher, who continued to march back and forth like a drill sergeant. Ms. Wright had swapped out her business attire and high heels for long black pants and a navy-blue top along with a silver whistle around her slender neck and a stopwatch in her hand. She fit the role of gym teacher quite well — a far cry from her earlier attire.

She stomped the grass into submission with her white sneakers as she gave her orders.

"Today, we're going to evaluate each of you to see how well you can use your element. This will be a rather simple exercise, so try not to overthink it; I simply need to see what level everyone is at to start the year." She had the group captivated, if not scared, every time she opened her mouth.

The class stood in a mile-long grass field with a steel chain-link fence stretching as far as the eye could see.

"I'll give you one demonstration, so make sure to pay close attention. I will not be doing this again."

Ms. Wright snapped her middle finger and thumb on her right hand together. Sparks ignited, bursting out a tiny reddish-yellow flame that swayed a few centimeters above her bony index finger.

Next, a wooden square target appeared, shooting up from under the grass. It had four painted circles going from large to small as it closed into the center. The outer ring was white, the second blue, and the third black. The innermost and hardest color to hit was red.

The class waited with bated breath as their teacher continued her demonstration. Using a graceful flick of her wrist towards the target, the fireball sprung to life and danced through the air with blazing speed. It struck true, and a puff of smoke engulfed any vision of the innermost ring.

Seconds later, a heavy breeze dispelled the smoke, revealing a small burn mark placed in the center of the target. The inner circle lit up to a bright red, signaling that it had been hit.

The class was left with their mouths agape. It was evident the sheer speed and accuracy of the flame were seemingly unattainable for most. Minisc had seen that sort of display from his father on more than one occasion, but to see it from a teacher felt somehow strange. In his mind, he was still in an ordinary school, but this served as a small reality check. Craning his neck to look around, he could see stunned expressions abundant. Even so, for Minisc, one reaction stood out among the crowd. The steel-haired student Jules had mentioned at lunch: Coro. His face remained cold, lifeless, and most importantly, unimpressed.

"Elements are not unlimited. Everyone has a limit to the amount of power your body can produce. This is why it's key to remain precise while maintaining speed in battle. Now, each of you will be tested with ten targets; your goal is to hit all the targets to the best of your ability. You will be graded on time taken to strike all ten targets, along with your degree of accuracy. Do we have any volunteers?"

Silence fell over the group. After seeing the display of their teacher, nobody wanted to embarrass themselves on the first day. So Ms. Wright turned her harsh gaze toward Minisc.

"Minisc, why don't you start us off — I'm sure your father has taught you something in fifteen years."

Minisc sighed; he'd had a feeling he would end up being used as an example a lot. He had faith that the drill was not overly difficult but also had a feeling that if he went first, it would make him a target for the rest of the class. Many would wear it as a badge of honor to beat him, thinking of it as equivalent to surpassing him in line as the next Hero of Light. The last thing he wanted was everyone trying to prove they were better than the Hero of Light's son on day one. Even so, regardless of the trepidation, Minisc remained far too scared to put up any sort of argument toward his new teacher.

He stepped forward, making sure to put some distance between himself and his classmates.

"On my whistle, you can start," Ms. Wright instructed. She held the whistle to her pursed lips.

Minisc inhaled a deep breath, gradually exhaling as he readied himself. Although he had grown accustomed to using his element, the unrelenting pit in his stomach came from performing in front of a crowd. He took another deep breath, making sure he stayed calm, the wait for Ms. Wright's whistle lasing an eternity.

"Start!"

Simultaneously with the whistle, Minisc's hands began to glow a sparkling yellow. He fired his arms out like a boxer throwing a flurry of punches. Four Lum Bombs exploded out of the boy's palms, racing toward their destined targets. The orbs hung low, grazing the tips of the grass blades, trails of gold light lagging behind. When they inched closer, the spheres sloped up like they had hit a ramp, and with a shattering echo ringing out, the attacks collided with their intended targets. A quick wind blew the veil of smoke away, revealing Minisc's score. The closest target had been a bullseye; the other three had the second-innermost rings glowing. Not a bad start, but he knew he would need to keep that pace to score high. Three targets sprung up ten meters behind the original four, and they fit perfectly between the gaps left from the first wave. Minisc paused for a second. The distance looked far too great to fire off attacks freely for a second time. He would more than likely only hit the outer ring if not miss altogether.

Gripping the grass, he pivoted his foot, aiming at the first target on the left. He grabbed his left wrist with his right hand to keep it steady before one singular blast rocketed from his palm. Lum Missile. A targeting attack Minisc had developed late in the summer thanks to his father. It was far more potent than his Lum Bomb; he could not fire multiple shots at once without straining his body, but its accuracy dwarfed his usual Lum Bomb. Unfortunately, there were still some kinks to be worked out, and the recoil from that much energy was just enough to send the attack off course, mildly grazing the outer left edge of the biggest ring. He quickly pivoted to the middle target.

Well, that was awful. Too bad, I need to move on to the next one. Arching his knees to get a better center of balance, Minisc repeated the same attack. Screaming through the air this time, it made direct contact with the center of the target. He then adjusted his angle for a clean third shot. Repeating his motion, he landed a perfect third hit. Ms. Wright watched with a keen eye, analyzing her student's every movement.

He's unpolished for sure, almost like he's new to using his element, but you can't argue the raw talent is incredible. He certainly takes after his father in that regard, but will he work the way his father did? Only time will tell, I guess.

The next two targets soared fifteen feet into the air, high above the rest. They looked to be at about the same distance as the back targets, but Minisc had no way of being sure. He had only used a total of five attacks, spending little energy in the process, so that left him with plenty of stamina remaining. Before his training, five attacks would have been as much if not more than he could muster, but with his newly developed strength, he could afford to be less cautious. Deducing that the best way to make sure he hit the targets would be a multi-blast attack, Minisc raised his hand in line with his objective. A majestic gold aura outlined his body as a barrage of five balls of light launched from his fingertips. Another Lum Bomb scattershot.

Interesting – sacrificing accuracy to cover more space and ensure he hits his target. Ms. Wright took notice of the laser focus in Minisc's eyes. It was reminiscent of the boy's father within him.

Both barrages landed on the intended targets, the left a bullseye while the right hit the third ring. Minisc stopped to catch his breath. A small tingle built up in his left hand.

"Might have overdone that one." He chuckled. The final target shot high into the sky like a rocket. It hung hundreds of feet in the air, looking like the size of a pea. Keeping his eyes glued as it rose, he saw a blinding light fall from the gods. Minisc squinted as he threw his right arm up to shield against the light.

"Lovely, I can't even see the target, let alone try to hit it," he muttered under his breath. *I could use a barrage attack again, but hitting a target that far away before the blasts spread would be next to impossible. My best shot is one focused attack.*

Inhaling, Minisc raised his left hand, upholding it firmly with his right. He squinted so vigorously that his eyes were almost shut. Only able to see a sliver of his target, he took a wild stab as to where he should aim.

Ms. Wright smirked in anticipation, knowing all too well that the last target caused more than a few of her students headaches. This drill was specifically designed to test not only speed and accuracy, but intellect. With the sun in the way, even the most veteran Elementalists would struggle to land a hit from this distance.

Minisc closed his eyes, calming himself. He channeled his energy and released a blast of light from his palm with a ferocious boom. Since he could not see the target as it soared into the sun, he listened intently, hoping to hear the faint echo of an explosion. But nothing ever came... until finally, he heard the high-pitched screech of his teacher's whistle. Eyes snapping open, Minisc whipped his head to his left, looking at Ms. Wright, who lowered the pipe back around her neck.

"Huh?" Minisc questioned.

"Forty-three seconds; your accuracy was a little spotty, but overall, not horrible." Ms. Wright nodded.

Minisc stood stunned. The target that had once looked like the size of a pea fell glacially back down into focus, and as it slid back, Minisc noticed the outer rim lit up. On the far-right corner he could see a faint mark from his blast. He had grazed it by a paper-thin margin.

Minisc could not resist the urge to smile, realizing that he had received a compliment from his teacher. Not bad might as well have been amazing coming from the disciplinarian.

He turned back and filled the empty spot in line.

"Who's next?"

The rest of the students each took their turn at the target course, with varying success.

"Jules, 1:15 seconds."

"Ivan, 1:45."

With each passing student, the sun started to dip in the afternoon sky. Only two students remained. Lily and Coro.

"Lily, you're up next," Ms. Wright called, readying her whistle again.

Hearing her name called, the brunette stepped out of the line. She looked so frail and innocent, it was hard to believe she could generate any sort of element, let alone fight with it. Not that such trivial things mattered to Minisc. He still stood in line, love filling his eyes as he watched the girl. Jules tried to nudge him but that resulted in nothing more than a failed attempt to bring his friend back to reality.

"Dude, what is with you?" he whispered.

No response.

With the stage all set, Ms. Wright blew her whistle, and the first four targets sprung to life. Lily stood stock-still. She seemed like she was concentrating hard, but with pitiful results. She flung her hand forward and a whimpering stream of water shot out. It failed to even come close to the first target. She turned around with an embarrassed expression.

"Umm, that's sort of the best I can do."

Everyone stared in awe, with murmurs starting to roll through the group.

"That's it? Lily… how did you get accepted to EA if you can't even use your element?" Ms. Wright asked, having never experienced a student with such meager abilities. There was no way she could have passed the entrance exam like that.

"I am rather good at being defensive, I just can't fight very well." Lily spread her arms apart, creating a wall of crystal blue water that acted as a shield. "See?"

"Who is this girl?" Ms. Wright murmured under her breath. "Umm, okay… well you can go back in line, I guess."

I'm going to have to look into that girl. There's no way she made it into this school with such trivial abilities.

Lily retook her place at the end of the line, trying to avoid any awkward stares directed at her.

"That was strange," Jules whispered. He took one look at his friend, seeing Minisc still off in his own world.

"I guess last up will be Coro."

The special exception student stepped forward, his scowl continually etched onto his face. Silence fell over the onlookers. Much like at a typical high school, word of the boy's unique acceptance had spread like wildfire.

Finally, Minisc took his attention away from Lily and stared at Coro, trying to read his hollow expression. He could relate to the boy, the expectations of greatness thrust upon him. Being a special exception student could not be easy. Still, even with those similarities, that did not stop Minisc from being interested in the boy's ability, much like everyone else.

Readying at the whistle, Coro crouched down. A brilliant icy blue glow cloaked his entire body.

"Did it just get colder?" Jules whispered, wrapping his arms around himself. A visible shiver ran up his arms at the noticeable drop in temperature.

The grass underneath Coro's feet froze solid. Even Ms. Wright began shaking.

"This is going to be intense," Minisc whispered.

"Start!"

Before the sound had a chance to fade, a tidal wave of ice darted toward all four targets. If you blinked, you would have missed the action. But you could not miss the aftermath. Glistening ice shimmered as the sun beat down across the newly made ice rink. All four targets were frozen solid.

"Unbelievable," Minisc whispered.

"He's so strong," Jules gawked.

Next, the back three targets sprouted from the ground, ready to accept the fate of their predecessors. Making it look effortless, Coro arched his knees again, releasing a fifteen-foot tidal wave of ice toward its target. Leaving everyone to pick their jaws up off the frozen grass, Coro completed his test. Even Ms. Wright looked stunned. For the second time in minutes, she found herself seeing something like she had never seen before, and from an underage student no less.

How do I even grade that? The entire target is frozen.

The woman hesitated a second, deciding how to proceed. Most students learning to use their power barely had enough energy to hit all ten targets. Students like Minisc and a few others were a rare sight, showing a display of skill and wits at such a young age. However, Coro looked to be on a completely different level. He did not even appear out of breath. It was a surreal display of ability. Having gained sufficient information from her little exercise, she called it a day.

"That's it for today. Go get changed; class dismissed."

CHAPTER 5
HATE RUNS DEEP

THICK BLACK CLOUDS PAINTED THE MORNING SKY AS darkness stretched in all directions. Apple-sized blots of water continued to bounce off the blurry glass while students waited patiently for what had been deemed a big announcement by their teacher. It was just over a week into the school year, and Minisc was slowly trying to adjust to his new way of life. So far, the training portions of class had been basic and easy enough to grasp, but that would only be the beginning.

"What do you think this big announcement is about?" Jules asked his friend and desk neighbor. Minisc, however, answered in silence, paying no attention to his friend, off in his own world.

"Minisc?"

"Huh? Yeah, I'm sure it's just some announcement about classes, nothing that big."

Before Jules could make a rebuttal, the two were interrupted by a twist of the doorknob. Walking in with haste, Ms. Wright wasted no time using her patented deadpan stare to capture everyone's attention. The students fell silent.

"Class, today I will be administering your second test," Ms. Wright announced, taking her rightful place at the head of the classroom. She turned toward the doorway and said, "Come in."

A group of five students walked into the classroom — two girls and three boys, all roughly the same age as Minisc. They stood in front of the podium, both girls on the outside and the boys in the middle. Four of them Minisc did not recognize, but the fifth one, standing in the middle, sent a chill up his spine. He had grown a few inches over the summer, and his hair was not in the pointy black style that it once had been, but instead long, with a minimal gap between hair and shoulder. The change in style had been drastic.

A soft nudge of his shoulder brought Minisc's attention to his best friend.

"Is that Ignis?" Jules asked.

Minisc paused for a second, taking a second look at the boy in the middle.

"Yeah, that's definitely him."

Ignis had been the third boy accepted from Minisc's past school. Luckily they had ended up in a different class, so both boys had been hopeful they'd seen the last of him, but they'd known that was unlikely. Ignis was far from someone to be trifled with. Mostly known for being a bully with a genuine mean streak, he held a particular animosity toward Minisc especially.

Feeling the fiery gaze of his former classmate, Minisc locked eyes with Ignis. Although Ignis had been a menace to the class and to Minisc in particular, Minisc held no hatred toward the bully. When he looked at Ignis, he could see what he believed to be sadness plaguing his eyes. That look of hate was nothing more than fear. Minisc knew that because when the two were young children, he and Ignis had been the best of friends.

****

Shadows grew long as dusk came closer to ending the day while squeaks of rusty steel chains bounced out through the vast open field.

Surrounded by gravel, two kids continued to swing at a modest pace. The playground was quaint, with a dull gray metal swing set fit for two right on the edge of the gravel pit. Off to the right was a rustic slide with patches of the interior looking like they would crumble under even the slightest pressure, and behind them were a small set of monkey bars. Once a bright, metallic red, now they were nothing more than a bronze orange and more of a hazard than a child's plaything. The playground's appearance, ravaged by age, would have kept most children away, but that did little to deter Minisc and Ignis from crowning it their favorite spot. Open grassy fields, the freedom to roam, and a working swing set. What more could two kids ask for?

Besides that, there was a winding cobblestone path that led through a small alley where a gambit of rickety houses resided. It was far from the nicest of areas, but they knew no better. To them, it was a paradise that provided serenity.

Both children's parents were often working with the Elemental Council, spending many days debating laws and regulations for Elementalists. That meant the two kids would spend hours running around, enjoying the freedom of childhood.

One brisk afternoon, the pair were gleefully swinging away when Ignis leaped through the air at the apex of his swing, landing flawlessly with the crunch of gravel bellowing underneath his tiny white sneakers.

Minisc, much more cautious, stuck his feet firmly on the ground, halting his momentum gradually. Chains rattled as the boy sat on the uncomfortable plastic seat.

"Why'd you get off?" Minisc asked in confusion. He took a quick look around to see if his mother or father were coming, but saw neither.

"Hey Minisc, do you ever think about what our parents are doing in there?" Ignis asked, taking his finger and pointing at the posh building.

Minisc looked over with wide, innocent eyes.

"Nope." He shrugged.

He had no interest in the building. The only thing he knew was that his parents went there often, and it meant that he got to go to the rusting playground he had become so fond of. Added to that, it gave him a friend in Ignis.

When it came to personality, Minisc and Ignis were polar opposites. Minisc had always been more timid and cautious, able to find fear in the smallest situations as a child. Never straying too far from the line of good, Minisc would never disobey his parents or act up. Ignis, on the other hand, was a known troublemaker and a reckless risk-taker with a talent for finding trouble.

However, the most significant difference between the two was a subject that Minisc differed on with most being an Elementalist — their interest in elemental abilities, or in his case, lack thereof. Ignis was a budding young star with a fire element to mirror the boy's personality. He also came from a talented family of Elementalists. His mother and father were two of the most powerful original Elementalists in the city. At home, every chance Ignis got, he would practice his element with his father. For his age, he showed exceptional skill.

Minisc himself hailed from the legend of all legends but lacked much desire. He spent much of his time with his mother, who had no element. Although Minisc showed as much potential as Ignis, he just wanted to be a child. That meant no rigorous training or elemental lessons. Sure, he would do a couple with his father to spend time with the man, but he had no desire to work on it every day.

Ignoring his friend's lack of interest, Ignis remained fixated on the building.

"When I grow up, I'm going to work with my daddy," Ignis bragged, opening up his tiny palm to reveal a candle-like, red-and-yellow gradient flame. It swayed mesmerizingly back and forth in the calm wind.

"What are you going to be when you grow up?"

"Don't know." Minisc shrugged his shoulders again. He playfully flung his legs back and forth. "I want to help people like my mommy." Minisc smiled, the innocence of the young child on full display.

"I'm going to beat up bad guys and kick butt."

Ignis swung his fists back and forth like a boxer. Minisc laughed at the boy's brashness.

"We can work together!" Minisc cheered, throwing his fist in the air.

****

Snapping out of his trance, Minisc managed to catch the tail end of his teacher's words.

"You'll be splitting into groups of two, and sparring with a group from one of the other first-year classes."

Jules and Minisc met with the same ecstatic look in their eyes. They would undoubtedly be an unstoppable duo as a team.

"Your groups will be based on your scores in the target exam."

Joy wiped itself off of the friends' faces, their hopes dashed.

Ms. Wright pulled out a list. Going through it name by name, she paired off her students.

"Jules, you'll be with Yuliana."

The woman continued to run down her list until she finally came to a name and hesitated.

"Lily, I don't have you with anyone since you demonstrated no fighting ability. So I guess you'll have to sit out—"

"I'll partner with her," Minisc volunteered, taking everyone by surprise. Lily gracefully spun around in her seat, laying her sea-blue eyes on him. She greeted him with a friendly smile, painting a scarlet-red stroke across Minisc's face.

"Are you okay with that, Lily?" Ms. Wright asked stoically.

"Sounds good to me."

Minisc tried to shake off the embarrassment, averting his eyes back to the front of the room. He caught a glimpse of Ignis, whose expression had not changed since he'd entered the room.

"Now... due to a side bet gone wrong, Ms. Gann's class has the honor of choosing which group they would like to spar with." Her bitter contempt was obvious as she dictated the instructions.

At last, for the first time since arriving, Ignis cracked a sinister grin. It did not go unnoticed by Minisc, and he anticipated what was about to happen next.

"Let's start with Ignis. Who would—"

"Minisc!" the boy shouted, aggressively pointing his finger at his chosen opponent.

Minisc gulped; he knew without a doubt Ignis would choose him if the chance arose. Any opportunity the feisty teen had to take out his frustration on Minisc, Ignis jumped at it.

To make things worse, Ignis was the last person he wanted to spar with.

The rest of the class went off without a hitch. Opponents were selected, and everyone began readily anticipating their post-lunch matches.

Sitting in the middle of the crowded cafeteria, Minisc held his head in his hands. A sense of gloom and doom floating over him.

"Come on, you trained with your father all summer; this will be a good test. Besides, don't you want to get some payback? I mean, he was such a jerk to us."

Jules spoke the truth. Minisc had often been the target of Ignis's rage, but never once had he wanted revenge on the boy. He felt bad for his former friend. Minisc was one of the few people who had memories of Ignis before he'd changed. Unfortunately, words failed to connect with the troubled teen, and seeing eye-to-eye was out of the question.

Minisc picked his head up, displaying a melancholy look. "I don't want revenge; I'd rather just not deal with it at all, frankly."

Before he could drop his head back on the table, Minisc felt a light tap on his shoulder. Sluggishly turning in his seat, he was met with a flawlessly white smile.

"Hey, Minisc," Lily chirped enthusiastically.

"Hello," he mumbled back, hardly recognizing who he was talking to.

"I just wanted to thank you for volunteering to be my partner; it was really sweet of you."

Doom and gloom for a brief moment were replaced by lovestruck beauty once again. Minisc feverishly tried to hide the change in his cheeks' color.

"Why don't you sit and have lunch with us?" Jules piped up, kicking back a nearby chair.

"I'd love to! I don't think I've formally introduced myself. I'm Lily Martel."

The brunette took a seat at the circular table before neatly placing her teal backpack in her lap. Stretching in to grab the contents in the bag, she revealed a series of fruits and vegetables before glancing at Minisc. She noticed the lack of food in front of him and his sad, unconvincing smile.

"Is everything okay?" Her voice sounded like that of a concerned mother — soft, sweet, and nurturing.

"He's fine; he's just nervous about the sparring match after lunch," Jules laughed, brushing off his friend's anxiety.

"We're facing that guy with the scary scowl... Ignis? He seemed really eager to fight with you. Do you know him?"

"Eager is probably not how I'd describe it," Minisc sighed.

"We went to the same school as him. He was a bit of a bully to most of the students, but your poor partner here found himself as the favorite target in class."

"That's terrible; why would anybody do that?"

"It's a long story," Minisc moaned, still wallowing in his misfortune.

"Well, I'm all ears."

Minisc picked his head back up, confused. That warm smile was once again directed at him. Figuring no harm would come from Lily knowing, Minisc decided to explain the bitter past.

"Umm... okay, well it's like this."

****

"You don't know what it's like! He could have saved them; he's supposed to be a hero, why didn't he save them!"

Minisc hit the dirt. Ignis loomed large over him, tears streaming down his puffy red cheeks. The boy's fists were curled up in rage. All Minisc could do was stay on the ground, at a loss for words. He was frightened, but even more so, he was broken. Words were being shouted at him through a stream of tears, and his best friend hated him for an incident he'd had no part in. Minisc did not know how to respond to it all.

"I hate the Hero of Light; I hate him and I hate you!"

The words cut Minisc like a knife, and he was powerless to defend against it. He remained frozen on the ground while Ignis bolted down the cobblestone walkway, disappearing around the corner of the alley.

Left all alone, Minisc found himself spinning around on the swings. Thick gray rainclouds started to mask the once-beautiful blue sky. As he fought off the tears while his mind raced around, raindrops slowly fell, splashing on the boy's drooping face. Minisc would stay there, swaying back and forth as he gradually became soaked from head to toe. His blond hair fell in front of his eyes, hiding the sadness that filled him.

A few days prior, an incident had taken place along the Toronto lakefront. A gang of rogue humans had set up an ambush to lure the Hero of Light to his untimely demise. However, before the rogues could execute their plan, the EC had caught wind of the attack and set up a counter unit. Minisc's father, along with both of Ignis's parents, had been part of the group. Unfortunately, the battle that ensued had produced several casualties on both sides, and Ignis lost both of his parents in the struggle.

Devastated, scared, and alone, Ignis started looking for someone to blame his sorrow and anger on. That burden turned to Minisc and Minisc's father. Ignis held an unwavering belief that the Hero of Light could have, and more importantly should have, saved his parents. But Don had not; he could not. Still, that fact would not bring any peace to the newly orphaned boy.

****

"Ignis was forced to live in an orphanage that despised Elementalists. I know he was treated horribly. The family was abusive to him, and he holds my father personally responsible for the death of his parents. I guess since he couldn't take out his anger toward my father, he started to take it out on me."

Lily flashed a sad smile at her new friend.

"That's horrible; it's not like it was your fault, you were just a child. I can't believe someone would hold that much of a vendetta against you."

Minisc let out a heavy sigh.

"Well, believe it."

"One question, though. Who is the Hero of Light?"

"Who is... what?"

Minisc's jaw hit the table, while Jules nearly fell out of his seat from shock. The duo stared at the girl like she had grown a second head. Lily responded with a puzzled look of her own.

"Excuse me!" Jules exclaimed as he pulled himself back into his seat.

"Wait... do you really not know who the Hero of Light is?" Minisc asked in disbelief. He had never met someone who had not heard the tales of his father's heroics.

"Nope." She gave an innocent, if not ignorant smile.

"Have you been living under a rock your whole life?" Jules asked, still trying to wrap his head around what he felt was a grave injustice to the history of the world.

"No, my parents just didn't like me talking about anything Elemental. They just wanted me to try and fit into society most of my life."

Minisc decided to interject before Jules fainted from his surprise.

"Still, don't you read books, or papers?"

Lily shook her head.

"So you know nothing about Luminosa, the Hero of Light, or even really Elementalists then?"

"Nope. That's part of the reason I came here, I wanted to learn more about who I am as an Elementalist."

Seriously, how did this girl ever get accepted?

"Well I'll sum it up for you real quick," said Minisc, "Back when Elementalists were first being born, and starting to populate the world, humans treated us like monsters. They would attack us, enslave us, and even try to kill some Elementalists. That's when Luminosa started to form. They were a group of Elementalists who had grown tired of being looked down upon, so they decided to revolt. Led by their leader, Dusk, who had created the idea of a world without humans, eventually Luminosa started to eradicate humans all over the city, and the government had no way to stop it."

"That's where the Hero of Light comes in." Jules jumped back into the conversation. "He banded together with other Elementalists to stop Luminosa, and the Hero of Light defeated Dusk, sending Luminosa packing! After that day, humans started to see the error of their ways, and the two races over time managed to mend fences and work as one cohesive society. More or less, anyways. That's why the Hero of Light is beloved. And best of all... he happens to be the father of your partner."

Lily shifted her focus to the other side of the table, where Minisc sheepishly nodded his head.

"That's so cool! Your father is a hero," Lily squealed.

Minisc nodded in embarrassment, not sure if he should be happy that Lily had never heard of his father or worried that now that she knew, she would become like all the others.

Jules, reading his friend's lack of interest in the current topic, decided to throw him a lifeline.

"So you can't use any offensive attacks with your element, and you didn't know about the Hero of Light. How did you end up at this school anyway?"

"My mother is a human and my father has a tiny bit of earth element, so they couldn't teach me much. I learned a small number of defensive skills, but my mother did not condone any forms of violence. So I was never taught how to use my element in that way, but I really wanted to come here and learn more about Elementalists and how to be a better one. So I took the exam and I guess they saw something in me that made them accept me." Taking a look at her watch, she reached for her bag. "Oh, I almost lost track of time. I'm going to get changed for class. I'll see you guys in a bit." With a wave and a smile, Lily headed off.

"Well, that was weird. She seems interesting, though. At least you have good taste in people," Jules joked as he got up from the table.

"Yeah, she's nice... Wait, what do you mean at least? I chose you, didn't I?"

"That's definitely not how I remember it. Regardless, we need to get to the gym — Ms. Wright will have us in detention for a week if we're late."

"Yeah, that's not a bad idea." Minisc nodded in agreement.

The gym resided in a separate building next to the central school, but it was only a quick walk up the blacktop road to the luxurious building.

Trees lined the path before branching out into the squares of freshly cut grass that filled out the front. About half the size of the primary school, it had a sleek design, a far cry from the school itself. Two triangular roofs came together with a small gap between them, and outlined in a solid white trim were square glass panels reflecting the now-cloudy sky as they stacked up against the sides of the roof. Steel beams sliced each panel in half to form patterned triangles mirroring the shape of the roof, and a steel coat of paint covered the exterior of the base. Bright white pillars lifted up a small awning that shaded the entrance of the facility. Hanging off the awning were the customary flags that Minisc had seen on his first day. They represented all the elemental types.

Minisc and Jules looked the unique structure up and down.

"Are you sure this is the right place?" Jules asked.

"Do you see another building behind the school?"

"But this place is so huge; I thought we were just going to the gym?"

"Well, only one way to find out. Come on, let's go."

The glass doors slid open, revealing a magnificent stadium waiting room. To the boys' left were changing rooms and to the right were large doors that led to another locked-off section of the gym.

Minisc and Jules walked forward to a viewing section at the north end. Peering over the railing into the lower bowl of the building, they saw that the massive drop below led to a humongous rectangular arena. It reminded Minisc of the makeshift stage he'd trained in all summer. This one, however, was far more glamorized, with thick white chalk outlining the boundaries. The field was made of dirt but was maintained to the point that it looked more like brown cement. Added to that, spotlights circled the steel rim of the roof, lighting every square foot of the battleground in bright white rays.

"Imagine fighting in an arena like that; it would be so cool!" Jules exclaimed, making no effort to mask his enthusiasm.

Minisc and Jules turned back into the lobby just in time to see Ms. Wright walk into the building. She was accompanied by another woman. The unrecognizable teacher was a good head taller than her counterpart, with short blonde hair and a much wider smile.

"Hello, Ms. Wright," the boys chimed in unison.

"Boys, this is Ms. Ganns, and we'll be sparring with her class today. Ms. Ganns, this is Jules, and that would be Don's kid."

"You got Don's kid? Come on, why do you get all the good students?" Ms. Ganns pouted, folding her arms. She appeared to be the polar opposite of the stoic statue of an instructor they were stuck with.

"Have you boys been here before?" the peppy woman asked.

"No, actually we were just checking out the giant stadium over there." Minisc gestured to the viewing area they had left.

"It's so cool; I'd love to get down there," Jules said, beaming with excitement.

"Well then, I have good news for you. Go get changed and take the door beside the girls changing room down underneath, because that's where class is taking place today," Ms. Ganns instructed. She had the same glow as Jules, who looked elated.

Looking around the stadium from the inner dome provided a spectacular sight for the class. The lights seemed to shine even brighter when on the field of battle, and fifty feet up and climbing were rows and rows of seating, just like a sports stadium.

Minisc stood in unison with his classmates, Lily on his left and Jules on his right, while ten feet across from them were their sparring partners for the day. The enemy uniforms were inverted, with white trimming around a red base shirt and shorts. Ms. Wright addressed her class sternly as Ms. Gann's class did a corny cheer. Minisc, paying no attention to the words of his teacher, focused across the gym. He took notice of the one person who remained separated from the other class's group, leaning up against the wall. As expected, Ignis did not take part. The boy had no interest in camaraderie or relationships. He had one goal, the desire to avenge his parents permanently etched in his mind. In a way, Minisc found the boy's convictions admirable. The troubled Ignis had a belief and refused to let go of it. Minisc just wished it did not involve him.

"Minisc and Lily, you'll be up first."

Minisc heard his name and snapped his head back to look at his teacher. He winced seeing the daggers posing as eyes staring back at him.

"Go stand at the center of the gym." She pointed to the large circle outlined in chalk.

"As for the rest of you, take the elevator up to the stands. Make sure to pay close attention to this match — you can learn a lot from your fellow classmates."

Jules bumped fists with Minisc and said, "Don't overthink this," before following the other students to an elevator stationed in the far-left corner of the floor.

Following Ms. Wright's instructions, Minisc and Lily stood in one half of the circle while Ignis and another shorter boy mirrored them on the other side. Ignis stood confident, his chest puffed out and fiery sparks in his eyes. His partner, on the other hand, showed no such confidence. Short and a little pudgy, the boy's knees were cackling together. A look of petrification expressed his fear perfectly.

Ms. Wright took charge in explaining the rules of the bout.

"Okay, listen up— Ms. Ganns and I will be the referees for this match, so no going overboard. The rules are simple: if either you or your partner exit the ring, you lose. We will step in if things get out of hand. We don't need anybody dying on us."

"Um, Ms. Ganns, has anyone ever died here?" the ghostly pale kid asked with unmistakable concern in his voice.

"No Jacob, nobody has ever died in a class before," Ms. Ganns assured.

"Well, there was that one kid…" Ms. Wright trailed off, watching the eyes of her students grow to the size of saucers. Jacob lost all color in his face.

"I'm kidding. Jeez, can't take a joke anymore?" she mumbled as the students breathed a sigh of relief. "Now go take your positions."

Taking their place, Minisc stood a half-step ahead of Lily. He turned around to see his partner wearing an enthusiastic smile.

"You ready, partner?"

"You're rather cheerful for someone who is about to be in a fight," Minisc replied, confused by the girl's blissful ignorance. She had no clue what she was about to be swept up in. Still, her positivity was a welcomed boost for what Minisc knew would be a less-than-enthusiastic experience.

"It'll be fun!"

She realizes she doesn't know how to actually fight, doesn't she? Minisc thought to himself as he turned his attention back to his opponents. A decision he would regret. He looked at Ignis, who had rage in his voice.

"I'm going to destroy you, Minisc."

"Lovely."

"Each team will have three minutes to create a strategy. Think wisely about your element, your physical strengths and weaknesses, and your opponents' strengths and weaknesses," Ms. Wright advised as she took her spot off the arena floor at the halfway point.

"Good luck, and remember to have fun," Ms. Ganns cheered.

Minisc and Lily huddled up to discuss their strategy.

"So what do you think we should do, Minisc? You know Ignis well, so you must know some of his weaknesses?" Lily whispered.

"Well, to tell you the truth, Ignis doesn't have a lot of weaknesses. He's pretty good at everything. However, the one flaw I could see working in our favor is that I don't think he is going to work with Jacob. Ignis is not about being part of a team. If I had to bet, he'll attack on his own accord—ferociously, but recklessly. Ignis knows how to make use of his fire element, but because you can use water, we might be able to counter it." Minisc put his hand to his chin, thinking of how best to utilize the duo's skills. Having a partner who had no actual battle experience acted as a handicap, but that did not mean Lily would be useless. Minisc just needed to think of the best way to utilize what she could do, and he would have to take care of the rest.

On the other end of the arena, Jacob said, "Shouldn't we think of a plan?" He stood a few steps behind Ignis, his knees still shaking violently.

"Stay out of my way; how's that for a plan?" Ignis fired back, not even turning to face his partner.

"Time's up."

Ms. Wright blew her whistle, signaling the fight was about to start. Each team took their positions and waited intently for the go-ahead. Ignis glared at Minisc, who attempted to avert his eyes from the boy at all costs.

"This exercise is to teach you to work in conjunction with your partner. So be sure to make use of your element, along with your partner's," Ms. Wright bellowed out from the sidelines.

"Yeah, whatever," Ignis spat as he crossed the centerline.

"Let's do this!" Lily cheered, giving her best look of intimidation. Minisc cracked a small smile, seeing what amounted to no more than a cute, goofy grin on his partner's face.

"On my count. Three... Two... One..." Ms. Wright blew her whistle.

The fight began with Ignis baring down, his hands bursting into raging flames. He flung a fireball the size of a basketball at Minisc, but before it could present itself as a threat, Lily slid in for the save. She clapped her hands together, creating a watery barrier all around the two. With a sizzling singe, the fireball was doused as it made contact with the shield, leaving a trail of steam behind. Even though Lily could not attack, she clearly had some power to her.

Ignis came to a screeching halt, watching his opening move doused.

"Good job Lily," Minisc said, encouraging his partner. She might not have been able to provide offensive support, but Minisc still figured she could prove to be a valuable asset defensively. Ignis defined hyper-aggressive, using an all-out attack mentality. With his fire element being so overwhelming, using Lily's water element to even the playing field was the best strategy Minisc could think of on the fly.

"Now it's my turn to go on the offensive."

Taking the lead position, Minisc rushed headlong into battle, returning fire with a series of Lum Bombs scattered at Ignis's feet. Tiptoeing backward to avoid being hit, Ignis could not find time to regain his balance. That was Minisc's part of the plan; he wanted to keep Ignis off balance at all times. Forcing him to expend his energy on the defensive side of the fight would ensure that his incredible offensive ability would not factor into the match.

Finding himself pushed back to the edge, Ignis thrust his right arm out, casting a raging horizontal flame. Minisc did the same, and the two attacks clashed with an ear-wrenching boom.

"I really think we should have come up with a strategy," Jacob mumbled, still standing at the edge of the ring.

"Shut up and stay out of my way, got it?" Ignis spat back. The boy's arm began to glisten a twilight red.

Jacob sighed, but it was one of relief. He seemed content with not participating in the match.

"Ignis has incredible potential," said Ms. Wright, watching the battle unfold. "He's tenacious and relentless, but far too careless with his strategies. Brute force will only get you so far without a plan of attack."

Ms. Wright looked over at the other woman, who maintained a goofy energetic smile, before nodding her head.

"Ignis has all the potential in the world, but he doesn't fight using his head, only his fists. Rage can be effective, but eventually, that fire runs cold. Refusing to work with his partner will prove troublesome as the fight drags on."

Ignis burst forward, sparks flying off his shoes as he moved. Before Minisc could blink, he wound up dodging for his life. Powerful swings came at him over and over—left jab, right hook, uppercut. Dancing like a boxer, on instinct he bobbed and weaved, trying to keep up with Ignis's overwhelming speed. The two exchanged glancing blows at high speed.

Looking for an opening, Minisc ducked under a high fist and landed a jarring blow to Ignis's rib cage. Flipping through the air, the other boy managed to land on his feet, though staggered. His eyes became even more cross, a fit of rage boiling up in him. Both his arms became engulfed in fierce flames. He gritted his teeth, letting out a ferocious roar.

"I'll never lose to the likes of you!"

A marvelous stream of fire roared toward Minisc, but jumping in front again, Lily enveloped the flames with a liquid barrier. Unfortunately, unlike last time, Ignis continued the stream, gradually raising the intensity of the fire with each passing second.

"Let's turn up the heat!"

Lily gritted her teeth, trying to hold steadfast. Her legs were beginning to wobble.

"Minisc, I can't hold this much longer; it's too powerful," Lily cried, her arms beginning to shake.

"I'm on it! Just hold it a little longer."

Stepping out from behind the left side of the shield, Minisc gripped his left wrist tightly in his right. A blinding flare of light encircled his hand.

"Predictable!"

Pivoting his left foot, Ignis quickly crossed his right hand over his left, discharging a second raging firestream.

"Oh crap!" Minisc yelled, panicking as the gap closed between him and third-degree burns. Even though he had not drawn up the amount of energy that he would have liked, Minisc had no choice but to counter with what he had. Inches from the flames burning him to a crisp, he launched the sun-like energy sphere. Flames ricocheted in all directions.

Sweat dripped from the tips of his hair; the flames were scorching.

If I don't figure something out quick, I'm going to have a wicked sunburn.

Fighting off the flames, Minisc caught a glimpse of Jacob out of the corner of his eye. The boy had not moved an inch off the starting spot, still scared stiff. An idea popped into Minisc's mind, and he immediately started mentally kicking himself for not realizing it earlier.

We've been going about this all wrong — Ignis shouldn't be our target, Jacob should be!

Ideas started to bounce back and forth in the boy's mind, but as he readied himself to switch targets, he heard a voice cry out.

"Minisc, I can't hold the flames off any longer," Lily screamed in agony.

Out of his peripherals, he could see the girl trembling, pain filling her eyes.

No, this isn't good. What do I do? Lily's hanging on by a thread... but if I hit Jacob once, we win.

Time felt like it was slowing down, but Minisc's mind started racing at double speed. He had no time for indecision; he had one opportunity.

"Minisc, I'm... sorry," Lily said, letting out an audible gasp before dropping to her knees. The once-fortified water barrier shattered, creating a rainstorm around the battlefield.

A crashing thud bellowed out as Minisc smacked the ground, with his left shoulder taking the brunt of the force. Bouncing off the unforgiving dirt, he rolled through the air, skidding to a stop inches from the out-of-bounds line. A few feet away, Lily lay motionless.

"What just happened?" a student asked, looking at the carnage below.

Jules watched his friend, trying to answer the same question.

"Minisc not only managed to shed the flamethrower that had him pinned, but also grabbed Lily and dove out of the way before they were both engulfed in flames," Jules whispered under his breath, "That was incredible."

Lily's eyes fluttered open. She found herself staring at Minisc, who looked to be in rough shape. The left side of his shirt was singed, with a beet-red burn mark on his arm.

"Minisc?" she called out weakly.

Minisc pushed himself to one knee, his arms tender as he applied pressure. He glanced at Lily, seeing her maintaining that beautiful smile despite the pain.

"Are you okay?" he asked.

"Thanks to you I am, but I don't think I'll be much help anymore."

Even as weak as the girl was, she still had an upbeat tone. She attempted to lift herself up but could not muster the strength.

"That was a close one." Minisc's voice was raspy as he tried to catch his breath. Looking back at Ignis, he could see a pained expression. Minisc recognized it right away. Muscles tense and bulging, shortness of breath, and sweat dripping slowly off his brow. It matched the look of someone who had overexerted themselves and now suffered the consequences.

Ms. Ganns smirked as she side-eyed her stoic companion. "Don's kid is pretty impressive, I must say. To have the wherewithal to use his blast and shield himself just enough to save his partner? Not too many people would think to even try that."

Ms. Wright remained silent for a moment, analyzing the stunt Minisc had pulled. Then she spoke. "He directed his attack in unison with the movements of his body to cut off the stream of fire, almost like a shield of his own, and he maintained it just long enough for him to make it to Lily. Then, while grabbing her with his left arm, he fired off a brief but effective blast, stalling Ignis's flamethrower with his right. That bought him just enough time for both of them to hit the ground. It could not have been more than a few seconds that he had to come up with an idea like that, and fractions of a second for his margin of error. Not only that, but the unwavering desire to save his partner. This kid... he's more like Don than I gave him credit for."

Minisc stared down Ignis; he knew the both of them were battered and bruised, but he held the advantage. Ignis had spent an exorbitant amount of energy. Hastily attacking both Lily and him at once was a reckless, if not an outright dumb strategy. His tank had to be running on empty. Minisc still had a little bit of energy left, and when it came to willpower, he had plenty left. Even knowing that, Minisc did not want to show his hand quite yet. Instead, he opted for hand-to-hand combat, charging full-tilt at Ignis.

"What do you think you're doing!" the other boy shouted, holding his hands out, ready to uncork another wave of flames. Nevertheless, Minisc showed no worry; he knew Ignis was bluffing.

Ignis stood like a statue; his attacks wouldn't form. A look of terror overcame the boy as Minisc closed in.

"Face it, Ignis, you have nothing left—you used all your energy on Lily's shield."

Throwing his left arm up instinctively, Ignis blocked the incoming punch. He gritted his teeth from the tenderness of his forearm, seething pain making every nerve in his body scream.

Minisc continued relentlessly, watching as Ignis winced with each glancing blow.

Now's my chance! Minisc thought as his opponent came dangerously close to the left corner of the arena. He reached deep within, drawing on all of his energy. Finally, he would beat Ignis.

As he went to unleash the finishing blow, Minisc's body went numb. A surge of electricity coursed through his muscles, dropping him like a stone. The boy splashed into a small puddle of water, his senses disappearing as the room faded to black.

CHAPTER 6
WITHOUT A SHADOW OF A DOUBT

MS. GANNS QUICKLY WHISTLED THE BATTLE DEAD, throwing her hand in the direction of Ignis.

"Ignis and Jacob win."

All the students went silent. A pin could have dropped, and it would have sounded like a boulder. Minisc lay flat on his stomach in a puddle of water. Motionless. Lily let out a gasp, covering her mouth with her hands as she saw her partner down.

Calls from the students could be heard before applause erupted.

"What just happened?"

"I thought Minisc was going to win for sure!"

"That was exciting, I can't wait for my turn."

Ms. Ganns turned to her friend with a sly smirk.

"Looks like you get to teach health class this year... Have fun."

Without missing a beat, Ms. Wright shot a petrifying look at her co-worker.

Tick tock... Tick tock...

The clock hanging on the wall read 4:45 p.m. Classes had ended almost two hours prior, and everyone had gone home for the night. At least almost everyone. Minisc lay peacefully on a narrow bed, his hands intertwined together, resting on his chest. An arch at the top of the bed supported the boy's head, which rested firmly on the single pillow allotted. Next to the bed was a small white table where two orange capsules and a glass of water resided.

Eventually, a nurse clothed in all white walked into the room. She looked to be in her early sixties, with short silver locks covering her oval ears. As she closed the door, Minisc's eyes snapped open.

"Well look who decided to finally wake up, I was getting worried I'd have to be here all night," the nurse joked as she picked up a clipboard, flipping through the pages. "Minisc, was it? Well, good news—you should make a full recovery. You young folks have it so easy. If I had electricity surge through these withered old bones, I'd be dead." She let out a hearty laugh as Minisc stared at her in confusion.

He tried to think back to what had happened prior, but his memories continued to escape him. He remembered being in class, and then he was fighting Ignis. He had the match won, and then the next thing he knew, he woke up in a hospital bed.

"Excuse me, but do you mind explaining what happened? How did I end up here?"

"You died," the woman deadpanned.

"I did... what?" Minisc blurted, sitting straight up, his eyes nearly popping out of their sockets.

The woman started to laugh at the frightened expression she had caused.

"I'm kidding. Gee willikers, you kids need to lighten up. You're just fine. Took a little jolt through the body, and you didn't have the strength to withstand it, so you blacked out. No big deal."

Minisc dropped back down onto the pillow again, muttering coldly.

"Woman tells me I'm dead, then tells me to relax like it's not a big deal... Who is this nurse, anyways?"

Paying the boy's mumbling no mind, the nurse walked over to a desk across from Minisc's bed. Pulling a drawer out, she reached in and grabbed a stethoscope.

Minisc let his heart settle back into his chest before glancing at the clock, which now read 4:50 p.m.

"Oh crap, I'm going to miss my train!"

Throwing his legs over the side of the bed, Minisc hastily prepared to leave, but before he could escape, a stern voice stopped him.

"Not so fast, bucko — you're not going anywhere." The nurse spun around, crisply eyeing Minisc. Chills crawled down the boy's spine.

"Huh?"

"Lift your shirt up."

Before Minisc could process the words, the nurse yanked his shirt up, revealing a heavily bruised abdomen. He flinched as the cold touch of steel pressed against the left side of his chest.

"Hey, that's cold!" Minisc whined.

"Hush up. Now breathe in as deep as you can."

Minisc inhaled following the instructions, his chest puffing out to its full size.

"Exhale."

He let out a long, drawn-out breath with the nurse listening to the steadiness of airflow. Once done, she nodded in confirmation, removing the metal tool from around her neck.

"Okay, you seem to be breathing fine, and your heart rate is good. Just take the pills on the bedside table and you're free to go."

Minisc hopped off the bed, puzzled.

"Umm, thank you?"

He looked back up at the clock again, taking note of the little amount of time he had until the next train. If he missed it, he would be waiting at least another hour or so.

Following the nurse's instructions, he grabbed the pills and tossed them down the back of his throat, following it up with a swig of water. A hearty gulp later and he was on his way.

Minisc made his way through the deserted halls. It was hard to imagine such a heavily occupied building during the day could be so barren in its after-hours.

Reaching his locker, Minisc cracked the combination, but to his surprise, and panic, the storage unit appeared empty. Backpack, wallet, phone, all missing.

"I cannot catch a break today," Minisc said, bitterly slamming the locker shut. He slumped as he made his way toward the entrance of the school.

"First I lose to Ignis and embarrass myself in front of Lily, then I end up in the infirmary, and now I lose my phone and my wallet. How am I even supposed to get home?" Minisc sighed. This new chapter of his life had not started on the right foot.

As he reached the entrance of the school, he continued looking at the ground, moping, until he heard his name called.

"Minisc!"

Before he could look up, Minisc became engulfed in a violent but caring hug. Still confused about what was happening, he heard the same voice start to pepper him with questions.

"Are you okay? Please tell me you're not hurt? I'm so sorry!"

Minisc finally looked up to learn that the girl in question was his partner and new friend, Lily. Minisc stood stunned, failing to free himself from the girl's bind.

"Lily? What are you still doing here?"

She finally released him, wiping away tiny pools of water into her jean jacket sleeve.

"I was waiting for you; I was worried that you might have been seriously hurt. I didn't want to leave until I knew you were okay."

For a second Minisc could not help but smile, and a warm, comforting sensation filled his body. He had been worried that Lily might act differently, realizing who his father was, but clearly that was not the case. She showed genuine kindness toward him, and for a brief moment, despite the disastrous day, he had found a sole bright spot.

Minisc returned the kindness with a sheepish smile. He still got nerves when talking to Lily, but something about communicating with the girl seemed natural. Like they had known each other forever, even if it had only been a day or so. She had a kind, easy-going personality, endearing herself to everyone she met.

"Well, thank you, but you didn't need to wait for me. I'm fine."

"That's okay, I did all my math homework while I was waiting!" Lily chimed, "Oh, I have your school bag and clothes as well."

Moving out of Minisc's line of sight, she revealed his black-and-blue backpack leaned up against hers. Minisc let out a sigh of relief, anxiety plummeting as he saw all his belongings neatly placed on the top step. He looked down to realize he was still wearing his tattered gym clothes. He'd never noticed.

"And I also have your phone." Lily reached into her jacket pocket and pulled out the device, handing it to Minisc. "Your father called as well. We had a nice talk. I told him you were going to be late."

"Wait. You talked to my father?"

Lily let out a cute, airy laugh, looking at the boy's frantic face.

"He called, and I picked up. He was worried that you hadn't come home, so I explained what happened and told him I was waiting for you. For being a famous hero, he was very nice."

Who is this girl? Minisc thought to himself, taking a few seconds to process what was no doubt one of the more bizarre exchanges he had been a part of.

Checking his phone again, Minisc knew he had to hurry if he would make the last train. As if reading her friend's mind, Lily made a new suggestion.

"We should head to the train station. The last train will be arriving soon."

"Sounds good." Minisc nodded, picking up the blue bag and handing it to Lily.

He swung his own bag around his shoulders, and the two walked down the sidewalk, EA fading into the distance. Despite the hellish afternoon, Minisc felt much happier now that he was walking down the street with Lily.

The train flew down the tracks like a speeding bullet as the sun began to set. A deafening silence filled the cabins, with most riders longing for quiet after a long day of work. Minisc and Lily sat across from each other in the back of the middle cabin. Minisc struggled to stay awake. His body was beginning to realize the extent of his activities, and the pills seemed less than effective. On the other side, Lily sat quietly looking around the train. Eventually, she made her way to the poster plastered on the far wall, one with a muscular man giving a thumbs-up. She read the words underneath it.

"Always ride with the Hero of Light," she whispered under her breath. She turned to look at a sleepy Minisc. "Is that your father on the poster?" she asked, signaling to the picture.

Without the need to look where Lily pointed, Minisc knew exactly what she had seen.

"Yeah, that's him," he nonchalantly responded.

"You didn't even look?"

"Trust me, it's him, he's on every poster in the city."

Lily furrowed her brow, sensing a bit of frustration coming from Minisc.

"Do you not like your father?" she asked softly.

Minisc's head snapped up to see the girl's worrying smile.

"What? No, it's not like that," Minisc fretted, "Sometimes I just get tired of his fame, that's all. In case you haven't noticed, everyone sort of expects me to be him. All the training, the autographs, the spotlight, fake friends, strangers—some days it just grows old. Or you get people like Ignis who want to prove how much better they are than me. I'm not really one for the spotlight. That's all."

"Oh, I guess I didn't think about it like that. Well, try to look on the bright side—I'm your friend, and I had no clue who your father was!" Lily gave Minisc a bright smile, making his frustrations quickly evaporate.

"Yeah, I guess you're right." Minisc returned the gesture.

Placing his hand on the armrest as he tried to readjust, he let out a feeble wince. Quickly, he reached for his right arm. The same one that had been grazed by Ignis in battle. He rolled up his sleeve to reveal a nasty red bruise and burn.

"That looks painful."

Lily tugged the ribbon in her hair. The small strand of cloth came undone, causing her hair to fall past her shoulders. Holding the fabric over her right hand, she took her left and sandwiched it together. A faint blue glow coated her palms, fading away a few seconds later. The cloth let out a teardrop of water onto the floor.

"Here, keep this on the burn; it should help." She tied the cloth tightly around Minisc's bicep. He winced again as she pulled the string to create a cute bow.

"Thanks; it feels better already."

"It's the least I could do; after all, none of this would have happened if you hadn't tried to rescue me," Lily lamented.

"I wouldn't worry about it too much. I got so focused on Ignis that I didn't even notice Jacob, or the water. My father would have expected better than that."

A brief silence fell over the two.

"Still... thank you. If I came home looking like that, my mother would pull me out of school before sunrise."

"Well, I'm glad that won't happen." Minisc laughed.

Lily, growing more curious about her newfound friend, decided to flip the subject.

"So everyone talks about your father, but what's your mother like?" she inquired.

"Actually... my mother passed away when I was little."

Minisc whispered the words, watching the color drain out of Lily's stunned face.

"Oh my gosh; I'm so sorry, I didn't mean —"

"Lily, it's okay. You didn't know," Minisc tried to reassure the mortified girl. "I don't have a ton of memories, but the ones I do have are some of my fondest growing up. She was always so kind and loving. We used to go on lots of adventures when I was young. My father was often busy working with the Elemental Council or the police force, so my mother would take me out to explore places around the house. Our home backs onto a forest that my mother and I would walk through all the time. Lying under the trees, listening to the birds, it was so peaceful."

Minisc reminisced, a smile overcoming him as he thought back to those memories. He looked back up at Lily, her fair complexion restoring from the pale, terrified look of moments ago.

"That sounds really sweet."

"She also worked endlessly to stop prejudices toward Elementalists and humans after the whole Luminosa disaster as well. Her dream was to have everyone live in peace together. Actually, she's the reason I chose to go to EA in the first place. I wanted to fulfill her dream of making the world a better place. To be able to help people in need. Human or Elementalist."

"That's wonderful." Lily paused for a second, "Actually, I think that's why my parents never let me practice my element growing up. They were worried that I'd be looked at differently or picked on and bullied. When I was first going to school, I started at a human-only school, but the teachers didn't want to teach me because I was subhuman. I was shunned for a long time, until my parents decided to pull me out of school. So I never really got to experience the good parts of what it's like to be an Elementalist." Lily looked sad for the first time since she had started school. She always seemed so chipper, but she had been carrying a fear with her all along.

"I guess because of who my father is, I never really had to worry too much about the negatives of being an Elementalist. I knew that even after the events with Luminosa were over, many Humans were still fearful of us, but I didn't realize it was that bad."

"It's okay—now I get to start a whole new adventure with new people. I already made a friend, and that's more than I could say at my last school. And I finally get to use my water element. I was born with it. I never understood why it was such a bad thing to use it." She cheered up.

Unfortunately, as the two continued to talk, a robotic male voice interrupted the conversation.

"Aurora, next stop Aurora."

"Oh, that's my stop." Lily sighed; her face drooped while those around her piled out.

Minisc echoed those sentiments. He would have ridden the train all night to keep talking to Lily.

With the train screeching to a halt, Lily stood up to make her way to the doors.

"It was fun getting to talk to you, Minisc; I'll see you on the train tomorrow?"

"I'll be waiting for you."

And with their parting words, she was gone.

After the rest of his train ride and a short walk, Minisc could see his cozy home over the horizon. A thin veil of clouds cloaked the soft moonlight. He was once again begging for the sight of his bed and a nice weekend rest. It had been a long and taxing week of school, and he could use some rest and relaxation, especially trying to let the annoyance of losing to Ignis fade from his mind. However, when Minisc reached the door, he saw a flash light up the sky.

"Was that lightning? Odd, it doesn't feel like it's going to rain."

He walked through the door, noticing that none of the lights were on, an unusual occurrence. In fact, the house was silent. Minisc stopped in his tracks, a strange pit forming in his stomach.

Minisc called out, "Father? I'm home... are you here?" to no reply.

"Alright, that's strange." Minisc flipped a switch, lighting up the empty hallway. With each step farther into his home, that pit in his stomach sank further.

The eerie silence unnerved the boy more and more. He took cautious peeks into each room down the hall, failing to find his father in any of them. Anxiously making his way to the kitchen, he caught another glimpse of blinding light through the patio door.

That wasn't lightning, it was an attack. That notion was more than enough to set Minisc into a panic, his mind jumping to the worst. The boy flung his backpack to the ground and ripped the back door open.

Another unexpected flash lit up the night sky and the ground shook like an earthquake, staggering Minisc in his sprint. Feeling his heart leap into his throat, he picked up his pace, speeding through the ghostly forest.

"Father, please be okay..."

Skidding to a halt at the makeshift arena, Minisc threw up his arms as blinding pillars of light rained down through the clouds. Getting a better look at the action, Minisc could vaguely make out a distant figure. The man moved faster than his eyes could follow, weaving in and out of the pillars of light with ease.

The man thumped the ground, kicking up a storm of dust, before firing a flare high into the sky. Four large orbs began hailing down rays of light, like shooting stars. He stopped just long enough for Minisc to make the man out to be his father.

Minisc stood star-struck, watching as his father eloquently tap-danced around each stream. He had sparks flying off him and a glow of light that Minisc had never seen before. Analyzing the man's movements, Minisc started to notice the nuances of each motion. It was not just the sheer speed that made the man fast. Each move was calculated, body position compact and agile, no wasted motion in each step he took. It was an exemplary display of talent and ability matched with relentless hard work and determination. Minisc could not believe what he was witnessing. Was this the real power that lay in the Hero of Light? It was too much for Minisc to fathom — truly a level of its own.

The fireworks display dissipated, allowing Minisc to finally see his father standing in all his glory. He remained in the forest opening, rubbing his eyes, trying to make sure he had not been dreaming.

Finished, Don glanced over, noticing his son's shadowy figure looming.

"Oh, you're home."

Minisc tried to express the overwhelming shock running through his mind.

"That speed... I couldn't even follow your movements. How can you... how can anyone move that quick? It's impossible."

The man let out a low, rumbling laugh.

"Yeah, I thought I'd get a little bit of training in while I was waiting for you to get home. Come on, let's get you some food."

After returning to the house, Minisc sat waiting for his meal to be served. The medication had started to wear off, and the pain through his body came back with vengeance. He was looking forward to getting some much-needed food in him and then collapsing in his bed.

Don slid a plate in front of his son with a thick juicy hamburger trapped between too-soft round buns. The steamy smell penetrated Minisc's nostrils, causing his stomach to let out a feeble growl. He picked it up with delight, taking a sizable bite.

"How're you feeling? Your girlfriend told me you took a nasty hit in training today."

Minisc's face turned a deep shade of red.

"She's not my girlfriend," he tried to exclaim, forgetting the food in his mouth. He went into a furious coughing fit, choking on his half-chewed burger. Thinking quick, he chugged back a tall glass of water to help down the food.

"Too bad, she seemed sweet."

Minisc ignored the comment. He was not prepared to start being hazed by his father about a girl he had just met.

"I feel fine; I just let my guard down for a moment and got shocked."

"What have I told you about staying focused? When you lose focus, you are all but guaranteeing defeat in battle."

"It was a mistake; I won't let it happen again." Minisc lowered his head, trying to hide the look of frustration overcoming him. A noticeable shift in tone filled the room.

"Minisc..." Don picked up on the frustration in his son's voice. "It's okay, you don't need to beat yourself up over it. Lily explained the match to me. You sacrificed winning and beating Ignis so that you could protect her. It's just like back before the summer, when you ran in to save that little girl. You want to help people in need. To be able to protect people. That's what you told me, isn't it? That's much more important than winning a sparring match." Don tried to cheer his son up. "I know sometimes people look at you and they expect me, and that's unfair for you to have to deal with, but you don't have to put that sort of pressure on yourself. When you decided to go to school, you wanted to help make your mother's wish for this world come true, correct?"

Minisc looked up at his father, nodding slowly.

"And you still feel the same way, don't you?"

"Yeah, of course I do. But—"

"Then there are no buts. Look, Minisc, you can't win against every opponent you come up against, and you can't save every person in the world, but just because that is the cold reality doesn't mean we should all give up. The world needs people like you. Someone who wants to help without reward or thanks. You continue to make me proud, and I know your mother is proud of you too. You just have to keep pushing forward and working hard. One day, when you least expect it, it will all pay off in a big way."

Don was known as a tough bruiser of a hero, the type one would read about in fairy tales and action movies. He never showed any fear, always ready for the next challenge ahead. At times, his parenting style could mirror that persona, but ever since his wife, Erika, had passed away, he had become much more understanding and sympathetic. His son was as strong and pure-hearted as anyone, and Don believed that he would achieve his goals, no matter what stood in his way. But he was still a teenager and had lots of growing and maturing to do. That would take time and patience — they both needed to remember that.

The next week went smoother for Minisc as he started to grow accustomed to his new school and new classes, even if he remained relatively secluded. The bombardment of questions about his father had died down, and hopefully as things progressed he would be able to go to school in peace. On top of that, he always had Jules by his side, and now Lily as well, with the three starting to form a rather tight-knit group.

After a long week, Minisc, Lily, and Jules were heading down the street back to the train station. However, that plan would soon be taken off course in a big way.

Jules was scrolling on his phone, looking at all of the articles depicting the rise in crime over the past six months in the city. Despite the EC's efforts, it continued — nothing seemed to slow down these criminals.

"Apparently someone witnessed two hooded people in black-and-silver coats before the latest attack on an EC-affiliated building."

"Jules, why are you even reading that stuff?" Minisc asked.

"I was curious. Ever since Yuri ran into that guy with the black coat, it seems as though people like that have been popping up more and more."

"It's a little concerning, don't you think? I mean nobody even knows who these guys are," Lily added.

Lily looked down the empty path they were on, noticing something off-putting.

"Hey guys..." Lily pointed to a man in a long black coat with his back turned to them. Minisc raised an eyebrow.

"You don't think—" Minisc stopped walking and then muttered, "I have a bad feeling about this..." He looked around the empty street as rain started to pour down. Praying that the cloaked figure had not seen them, Minisc grabbed his friends' hands and started to head in the opposite direction.

"Minisc, where are you taking us?" they whined.

"I don't know, but something tells me that guy is bad news. And we're not sticking around to find out." Minisc pulled out his phone, ready to call his father and inform him of the man, but first he wanted to make sure they were a safe distance away. He remembered the press conference over the summer and Dwayne even showing up at their door. Putting together what little information he had on the subject, Minisc had a feeling that the cloaked attackers were in some way related to Luminosa. He didn't want to send Jules or Lily into a panic, but he also needed to make sure they were out of harm's way. Minisc had pulled out his phone, ready to call his father, when the cloaked man appeared in front of them.

"Hmm, it looks like I might have missed a few stragglers. Can't have that now."

Minisc dropped the phone, terrified as it crashed onto the ground. He grabbed Lily and Jules, starting to run again before rounding the corner into a nearby construction zone. The place had a number of transport vehicles and other machinery like cranes and bulldozers around. At the least they had protection, but Minisc had hopes of being able to lay low and make an escape unseen.

"Minisc, who the heck was that?" Lily asked, huffing to catch her breath, "Do you know that guy?"

"Nope, and I'd rather not find out." The three crouched behind a loaded truck, hoping to stay out of sight and out of mind. Unfortunately, the cloaked man had no intention of letting anyone run free.

"Come on, running away really isn't going to solve anything," the same voice said again. All three of them looked up with horror and dread. Standing on one of the steel cross beams high above them was the cloaked man.

"Is this the same guy Yuri faced over the summer?" Minisc asked. Jules peered up at him. "No, he looks different somehow."

Lily and Jules both pulled out their cellphones, hoping to call for help, but the man wasted no time jumping down. He lifted his left hand up, and from his knuckles wolverine-like claws shot out, black blades made of shadow element. He swung with precision, slashing the phones into tiny chunks that crumbled in their hands.

"My phone!" they both cried. Now all three of them were without communication, and to make things worse they were in a dead-end construction site.

"Who are you, and what do you want with us?" Minisc demanded, inching forward.

"Don't flatter yourself, kid. I don't want anything with you three. But I know if I let you live, you'll just go blabbing to the EC about me, and we can't let that happen. It's really rather unfortunate timing on your part, but I can't really help that, now can I?"

Minisc inched forward again and Lily could immediately tell he was ready to fight back.

"Minisc, don't do it," she whispered. Her insides were beginning to shake despite her keeping a brave face. Next to her, Jules was gearing up for a battle.

"Don't worry Lily, we're going to be fine. I don't plan on fighting him for long." He looked back at the threat. "If I were you, I wouldn't worry about us telling the EC about you." Minisc raised his hand to the heavens and fired off a blast of light into the sky, acting as a flair. "It'll be easier for you to tell them yourself."

The cloaked man raised his hand to his head. "Why is nothing ever easy with kids these days? That's too bad. I was hoping we could do this with minimal bloodshed, but I guess if you don't plan on playing nice, then I'll just have to finish this quick."

The man lunged forward with his shadow claws, but Minisc leaped out of the way, dodging the hit.

Retaliating, Minisc fired off a small series of light blasts, but the man sliced them away with ease. Whoever the cloaked figure was, he knew how to use his element. Except, he was not as strong as Minisc had first thought. His speed and power were at best maybe a second-year EA student's level. Strange considering the other cloaked villains had given multiple EC members fits in battle. Or at least, so it had been reported. But it seemed like this one would not stand a chance against a top Elementalist.

"Jules, you and Lily should get out of here—I can hold this guy off on my own. Don't worry, I won't let you get hurt by this monster."

Thankfully, Jules had noticed the same thing Minisc had.

"No way, Minisc. This guy is nothing but hot air. We can take him together. I'm staying," Jules argued.

"Yeah, me too."

"Big mistake." The man laughed. He sped forward, but before he could make any headway, Jules caught him in a swirl of wind.

"Minisc, get him now!" Jules ordered.

Minisc held his hands out, drawing as much power as he could before firing off a blast. They needed to take this guy out before things became drawn out and they grew tired. Although they might have been on the same wavelength when it came to skill and power, stamina was where younger Elementalists always took the longest to develop. Even if the man was only a little older, that was hundreds of hours more practice and stamina development that they did not have.

"Take this, you creep." Minisc shot off his cannon-like blast, but before it could land a deciding blow, the man broke free of Jules's wind. He fell to the ground and the blast sailed over his head, colliding with some of the framework of the construction site. Part of the building began to crumble.

The villain pounced, slashing everything in sight with his claws. Minisc and company continued to dodge, but the construction site soon became a wreckage site. The cloaked man was reckless in his attacks, not caring what he damaged as long as he got his target.

Finally, the man swung his claws downward at Lily, cutting her and sending her flying back.

"Lily, no!" Minisc cried out. Jules ran over to his new friend, helping her to her feet.

"I'm fine, he only nicked me." Lily said, doing a quick examination of herself. She had a small gash on her arm, but it was nothing that a few bandages could not heal.

Even so, that close call provided enough for Minisc to let his power explode as his anger boiled over. He would not let Lily or Jules get hurt, no matter the cost. Much like when he'd landed the staggering blow on the robber, Minisc cocked his fist and readied his punch. The mystery man crossed his arms to block, but the punch still sent him flying back, crashing through the drywall and sending another part of the building tumbling down.

"Unbelievable. I didn't know Minisc was so strong."

"Neither did I."

But, that strength would still not be enough, as the man picked himself up and dusted himself off. "Huh, that actually hurt... okay kid, I'm done screwing around with you," the man seethed. But before he could make another move, he heard sirens fill the air and marching soldiers on their way. If the flair had not alerted authorities, the sounds of buildings crumbling certainly would have. "Damn, looks like I'm out of time." Taking a quick look around for his escape, the man sliced another steel pole, dropping the floor above him. The crash and smoke created enough of a diversion that he could escape without worry, not that Minisc had any intention of chasing him down. His body had started to shake from the power, and as it dropped, fatigue came with it.

Seven men and women stormed the area, all wearing EC uniforms, and they did not look pleased. They took one look around, seeing all of the damage that had been done, and then looked toward the three teenagers, who were the only people present.

"Oh, that can't be good," Minisc sighed.

The next day Minisc, Lily, and Jules all sat in a large office within the EC's main building. After the previous night's events, they'd had the unfortunate pleasure of waiting for their punishment. A meeting with the EC lead detective Thomas Cooper, along with Ms. Wright, had been requested. Which one frightened them more was hard to say. Lily and Jules, but Minisc in particular, had caused a serious amount of damage to what would have been a new hospital that the city desperately needed.

Thomas walked into the room, taking a seat across from the three at his desk. He gave an unreadable expression as he looked at them.

"So you're the EA students that went up against that cloaked man last night."

"We are," Minisc said. He figured as the Hero of Light's son, perhaps he could use that to his advantage. But, Sgt. Cooper had no care for lineage. His only focus appeared to be the law.

"Well, allow me to give you a lesson you should have already learned. When elements first started developing in this world, in order to help keep humans at ease, the government put strict laws in about using powers without proper authority. After all, we are trying to make a safer city for everyone, and allowing students to use their elements without repercussions in public would more than likely have disastrous results. That's why the EC are the only Elementalists allowed such a privilege. The only way that we have managed to maintain such unity is because the first generation of Elementalists have chosen to abide by these strict mandates. So whether you were fighting a criminal or not, what you three did was not only dangerous but incredibly illegal. On top of that, you destroyed the work site for a new hospital that this city is in desperate need of." He paused for a moment—the kids were stunned. This guy was pulling no punches on the damage done. "That means," he started again, "by the full extent of the law, you three should be heavily fined and even expelled from EA."

"Now hold on a second," Minisc tried to say, but Jules jumped in with more fire in his voice.

"We were fighting for our lives. We didn't go seeking out that cloaked guy, he found us. What were we supposed to do? Just let him kill us?" Jules growled standing up in frustration. "Nobody was coming to help us. We did what we had to do to survive."

"Jules, calm down," Lily said, trying to keep her friend from going over the table in a fit of rage.

"So let me understand what you're saying. You believe it's fine for the law to be broken as long as it goes your way. Is that it? This is why you are just children and not part of the EC."

"Why you —"

"Jules, pull it together," Minisc said. Before his friend could leap over the table any further, Ms. Wright held her hand out, urging Jules to sit back down.

"You're going to want to hear him out, Jules."

"Huh?"

"What I have said is the EC's official statement on the matter at hand; it will be released to the public in a few hours. That is, if you choose to make the news public."

"What do you mean, if we choose?" Minisc asked.

"I do not doubt that you are aware of the multiple cloaked attackers who have struck all over the city in the last few months. We here at the Elemental Council have been doing our best to keep the city at ease by holding most of these attacks under wraps. It's better for the citizens that way. So with that, we would like to keep this disaster from letting the public think we don't have this threat under control. Since nobody was around to witness the events, we will tell the public that the hospital was unstable and we were the ones to bring it down. I know that you three were fighting for your lives, and I know you had no other choice, but in order for you to avoid any punishment, we must keep these events a secret. That means you will not be allowed to talk about last night with anyone outside of the EC whatsoever. Personally, I know what choice I would pick, but it's up to the three of you."

"And what if we did talk about it?" Minisc asked.

"Well then you would be expelled from EA, and that's just a start," Ms. Wright jumped in. She shot the three of them a menacing look that sent more fear up their spines than any cloaked man ever could.

Minisc, Lily, and Jules looked at each other. The answer seemed pretty obvious.

"Alright, we promise. This never happened, and we will never talk about it again. Thank you," Minisc said.

"Good. I am glad we are all on the same page then," the chief said, "I am also happy to see that the three of you are safe and were able to defend yourselves. I know the damage caused is extensive, but it would pale in comparison to the irreversible loss of life." The chief took a bow.

"You know, if you had just started with that…" Jules said again, still frustrated.

"Jules, come on." Minisc smiled. He was just happy that they were still students and nobody had been hurt.

The three managed to escape with their lives, and although nobody ever found out about the incident, the EC would not be able to keep Luminosa's attacks under wraps forever.

CHAPTER 7
THE TOURNAMENT

THINGS CALMED DOWN OVER THE NEXT FEW MONTHS, and Minisc started to settle into school. Since he had avoided expulsion, he continued to attend EA while improving and expanding his skills alongside Lily and Jules. Only Ms. Wright knew about the battle with the cloaked man, but that did not mean the memories left Minisc or his friends. The city itself seemed to be more at ease, with fewer reports of the cloaked villains, but Minisc knew it could be a result of the EC trying to cover it up. Either way, those investigations were not for him to be a part of, so he tried to do his best and focus on school.

Even the students' infatuation with the Hero of Light gradually died down, with many becoming used to having his son in their class. Still, that did little for Minisc, as every opportunity to spar ended in him being selected first. It was some sort of strange way for his classmates to prove themselves. If they could beat Minisc, then they could imagine being the next great hero, most likely because Minisc had been labeled that by so many early on in his life. He had a permanent target on his back. But since he'd spent so much time over the summer with his father, he seemed to be growing a different outlook on the target. It just meant he would have to work harder and become better so he could embrace his mother's dying wish in the most impactful way possible.

The only person in the class who did not care to prove their skills against him remained to be Coro — the special exception student.

Coro remained a mystery to the class. If he were to speak, not one student would have recognized his voice. All they knew was he wore a disinterested scowl at all times. On top of that, he was often avoided in sparring sessions because of his unmatched ice element. Nobody could come close to facing him, even when grouped up.

Although he knew nothing about his classmate, Minisc held an appreciation for Coro. He could see some resemblances in their circumstances. They were both meant to be great. The only difference was Coro instilled fear with his strength, whereas Minisc was reasonably within his classmates' skill range. That made him a far fairer opponent when it came to training.

The dead of winter had taken over the school, with beautiful white snow drifting to the ground. Minisc watched as each flake stacked along the seal of the window, focusing on their glistening beauty while the rest of the class waited patiently in their seats, chatting among themselves.

The clock struck nine and a bell reverberated through the school. Silence fell over the room, a trained habit, as any second their dictator posing as a teacher would walk in. As they waited, seconds ticked by. Nothing. One minute passed, and then a second. Still no arrival. Minisc leaned over to Jules. "That's strange, she's never late."

Lily, occupying the seat in front of the boys, turned with a question in mind.

"Do you think she's alright?"

"I'm sure everything is fine," Minisc replied.

Another minute passed, with no sign of their teacher insight. Finally, one of the students decided to take action.

"Well, Ms. Wright's not showing up, so we get the day off!" The boy shot up, sending his chair sprawling back. His name was Devin, a rather talented earth Elementalist. He could easily have been near the top of the class, however he hated hard work and would often be rather lackadaisical in his training efforts. So of course he would be looking for a day off in the middle of the week.

Minisc often tried to ignore the boy, today being no exception. Devin had been the most persistent, pestering Minisc about the Hero of Light, asking him question after question during sparring. The student needed to know every detail of Minisc's father's life.

As if waiting for a revolt to start, the door slammed open.

"Sit down, Devin!" Ms. Wright commanded before she could even be seen.

She had her patented hardened look as she stormed into the class, hands gripping a pile of papers stacked to her neck.

"Sorry I'm late, class; I was getting confirmation."

"Confirmation on what?" Lily asked.

"I'll let him explain…" The woman turned her attention to the doorway. "Class, this is the president of the Elemental Council, Mr. Zale Osiris."

She gestured over to a sharply dressed man sporting a navy-blue suit jacket paired with a white dress shirt as he walked into the room. Thick, silver-brimmed glasses projected his large brown eyes, which matched the color of his freshly cut hair. It looked more like the man was preparing for an interview than to talk to a group of teenagers.

Most of the greater world knew of Zale Osiris and his impact on Elementalist society. Some would dare say he was second only to the Hero of Light. Minisc had seen him on television interviews many times, but in person, he gave off an even stronger presence. There was a tangible aura surrounding him.

"Hello, all. As Ms. Wright mentioned, my name is Zale Osiris, President of the Elemental Council. I'm sorry to disrupt your regularly scheduled class, but I have some news that I think will excite everyone in this room." The man spoke confidently, articulate and with clarity. "In three short months, we'll be holding the Tournament of Elements. Now, most of you probably know about this annual event hosted by the EC every year, but for those who don't, it is a showcase to demonstrate your exceptional abilities to the world."

Minisc looked over to Jules, who beamed with excitement.

"What's the Tournament of Elements?" he whispered, trying to avoid disrupting the speaker.

"Are you serious?" Jules looked at the blank expression on his friend's face in bewilderment. "Holy crap, you are serio—"

Before Jules could finish his thought, an obnoxious cough from the front of the room interrupted him. The two redirected their eyes, only to be met by the icy cold stare of their teacher. Both averted their gaze, slumping back into their seats.

"This year's tournament will be hosted at Scotia Coliseum. I'm sure you all have seen the building many times. The Tournament of Elements is the biggest stage for young Elementalists to display their skills, with a city-wide broadcast. Your teachers will all collaborate together to decide which eight students from each year will get to compete. As for the champions of each division, the student that wins will be granted a position at the Elemental Council upon graduation. This is a once-in-a-lifetime opportunity, so make sure to take advantage of it. Train hard, listen to your teachers, and give it your all!" Zale bowed to the sounds of trained claps of appreciation.

As Ms. Wright escorted him out of the classroom, quiet chatter developed. Most of the students were gleaming with excitement. A chance to compete in a tournament broadcast on television, and a position at the Elemental Council? For almost all of the students in the school, that would be the dream. They had all come to EA to join the EC, after all. Nobody could pass up such a great opportunity.

"So, who do you think Ms. Wright will pick to join the tournament?" Lily asked.

"Hard to say really, but I know for sure of one person who will get picked." Minisc gestured over to the boy sitting in the front row, looking straight ahead, his lifeless eyes staring at the void of a black chalkboard.

"Yeah, Coro will definitely get in. I hope she picks me. I want to fight so badly," Jules said.

The conversation was abruptly interrupted by the clacking of high heels re-entering the room. Ms. Wright took her place at the front before turning to address her class once again.

"I am sure everyone is eager to know which of you I have selected to enter in the Tournament of Elements, but first I would like to say that over these last few months, I have seen significant strides from all of you. Unfortunately, you can't all enter, but remember, just because you were not picked this year does not mean that you can't be picked next year. So do not stop working."

The class waited with bated breath, almost annoyed that their teacher was dragging her unusually sentimental speech on for so long.

"So... I guess without further ado, I should announce who I selected. Our class will have four participants this year, the first of which will be Coro."

No one in the class batted an eye. Coro regularly outperformed the class with not so much as an effort. He not only would be in the tournament, but everyone knew he would be the favorite to win the first-year division.

"Second to participate..." She paused, letting the class sweat. Ms. Wright seemed to be enjoying the torture a little too much. "...Will be Jules."

"Yes." Jules pumped his fist, making a bit of a scene. He did not care in the slightest—he was just excited to participate.

"The third contestant is Minisc."

Unlike Jules, Minisc sighed, head in hand. He knew he would be entered—based on his father alone, it seemed obvious. But that was not to discredit his own skills. He had been training with his father and he had been training in classes non-stop. There had been a noticeable improvement in his skills. Minisc had earned the confidence of his teacher and wanted to do his best. A national stage, as much as he hated the spotlight, would provide him an opportunity to lock in a spot at the EC, and that would only help him down the line.

"That means we are going to get to fight each other!" Jules gleamed.

Minisc blew off the comment. He hated to be the one to tell Jules that he did not want to fight his friend, but he would cross that bridge if it came to pass.

"And our fourth and final participant will be…" The woman looked in Lily's direction with a sly smile. "Lily."

Everyone turned their gazes to the girl.

"Me?" Lily said, pointing at herself.

"Yes Lily, you will be the fourth participant."

"She can't even use her element right," one of the students heckled.

"Yeah this isn't fair."

"That's enough," Ms. Wright snapped back.

The class fell silent. "I have made my decision, and I don't want to hear another word about it. Understood?" Even as harsh as Ms. Wright could be, the class had never heard her bark back like that. She was the type to speak in a calm manner, to the point it was almost off-putting. Hearing her raise her voice sent a clear message. Lily sat, trying to maintain a fake smile while her mind wandered.

But… why would she pick me? The others are right, there must be better students to participate than me.

One of the perks of living away from the inner city was the relaxing sounds of nature in the evening. No roaring traffic or chattering civilians roaming around. Only the peaceful howls of the wind and purring of wildlife.

Minisc sat on the front porch of his home. The sun had set a little over an hour ago, granting the boy a beautiful starry night overhead. He leaned back, taking in the crisp nighttime air. Minisc would often find himself sitting back and stargazing when he needed to clear his mind. The peace allowed him to organize his thoughts.

At least until the creak of the front door pulled him out of his blissful malaise.

"Hey." A beast of a voice echoed as Don took a seat beside his son. Clasped in his hands was a steaming cup of tea. The lemon scent quickly filled Minisc's nose as he took a hearty whiff.

"Here, I thought you might want a drink."

Minisc gripped the mug in both hands, taking a small sip.

"Thanks."

He got a strange feeling as his father eyed the brilliant white glow of the full moon.

"So… the Tournament of Elements," Don brought up awkwardly.

Minisc let out a small sigh, realizing the direction the conversation was about to take.

"Yeah? What about it?"

"I'll be presenting the champion trophy this year."

"Okay…"

"Imagine the Hero of Light getting to present his son with the championship trophy, in front of the world."

"What are you getting at, Father?"

"I'm not getting at anything; it's just a thought."

A momentary silence followed.

"I'll spare you this awkward exchange—yes, Ms. Wright picked me to enter, along with Lily and Jules."

"You don't sound overly excited by that honor?"

"It's not that. I'm just a bit nervous is all. I don't really want to be fighting on a big stage with thousands of people watching me. That sort of attention is your thing, not mine. What if I embarrass myself? I just wanted to help people like Mother, not be an icon for the world."

"Yeah, I get that. Honestly, I never wanted to be an icon for the world either. I only became that because people needed someone they could look up to. Someone they could put all their hopes on when things looked to be at their worst. That's why I accepted the title Hero of Light instead of fighting it. In fact, it was your mother who convinced me to do so. I was a lot like you, just wanting to do my part to help people, but it wasn't going well. Your mother was the one who came up with the name and made it famous. Sometimes I think she wanted me to absorb the spotlight so she could go about her business in the background, but either way, she was right," Don sighed, "Sometimes the world needs someone to look up to so they can feel safe, but that doesn't mean you have to be that symbol. After all, I'm still here. I will remain the Hero of Light, and you just keep doing your best while trying to stay in the background. You don't need to focus on anything else but achieving the goals you set out for yourself. None of the outside world's opinion matters. I know that isn't easy with the last name Premier, but if anyone can avoid the spotlight, it's you." The two laughed.

"I guess you're right," Minisc said, standing up.

"Where are you going?"

"I think it's time to step up the training."

Minisc always followed in his mother's footsteps more than his father's, but at that moment, hearing those words, Don could not help seeing himself in his son.

CHAPTER 8
THE PRODIGY

"COME ON, JULES; IT'S NOT THAT COMPLICATED." LILY let out a dejected sigh as she scrutinized her friend's worksheet. Tapping the tip of her pen against her chin, she started correcting all the wrong answers. The two were sitting at a long wooden table, and behind them were shelves filled to the border with books of all shapes and sizes. The room was split into two sections. The upper half was a library for studying and checking out educational materials, while the lower half was a common area for students to gather and hang out in.

While Lily and Jules worked on homework, Minisc weaved in and out of the rows of books, seeking out the one Lily had requested.

"This place has ten thousand books—how am I supposed to find anything in here? Come on..." He finally came across where he believed the book should be. "Hmm, what about this?" Sliding a thick black text out from between two smaller ones, he looked over the cover of it. "*Light, Dark, and Everything in Between: A Brief History of the Elemental World...* What on earth could Lily want with this?"

Regardless, he tucked the book under his arm and headed for his friends.

"Jules, you didn't get a single question right. How is that even possible?"

"It's difficult," the rattled boy whined.

"You know, if you studied even half as hard as you trained, you'd do so much better," Lily pointed out, much to Jules's dismay.

"Why are you so good at this stuff?"

"I actually study."

Minisc pulled up a seat beside the two, noticing the disgruntled look plastered on Jules's face.

"Math homework?" he joked, knowing full well the subject had been the bane of Jules's existence since they were children.

"Yeah, and it's not going well," Lily giggled. She took notice of the book in Minisc's hands. "Did you find it?"

He placed the text on the table. They looked at the weathered cover, which showed discoloration in the rustic gold title print.

"*Light, Dark, and Everything in Between*?" Lily read the title, examining the book before flipping to read the backside. "A comprehensive guide to everything elemental."

"Why'd you need this book anyways Lily?" Minisc asked.

"I figured it might help us if we did some studying before the tournament. I don't really know anything about the tournament after all. Ms. Wright said this book might help me."

"You mean neither of you have heard of the Tournament of Elements?" Jules groaned. "Who are you people? We don't need some book, I can tell you all you need to know about it."

"Huh? Really?"

"Yeah, I might not be any good at math, but I certainly know about the tournament. My brother told me all about it when he was in school. He is a former champion, after all."

"He is?" the other two said in unison.

"How did I not know that?" Minisc asked.

"Probably because until a few months ago, you refused to talk about elements with me at all," Jules quipped, seeing the befuddled look on Minisc's face proving him right.

Jules flipped the book shut and shoved his abysmal math homework out of the way.

"Anyways, unlike all the training we've been doing in class, this will be one-on-one only, so we can't rely on others. Each year, students have a set division they participate in, and since we're first-years, we will go up against the other first-years picked. They also usually have a twist in the tournament to help even out the playing field a bit. Normally it's a terrain change of some sort."

Jules thought back to the stories he had heard from his brother. He had forced Yuri to tell him every detail imaginable, especially of his heroic victory in his final year.

"If it's a one-on-one fight, why would Ms. Wright pick me? I have no hope of winning."

Lily's lack of confidence bled through, but as much as Minisc and Jules wanted to comfort her, they were just as perplexed by the decision. In months of training, albeit in pairs, Lily still lacked the skills of the others. She tried hard, and her smarts made up for a lot of shortcomings, but in terms of power, if she was not the weakest in the class, she was right next to it.

"I'm sure it will be fine, Lily." That was the best Minisc could come up with.

Trying to distract herself from the doubt, Lily grabbed the book she had requested and cracked it open in the middle.

"Well, regardless, I think doing a little studying on the other elements could go a long way." She looked down at the heading of the page. The title read *Dual Elements*.

"Dual elements? Like having two elements in your body at once?" Minisc asked, his curiosity piqued.

"I've never heard of someone who could use two different elements. Is that even possible?" Jules wondered.

Lily read the opening paragraph to the group.

"Although scientists have yet to solve all of the mysteries regarding how Elementalists came to be, many studies have shown a split in blood cells, with one type of cell being dubbed the element cell. Those cells are what are believed to give the race its elemental powers. When the species known as Elementalists became more common, scientists began experiments to see if an Elementalist's body could sustain multiple elements, known as the dual element power. With no other way to execute such hypotheses, infants were chosen at random to be experimented on from birth, in hopes of being able to extract and inject element cells. Experiments ceased upon creation of the Elemental Council, deemed unethical…"

Lily halted her reading, a look of disgust on her face. She slammed the book shut with a thud loud enough to draw the attention of everyone in the area.

"What is wrong with people? How could they experiment on babies just for their own benefit!" She was seething, and the boys were pretty sure they could see smoke coming from her ears.

"I don't know, but the Council put a stop to it, so you can calm down," Minisc advised, raising his hands in slight fear. He was not prepared to endure the wrath of an angry Lily.

Meanwhile, wedged into one of the compact cubicles a few feet away from Minisc and company sat Coro. The reserved, exceptional student made little noise, but he had been eavesdropping on the conversation, a low building frustration welling up inside him.

Later that night, puddles of sweat formed in the shadows of the sparsely lit basement. Bordered by concrete walls, the room was loaded with dumbbells, weight benches, and a dark workout mat. The area had the feeling of a castle dungeon more than a basement in a modern-day house.

Thundering thuds rang out as the sand-filled bag bounced back and forth, absorbing each blow with little give. The boy bobbed and weaved, shifting his finely toned body effortlessly as he swung at the cylindrical target. Each punch connected with a violent passion.

"It's time for dinner Coro," a motherly voice called from the top of the nearby staircase. Coro paused, listening to the words before taking one final KO'ing blow at the bag, nearly breaking it off its steel chains. He grabbed a raggedy white towel off of the rack, and with a quick wipedown, he headed up.

He walked into the kitchen and was hit with an infectious smell—the scent of a good home-cooked meal. Ready to eat, he took a seat across from his mother, a middle-aged woman with curly blueish-silver hair.

She had a few wrinkles slowly forming underneath her large maroon eyes, but other than that she looked good for someone her age.

"Is Father joining us?" Coro asked, stoically stabbing his fork into the meat, watching the juices bleed out.

"No, he's working late at the lab again."

Coro gave no reaction. The notion that his father was not home could be seen as more of a blessing than a disappointment. Coro's father was once known as a renowned scientist by the name of Dr. Jarrad Normanday. He had been one of the leading humans for more than a decade in the research of Elementalists. His desire to enhance and manipulate Elementalists' abilities had helped create many controversies over the years, but that had never stopped the man from pushing the boundaries of science. He'd also straddled the line of ethical decisions on more than a few occasions, all in the name of discovery. Dr. Jarrad was often loathed for wanting to create monsters of war more than expanding research but after multiple restrictions were placed on his studies by the EC, he'd had a drastic fall from grace.

Only the faint clanking of forks and knives kept dinner from being silent. After cleaning his plate, Coro cleared his spot at the table before heading back down into the basement. Training was the only suitable way to deal with the aggression built up inside him. On top of that, if he did not stay in shape, his father would chastise him.

Prepared to pick up where he left off, Coro started pounding the sandbag with vicious force. Small waves of air popped off the bag as it flew back. But after a few swings, he started to hear the distressed yelling of his mother from above.

"He's a child, our child; you can't keep using him for these sociopathic experiments!"

"That boy is my chance to re-establish my glory. I'll use him as I see fit. Now get out of my way."

The voice of the man was firm, but it was a far cry from yelling.

Coro attempted another swing, missing as he heard the frustrated cries of his mother once again.

"Coro is not some experiment; he's my son, and I won't stand by and let you treat him like some sort of monster creation."

Nothing could drown out the cries of anger, despite Coro's best efforts. He had grown used to the arguments but expected nothing to change. It never did.

The chain rattled vigorously, almost coming unhinged with another punch. The word monster was one that he had especially grown numb to. Coro had such overwhelming powers, and such exceptional abilities, that many viewed him as just that. A monster. It hurt, but in his heart, he knew it to be true.

"Science and my experiments have blessed that boy with a gift that could revolutionize the study of Elementalists. His power will be unmatched by all—the ultimate fighting machine, created by me. That boy is my ticket back to credibility, fame, and wealth; he holds the key to it all."

"Do you even hear yourself? Fame, fortune—those things never used to be important. You used to want to help push the boundaries of science, not create a fighting machine."

The man brushed past his upset wife, leaving her stewing in frustration.

Coro's ears perked up again, listening to the creaking of wood after each step. "Leave!" he spat coldly, refusing to turn around and acknowledge his father in the doorway.

Unfazed by his son's demeanor, the man reached into his pocket and pulled out a small clear bottle.

"Take these." He lightly tossed the cylindrical bottle in his son's direction. "You should be grateful. Thanks to me, you might actually make a name for yourself." The disdain for his son's uncooperativeness could be felt through the tense room.

As if he had eyes on the back of his head, Coro stuck his left arm out backward and caught the toss in the palm of his hand. He gave the bottle a once-over, seeing two small blue capsules no bigger than his fingernail. He popped the lid off and dumped the contents into his palm. The pills looked so innocent. It was tough to imagine something so small could have such effects on one's body, but Coro knew all too well of that falsehood.

At a young age, Coro had been forced into the role of the test subject by his father. From injections to serums to the pills in hand, he had gone through every method imaginable to ingest substances, with varying degrees of success. Begrudgingly, Coro tilted his head back and popped the capsules into his open mouth. It would be a day or two till he felt a difference in his body, for better or worse.

While that was going on, near the far outskirts of the city, a man cloaked in shadows swiftly darted in and out of the alleyways, a large gray briefcase clanking behind him with each step. He took great caution in making sure no one laid eyes on him. Striding out into the barren street, he took cover behind a dumpster.

Stormy clouds shielded the evening moonlight, and only the pointed shine of streetlights kept the night from being sheathed in utter darkness. Through the wasteland streets, the man took long strides toward a run-down house wedged between two equally destroyed homes, though far bigger than the one he wanted to enter. He peeked in through the window, seeing nothing but boxes and what looked like severe fire damage on the inside. Surveying the surroundings to ensure he was still alone, the man walked up to the dull gray door and pulled out a small key.

Once inside the abandoned home, he had the option of two staircases, one leading to the second floor and the other leading to the basement. The set leading up was filled with broken pieces of wood that made passage next to impossible. So was the price of hiding in a ruined house. Taking the only real option available, the man headed down to the basement and pounded on the door, loud enough to blow the hinges off. Not waiting for his knocks to be answered, the man swung open the door, startling the two others in the room. He felt particularly proud of his work today.

The space inside could only be described as ancient, layered with rotten wood flooring that looked as if any given step could puncture the planks. Crates lined the left wall, stacked to the ceiling and were labeled with various ingredients, none of which could be fresh. On the right side was a makeshift kitchen filled with a rusty oven, and a small cabinet hanging over the top.

The man had not come for any of that, though. He'd arrived to meet the two who sat around a decaying table in the center of the room. Their faces were sparsely lit by a single spotlight stuck in the rafters, raining down a dingy fluorescent yellow light.

Around the table on the left sat a young woman a few years younger than himself. Except, even though her child-like face gave off the impression of her youth, the sinister grin with sharp teeth indicated she should not be trifled with. Across from her sat another man around the same age, but he looked closer to his actual age. With tired eyes and messy white hair that had not been combed in months, he almost looked like a zombie more than a human given the lack of sunlight.

"Are you trying to scare us or what, you idiot! You're lucky I didn't blow a hole through you," the girl seethed.

"Funny Bex, you couldn't hurt me even with your little icicles," Bronx mocked, ignoring the violent glare directed at him. No comments were going to stop him from showing off what he had just snagged.

"Who cares about that? Did you get the material, Bronx?" the other man asked.

"You bet I did." Bronx skipped over to them, swinging his briefcase from over his shoulder onto the table. With two quick clicks of the golden locks, the top popped off to reveal their sought-after contents. Bronx leaned in, picking up one of the small vials between his fingers and scanning it briefly. Inside the clear, corked tube, no more than a few drops of thick blue liquid sloshed around. Those drops, however, contained the missing ingredients in their plan.

"That's it? You couldn't get any more than that?" the man asked.

Bronx shot a glare at his partner. "Yeah, it's not exactly in high supply — you should just appreciate that I managed to get this much."

Bex, intrigued, snatched the vial right from Bronx's hand, examining it herself. "So what is this supposed to do, Brooklyn?"

The teen named Brooklyn turned to a little radio sitting by the kitchen. He walked up to it and started jiggling the dial until the frequencies let out an ear-splitting static.

"We have all of the necessary supplies — you said these would help me get rid of the Hero of Light, so what's next?" he said to the radio.

The group waited patiently until they heard a static voice.

"Wonderful work — the chemical you have in front of you is called Bakari. It is a liquid that is drawn out of Elementalists' blood, which hospitals have been using to help temper newborn babies that have an overwhelming element they cannot control."

"How is that important to us, though?" Bex probed further.

"Combining this with the other chemicals you have gathered, you should be able to enhance the effects. Doing that would make the serum so powerful that it would begin to erode elemental cells in the body. Such a virus will allow you to erase the element in any Elementalist's body."

"Oooh, that sounds like fun. Can I use it?" Bex said, bouncing up and down with childlike glee.

"Settle down, Bex. Once the time is right, you will make the most of your hard work."

"What about the boy? He has still managed to elude us, and the EC has ramped up its security around the city. Getting him now will be next to impossible."

"Do not worry, he will not be able to stay safe forever. When the clock strikes, he will be in our clutches, and the pieces of the puzzle will all come together." The radio fell silent.

CHAPTER 9
TRIAL BY FIRE

AFTER MONTHS OF ANTICIPATION, RELENTLESS TRAINING and testing the limits of their elements, finally, all of it would culminate in one grand trial for the semester. The Tournament of Elements had arrived.

Each of the chosen participants had dreams of winning their respective divisions and locking in their spot at the Elemental Council. The harsh truth remained though. Only four fighters could prevail.

Elemental Academy was a four-year school program, and enrollment for each year dictated the number of classes. For Minisc, that meant he and his first-year class only had two separate groups. Although an unusually low attendance for the school in recent years, it still dwarfed the fourth-year students, who came in at half that number.

Minisc and his friends stood in line at a small booth outside of Scotia Coliseum. They were waiting patiently to be given credentials that would grant them access in and out of the building at will. Minisc walked up first, handing his admission slip over to the security guard.

Beep.

A quick scan was followed by a pleasant jingle, and Minisc gained access to the grounds. On his way out, a woman handed him a white-and-gold lanyard with his picture on it. Since the students had been registered beforehand, all the participants were given special lanyards to act as an ID.

Lily and Jules followed up the rear soon after. Minisc looked around, taking in all the activity. Food stands, mascots, and merchandise booths had been placed all around the premises filled with spectators. He hadn't seen so many people in one spot in his life. Even when his father would speak.

Humans and Elementalists alike would travel from all around the world to experience the spectacle. Even though the tournament participants were students, it still represented a grand sporting event for the world to see.

"This is going to be so cool," Jules said, getting a glimpse of the excitement. The energy all around was infectious, and he couldn't help but get swept up in the activity.

As they walked, some excited children ran past Minisc cutting him off. Wondering where they were going, Lily grabbed Minisc's arm and yanked him in the direction of a towering clown on stilts.

"Look at that."

The bright red hair and round matching nose were impossible to miss even among the crowd. Not to mention he loomed over everyone with the added length from his planks. He walked around, smiling at the kids while juggling three bright tennis balls.

Lily yanked Minisc's arm again.

"Oh, look over there."

His arm felt like it was popping out of its socket. At this rate, Lily would knock him out of the tournament before they had a chance to start.

"This is so cool," the girl cheered, doing a 180-degree spin while tossing Minisc around like a rag doll.

"She must be really excited," Jules joked, giving his buddy a sympathetic smile.

"It's like a giant carnival. I've always wanted to go to a carnival!" Lily squealed with glee.

She too had been swept up in all the excitement.

"Lily... remember why we're here," Minisc cautioned as his feet finally landed back on the ground. She loosened her death grip in embarrassment.

"Right. Guess I got a little carried away."

"Whoa, now look at that," Jules boasted, gesturing to the side of the building. His gaze was directed at a video board taking up nearly half the side of the building. On the board were the four divisional brackets with a slot for each of the thirty-two participants. Cut into quarters, the board remained empty for the time being, but soon it would hold the path to each student's dream.

The draw ceremony would be taking place in just over an hour, and through that, the matches would be decided upon. The other thing that caught Jules's attention was his name on the ticker below.

"This is going to be so much fun." Jules took his turn to become distracted.

Minisc sighed in defeat. He was happy his friends were enjoying the experience, but he lacked the same level of interest in such outside activities, at least for the moment. There would be no shortage of opportunities for exploring over the three-day event, but for the time being, he had one goal in mind. Win.

The three finally came up to the front of the building. It had been painted top to bottom in vibrant red and gold stripes, matching the EC color scheme. Hanging down parallel to the front doors on either side were two extravagant banners. On the left side posed a woman the three failed to recognize. She had a slim body and curly, dark green hair that fell in front of her eyes. The banner only showed half of her fit body, posed in a menacing fighting stance. Across on the right banner, holding the trophy above his head, happened to be a man quite recognizable to Jules. Short brown hair flowed to the back bangs parting to the sides, shaping his face. His eyes were a sharp black, piercing with one look.

"Hey, it's Yuri," Jules pointed out enthusiastically. The posters were bigger than life, and seeing his brother hanging high, Jules could already picture what his banner would look like one day, hanging up next to his brother's. It would be glorious.

Scotia Coliseum was a state-of-the-art building all around, from the marvelous inside to its outer architecture. It had been used for many years as home to all of the city's biggest events, including concerts, numerous other sporting events, and even a few city-wide meetings. The building was one of the more recognizable attractions in the city's history.

The inside of the Coliseum was as elegant as the outside. Granite rock tiles cut into perfect squares patterned across the floor, and placed at the center of the enormous room was a large round desk. Hanging above the desk were four huge flat-screen televisions, positioned together to make a square facing outward. The front one had the local news channel playing on it while the other three had empty brackets waiting to be filled out. Four receptionists stood below, each under a specific monitor, waiting to assist the small lines of people that had already formed. Behind the desk, the room slanted off in two directions, diagonally to the left and right. Posters, banners, and a trophy case housing different memorabilia filled out the rest of the area for tourists to relive the history of the building and its events.

The three stood mesmerized by the building, looking it up and down in awe. Before they could decide where to go, they were approached by a woman dressed in a fancy blue blouse and matching knee-high skirt.

"Is there something I can help the three of you with?" she asked with a cheerful smile.

"We're here for the tournament," Minisc answered.

"Are you spectators or competitors?"

"Competing," Jules chimed. He held up the lanyard around his neck.

"Head over to the receptionist table, they will help you from there." The woman gestured toward the small lines. Most of the competitors appeared to have already registered and must have been heading to the draw ceremony.

It took just a minute or two for the line to dwindle, leaving only Minisc, Jules, and Lily, along with one other boy. In short order, Minisc came face to face with a less-than-pleasant woman. She wore a hard scowl that said she wished to be anywhere but her current location.

"Name?" she said with a slow drawl.

"Minisc, Premier."

"Number 6... Next!"

She scribbled the number on an official piece of paper and stashed it away.

"Uh, okay, thanks." Minisc blinked a few times before deciding to get out of line.

With sign-ups all set, Lily asked, "Now what do we do?"

"I think we're supposed to go to the draw ceremony." Jules gestured to a plastered red sign on the wall accompanied by an eye-catching arrow pointing down the hall.

Scotia Coliseum had been designed to be a giant octagon with the center cut out, acting as an open-roof stadium with two main entrances, one on each end. The arena part of the stadium, where the matches would be held, sat in the center of the building, but at the moment the battlefield had been removed to make room for the thirty-two young aspiring Elementalists waiting to find out their fate.

A quiet wind swirled through the stadium as everyone waited intently, their undivided attention focused on the wooden stage that resided at the north end of the arena. Hanging high above the competitors floated another giant scoreboard. It shared the same empty bracket that had been on the jumbotron outside.

With a palpable excitement thriving through the group, that feeling only grew when three men walked out of the back tunnel making their way onto the stage.

"Hey, isn't that your father?" Jules pointed out, getting a glimpse of the burly Hero. He stood offset to the side of another familiar face.

"President Osiris is here as well," Lily added.

Zale stepped up to the microphone ready for his opening remarks. Much like when he'd spoken in Minisc's class, his composure and presence were at the forefront, the only difference now being how his voice boomed out from the mic.

"Thank you, everyone, for coming out today to our annual Tournament of Elements. A place where EA's finest students can show off the fantastic training and skills they have learned to the world. From what I've been told, this year's tournament will be the most exciting one yet, and I would like to wish each and every one of you the best of luck in your bouts. I have no doubts you'll make your school proud." The man finished his opening statement to applause from the students.

"I'd now like to invite our referee to speak on the rules for the event."

Zale stepped back, and a short stocky man looking almost like a dwarf dressed in all white took his place at the podium. His pointed face and round jaw matched his bloated belly. He had a little bit of stubble and looked significantly older than the two men beside him.

"Hello all, my name is Law, and I have been appointed the tournament official for this event. I know everyone is excited, but I would like to touch on the rules before the tournament starts. All matches will be one-on-one bouts with no help from outside sources. That includes weapons or other substances that could aid in battle. You are only permitted to use your element and your own fighting techniques. With that in mind, there are three ways to claim victory. The first one is to score a ring-out on your opponent. That means the first fighter to step out of the ring will be declared the loser. The second way is for you to knock your opponent out for a ten count. The count will be administered by me. And the third way — I have the authority to call off any match and declare a winner if I see fit. As well we will have three separate officials on the ground level who can jump in and stop the match if I see things getting too dangerous. Nobody will be breaking through my ten-layer rock wall." Law stomped his foot, and just as he said, ten-foot walls of rock came springing up from the ground, encasing all the students. He smiled, stomping his foot again causing the walls to fall. "So if you try to kill your opponent, then I will be forced to halt the match and you will be disqualified — not to mention you will be dealing with the school. But anyways… Let's have a nice, clean tournament, and may the best Elementalist win."

The man finished to another round of applause. As he stepped back and Don stepped forward, the applause erupted to a defining pitch. The legend gave a heroic wave, playing to the audience. Everyone cheered with excitement—the exception, of course, being Minisc, who just shrugged in embarrassment.

So much for not loving the spotlight.

"Now, for the moment you've all been waiting for, we shall draw for first-round opponents. Please direct your attention to the video board above." Don gestured to the giant board hanging over his head as it lit up with every student's name, picture, and division. As the students waited breathlessly for what fate they would be dealt, the board started to pair off the pictures like a puzzle falling into place. In no time, everyone had been grouped up, and the board then displayed the order of each first-round match, starting with the first-year group.

Much to Minisc's chagrin, if not outright embarrassment, he saw his picture blown up to half the size of the jumbotron. Ignoring the fact his picture looked rather awkward to him, he also had the *privilege* of kicking the tournament off. Next to him, the picture taking up the other half was of a child-like boy with wavy blue hair and a deceptively happy grin. He also had small freckles under his round eyes. The name underneath read Trotz, and Minisc knew his fellow student as arguably the biggest Hero of Light fan on the planet. He'd continually bugged Minisc early on, but with Trotz being in the other first-year class, their interactions were limited.

"Hey, you're the first match in the tournament!" As Jules pointed out the obvious, an awkward anxiety came over Minisc. In the end, going first didn't matter, but he would have appreciated at least not being the first one out. He just needed to focus, ignore the hype, and relax. Trotz was nothing special in Elementalist terms. Minisc knew he should have the upper hand. Even so, he still had the nerves of stage fright. Lily noticed the trepidation of her friend and put her hand on his shoulder.

"You're going to do great."

The gesture helped put Minisc at ease, if only for a minute. But sadly, Lily's optimism would be tested when she saw her face appear. Or more specifically who it appeared next to.

"I face... Coro?" She gulped. Lily already had severe doubts as to why Ms. Wright had picked her, but facing Coro would be a mismatch of the highest order. Minisc and Jules both looked at her with shocked expressions. They couldn't hide the fear for their friend either.

"Don't worry, we'll make a plan," Minisc said, doing his best to return the reassurance he had just received.

The last to see his picture appear was Jules, and he was selected to face a student by the name of Reese. One of the top students in the other class, she had proven to be an obvious pick for such an event.

With their work cut out for them, the gang walked back to the reception hall, but were quickly stopped along the way.

A young lady looking to be a few years older than any of the students approached them. She dawned the same navy-blue uniform they had first seen when they entered the reception hall.

"Hello, Mr. Premier."

"Um, hello?" Minisc said with a puzzled look. He was plenty accustomed to strangers stopping him, but the address had caught him by surprise.

"I will be showing you to your changing room so you may get ready for your first match. Please follow me."

"Oh... okay." Minisc nodded.

After being led down a winding hall, the group stopped in front of a futuristic steel door. Just to the left, on a small gold plaque, were engraved the words: *Challenger Dressing Room*.

Minisc slid the door open.

"This place is huge," Lily exclaimed.

The room had to be as big as their classroom, but far more lavished with beautiful pots of leafy flowers, artwork, and a personal bathroom. Added to that was a large table stationed in the middle of the room and a TV hanging on the freshly painted white walls.

"There you go. Good luck in your match."

The woman waved goodbye as she left the three to their palace.

"Wow, this is way better than the school changing rooms," Jules boasted, examining the portraits. He failed to recognize anyone, not that he cared.

Minisc checked his phone for the time. His match started at 1:00 p.m. sharp. It was currently 12:45, which meant reality started to set in. And so did the anxiety. Minisc could feel his body becoming rigid with pressure weighing him down. Lily picked up on her friends trepidation.

"Just take a deep breath and relax—you know you can win this."

"Thanks, I guess I'm just nervous."

Jules turned his attention to the conversation at hand.

"All we can do is go out and try our best. Whatever happens, happens, right?"

"Right." Lily nodded, smiles growing among the group with each reassurance.

"It's almost time. We should leave you to change and get ready."

"But before we go…" Lily stretched her arm out horizontally. Jules quickly threw his hand over the top of hers, followed by Minisc.

"On three, do your best," Lily chimed.

"That's kind of corny don't you think?" Jules mumbled, before being greeted with a violent stare from the girl.

"Do you have something better?"

Jules said nothing more.

"That's what I thought." A sly smile formed on Lily's face.

"One… two… three… Do your best!" they exclaimed, throwing their hands up in the air, and just like that, Minisc found himself alone.

The tunnels leading to the stadium were hollow and concrete with the only constant light being small pot lights that hung every few feet. For a building as elegant as Scotia Coliseum, the tunnels to the field were anything but.

With each passing step, Minisc could hear the roars of the crowd reverberating. It sounded like thousands of stampeding elephants coming his way, louder and louder. His nerves grew along with the noise. He could see the entrance within sight. The light at the end beckoned him, calling his name. In a few moments, he would be on a stage like no other. There would be no turning back, no pauses, no do-overs. Only he and his opponent until a winner was proclaimed.

Minisc stood stagnant while time started slowing down. Seconds felt like minutes, and minutes felt like hours. He waited patiently for his introduction. Trying to keep his nerves at bay, Minisc took a deep breath, his chest expanding two-fold. As he gradually let it out, an eruption of cheers made the boy jump. The excitement from outside let him know the moment was upon him. All that remained was to go out and seize it.

"Hey, there are two empty seats," Jules pointed out.

"This crowd is insane!" Lily added, trying to be heard through the noise.

The stadium had three tiers of seating, in three separate bowls. Jules and Lily made their way to the second level, where a designated section had been blocked off so participants could sit and watch. The two got situated among the other competitors, ready to cheer Minisc on. Their section appeared to be the only one not full; it looked as if a hundred seats had been set aside for only around thirty people.

Jules looked down to the first tier of spectators, jammed with fans screaming and cheering. A few people even made signs with competitors' names on them.

Lily glanced at the arena floor. It was octagonal, but the sides were significantly longer than the back. Two small stairways, with three steps, could be seen at each end, and square white tiles filled the interior. Surrounding the elevated flooring was freshly cut grass that looked to have been made pristine for the event. As far as battle arenas went, this one had to be considered quite elegant.

A voice boomed out over the speakers in each corner. The third-tier seating was luxury boxes, but in the middle of those fancy suites sat the announcer. He spoke in an enthusiastic yet smooth voice, one fit to call the tournament's action.

"Welcome one, welcome all, to the Tournament of Elements. We thank you for coming out today for this spectacular event. We have the top young Elementalists here ready to duke it out for the right to claim the title of champion in this year's tournament. So without further ado, I'd like to introduce the first match of the day. Looking to follow in the steps of his father, the Hero of Light, please welcome to the stage Minisc Premier."

On cue, Minisc walked out to a chorus of applause. Then he looked around, taking in his surroundings. Much to his surprise, the moment felt surreal. Surreal, yet uncomfortable—a few thousand pairs of eyes staring and scrutinizing his every move. In one sense it filled him with uplifting adrenaline, but in another, it terrified him. The only question would be, which would control him? Upon exiting the tunnel, Minisc could hear some comments from spectators.

"That's Don Premier's son? He doesn't look that impressive."

"He looks nothing like his father; I could take him."

"That's the Hero of Light's kid? I wonder if he's any good?"

"Ignore them, just block out the noise," he muttered as he took his first steps into the ring.

Chants from the crowd slowly faded into the background. Minisc's head began to quiet, and a fierce look of concentration took over. In the time leading up to this, he had worked with his father more on mental concentration rather than skills and technique in hopes of easing the stress. Now would be the first real test of that training.

Minisc stood to the announcer's left, wearing the same blue-and-red training uniform he had used all summer. In a tournament of uncertainty, at least he could wear somewhat-familiar clothing. It was one of the few things he could control. On the other side, Trotz stood about ten meters away, sporting a black-and-red uniform. He looked far more intense than Minisc had ever seen him.

Since the two first-year classes trained against each other only on rare occasions, Minisc had never actually sparred with Trotz, but just from watching him the few times their classes did work together, Minisc knew the boy had some skill.

"I was so hoping I would get to fight the Hero of Light's son," Trotz said with a gleam. He looked innocent enough, but then his tone turned more sinister. "I'll have you know, I know everything about the Hero. I'm his biggest fan. Therefore, I know everything about you as well. Likes, dislikes, all your tendencies. This will be quick."

"Yeah, I'm aware... I got the hint the first ten times you told me, Trotz," Minisc said with some smugness. He put on a farce of confidence, if not arrogance that most would never associate with him. Even if it was a facade, Minisc didn't mind getting a chance to beat one of the students that bugged him the most.

"Added to this year's competition, we would like to introduce a new twist," came the voice of the announcer. On the big board, eight symbols appeared, all in a circle. They were the eight elements, all taking up a piece of the pie. It began to spin around and around, waiting to stop on the slice of pie that would dictate the added element into the battle. After a few seconds, it stopped on the symbol of a teardrop. Water.

The arena began to shake as the floor split in the middle. It slid back neatly underneath, stopping at the small boxed area in which Minisc stood.

Where the plain stadium floor used to reside, it had been replaced by a tank of sea-blue water. Scattered throughout the body of water, multiple platforms bobbed back and forth.

Oh come on... why does it have to be water?

"Please fighters, step forward onto the closest platform in the arena." Minisc followed the ref's instructions, hopping onto the platform that floated in front of him. He felt the green square dip below the water just enough for his feet to become soaked.

While Minisc tried to shove his hatred of water to the back of his mind, he suddenly realized he was in more trouble than just sinking.

"Ha, this is perfect. I'm going to fry you with my electricity," Trotz laughed, "Then I'll go on to win the tournament, and prove that I should be the one who will take up the mantle of the Hero of Light."

This is just my luck. As Minisc braced himself, he waited for the words all in the stadium wanted to hear.

"Let the tournament begin."

Almost simultaneously, with the sound of the flag, Minisc began his attack. He opened with a pair of Lum Bombs. Glowing balls of light rocketed out of his left hand, but with an effortless smack,

Trotz redirected the blasts into the water, creating a wave that violently shook the platforms. Minisc dropped down onto a knee, desperately hanging on for dear life.

"What is Minisc doing?" Lily asked Jules.

"Well, you see… Minisc sort of has a fear of swimming. A water arena is probably the worst-case scenario for him."

"Really? I didn't know that."

"Yep, and with Trotz also having electricity as his element, Minisc is going to be in tough if he falls in the water."

Trotz watched Minisc struggle. "What's wrong, scared of a little water?" he mocked. "Here, allow me to make it even less comfortable for you." The boy bent down, sticking his hands into the pool. His body began to glow, and so did the water. In a flash, sparks started to circulate in the pool.

You have to be kidding me, now it's exactly the way I lost to Ignis and Jacob… I need to be wary of any residual water, as well as this stupid electric pool.

Trotz stood up as the water steadied again, while Minisc braced himself for the boy's next move.

"You know, your father would never be scared of a little electricity and some water," Trotz scoffed.

His left hand was now enveloped in electricity, with sparks shooting out around him. His hair started to fly up from the generated static. Trotz showed much more power than what Minisc had seen in class. *I guess I wasn't the only one doing a little extra training.*

Minisc braced for a counterattack, watching as a blinding yellow flash filled the stadium. As it did, three lightning bolts zoomed toward him. He jumped to his left onto a new platform, avoiding the shocks but as he landed out of harm's way, he let out a wince.

"Okay… that was fast," Minisc said, grabbing at his right arm. Along his sleeve, he saw a narrow slice as if a knife had cut him. He had managed to avoid the full brunt of Trotz's attack but been grazed in the process.

"Oh, did that hurt your arm? Sorry, next time I'll aim for the heart." Trotz laughed in an almost sadistic voice.

This guy is crazy. Who would even let him into the EC anyways?

His arm still stinging, Minisc tried to maintain his balance against the shallow waves from his landing. He debated what his next advancement should be. Fighting hand-to-hand was out of the question, with the platforms barely big enough for both to stand on at once, and on top of that, his arm stung with the slightest breeze crossing it. Yet the recoil of firing accurate attacks with his element seemed dangerous as well. If he slipped or fell in the water, he would be done in for sure. For the moment, Minisc decided to let his opponent come to him and base his strategy on that.

"You don't deserve to be the Hero of Light's son," Trotz yelled, "I should have been his son, but after you're out of the way, I'll be his new apprentice, learning from my idol, fighting evil at every turn! I'll be the hero you could never be!"

Trotz bounced around quickly from platform to platform, neither the swaying of the water nor the pool of electricity fazing him. He fired electrical bolts at his opponent, one after another.

Minisc slanted his eyes, beginning to grow annoyed with the theatrics of the child. He blocked each bolt with a small amount of light energy as he snapped back. "Do you ever shut up?"

Meanwhile, Lily was beside herself. "Why is Minisc not moving?" she yelled, continually bouncing up and down, her actions growing more violent with each passing second.

Jules eyed his friend, watching the ridiculousness of the scene. He wanted to pay attention to the match, but Lily's exhibition was too distracting.

"They seem to be talking more than fighting," Jules said, watching the two combatants flapping lips instead of trading punches.

"I wish I could make out what they're saying!" Lily grumbled.

"I don't know, but Minisc looks annoyed."

Minisc continued to dodge strike after strike of lightning. He could feel the air whiz past his cheeks as each attack narrowly missed its target. He could also feel the tingling of electricity radiating just below his feet. It had an unnerving waft to it. Just as Minisc wanted to turn to the offensive, he slipped from the waves, rolling his left ankle and falling to the ground in a heap. He nearly tipped over into the water but managed to maintain his balance. Unfortunately, his recovery left himself wide open.

"Pathetic. Your father must be so ashamed to call you his son."

Trotz lifted his two fingers in the shape of a gun toward Minisc. "I can't wait to take your place."

In a brilliant flash, Minisc and his side of the arena were engulfed in a smoky explosion that vibrated through the stadium.

"NO!" Lily shrieked in terror.

Jules sat wide-eyed in shock.

With the crowd stunned, the ref prepared to throw up his flag. At least, until he heard a voice through the cloud of smoke.

"Phew, that was a close one, wasn't it? Stupid water never fails to make my life hell." The smoke blew away while Minisc remained on one knee, his hands stretched diagonal across his body. Woven in between his fingers were strings of light creating a glowing gold barrier.

"How... that should have finished you!" Trotz growled.

"I guess you could say I picked that little trick up from a friend. A good thing, too. That could have ended badly."

"Explain, now."

"Nothing special, really—at the last second, I created a shield to absorb the blow. It wasn't overly strong, but it was enough to take the brunt of the attack. Guess I'm a little better than you gave me credit for, huh?"

Now was Minisc's turn to frustrate his opponent through the power of speech.

Trotz's eye started to twitch, his anger boiling over. The diminutive wannabe set out for blood. On the flip side, Minisc looked calm and concentrated, a far cry from a minute ago. Being forced to protect himself in such a drastic and clever way had made his instincts take over. The benefits of all the work he had put in were beginning to show in a big way.

He snapped his hands shut and his safety shield evaporated into the air as the smoke dispelled from around him.

"Did he just use your shield move?" Jules asked Lily in confusion.

"I—I think so," she replied through deep, intense breaths.

Trotz roared, "Clever, but let's see if you can survive round two." He sent a flurry of electrical attacks at Minisc. This time, however, the attacks were sporadic, all of them continually off-target and uncontrolled. Trotz grew angrier with every failed attempt as Minisc easily deflected the blasts with his own light. He even managed to maintain his balance, putting his fear of water into the back of his mind for the moment.

Minisc could see the boy tiring out. Trotz's breathing had intensified, and his attacks were becoming sluggish.

"Why do all my attacks keep failing?" Trotz shouted as he watched Minisc remain still, almost mocking him with the effortless style. It was becoming apparent to the crowd that Trotz was going ballistic in his assault, but no longer anywhere near accurate.

Trotz fired one last spark. This one Minisc stood still for, taking the hit directly in the chest. A brief pause stalled the battle before Minisc smirked again.

"Is that really the best you can do? That's a shame. You think with wanting to be the next Hero of Light, you could add a little more punch."

Minisc felt a childish grin overtake him. He enjoyed the cocky streak he was displaying. Looking at Trotz, he saw the growing frustration in his opponent's hate-filled eyes. Jealousy ran deep, and the mind games and trash-talking Trotz had dished out at the beginning of the match were now rattling him. Minisc had used next to no energy as well, dodging and only squeezing in an attack when he could. On the other hand, Trotz had wasted all of his strength in his fit of rage, like a bull rampaging in circles till it tired itself out.

Angry and embarrassed, Trotz had seen enough—he started charging all his energy into one final assault. Sparks flew from his body, which began to glow a sparkling yellow, and his hair pulled to the sky as the static built up. Both of his hands stretched perpendicular to his body, with sparks flying back and forth between them. Minisc stood a dozen feet away, his feet firmly planted on the platform floating calmly in the water. He waited with confidence, letting Trotz charge everything he had into his attack.

"Why is Minisc just waiting? He should be taking advantage of Trotz's lack of mobility," Lily yelled, leaning over the cold steel bar that was guarding her against the lower bowl. Jules latched on to her desperately, trying to keep her from tumbling over.

Meanwhile, Don had been watching the battle from the press box while taking care of some arrangements for the tournament. Still, he would never miss his son's fight. He wanted to see how much Minisc had grown since starting school.

"That boy doesn't have any energy left," he said under his breath.

Don thought back to his early training with his son. *When we first started training, Minisc would run out of energy far too quickly and leave himself open. Trotz has done the same thing in his fits of rage. Minisc is as cognizant as anybody about that.*

"Try and dodge this," Trotz bellowed in hatred.

Sparks flew off his body in all directions, his energy skyrocketing. Minisc let out a small chuckle watching Trotz's intensity grow. It was an antagonizing laugh, as if he were keeping a secret joke from his opponent. That was the final straw. Infuriated, Trotz launched his all out assault at Minisc.

"Say goodbye!"

A twirling ribbon of sparks ripped through the air like it had been shot out of a cannon. But sadly, before it even traveled halfway to Minisc, the attack faded into a small puff of smoke, whisked away in the cold stadium air.

"Wait, what happened?" Trotz looked on, confused at the pitiful result of his finishing move. Minisc decided to let his opponent in on a lesson he had become all too familiar with.

"You wasted all your energy spouting off those attacks in your little temper tantrum. You see, your element is just an extension of your physical abilities. When you exhaust yourself, you can't muster up the energy your body needs to use your element. If you were really worthy of being the Hero of Light's sidekick like you claimed, then you'd have been aware of that small oversight. Too bad; I still have plenty of energy left."

Minisc began to charge up a ball of light. With an aura starting to radiate from his body, Trotz squeaked out a surprising response. "I surrender."

"Excuse me?" Minisc blurted out. He dropped his energy and turned to look up at the referee with a puzzled expression.

The burly man shrugged his shoulders. "By rule, Trotz has surrendered. Therefore, the winner is Minisc."

The crowd paused for a second, confused by the result, at least until the scoreboard flashed to Minisc's picture with the word *Winner* in white and red underneath it. Once they saw that, an eruption of cheers followed. Trotz quickly skirted out of the arena and down the dimly lit tunnel while Minisc remained stumped, standing in the middle of a booming crowd.

"Why do I always get the whack jobs?" he muttered, "Oh well, time to get me on dry land…"

CHAPTER 10
MISMATCH

WITH THE TOURNAMENT UNDERWAY, AND THE NEXT SET of matches not involving Minisc, Jules, or Lily, the three took in the beautiful weather on one of the many patio restaurants. Jules customarily stuffed his face with a trough of crispy golden French fries, while Lily and Minisc went over a pamphlet of all the fighters in the tournament.

"I'm surprised you guys didn't want to watch Ignis fight," Lily said, pointing to the boy's picture in the pamphlet. It had the tournament bracket on the left and each student's picture on the right.

"I've seen him fight enough times — besides, I could use some food after that match. Jules, pass me some French fries." Minisc looked over to see his friend's face stuffed past the point of disgusting. He then looked down and saw a bare tray of fries.

"Oh come on, Jules you ate that whole thing? You do realize you fight in less than an hour, right?"

Jules took a large gulp and swallowed his food. "Don't worry, I'll be fine. I've seen Reese fight lots of times — I'm not worried."

Lily and Minisc both shrugged. If Jules sounded confident, they would just have to assume he was prepared. Hopefully, his overconfidence would not be his undoing.

The other matches flew by, and in no time Jules found himself waiting in the locker room. Finally, the moment he'd dreamed about since childhood was upon him. This would be the first step in winning the tournament, joining the EC, and working with his brother.

Jules made his way down the long, winding hall to the underground tunnel. From there, he would only be a few steps away from his grand stage. Excitement bubbling up inside, a gleaming plaque on the wall called out to him. He stopped along the way to admire the display. Engraved in elegant silver lettering were the names of all the past tournament champions. For Jules, having his name engraved on the plaque would be a dream come true.

 Scrolling down each name, he paused as he came across the one he had been looking for.

"Yuri Embroider," he murmured to himself, running his finger across the gold nameplate.

"I'll make you proud, bro."

Continuing along, Jules readied himself for battle. Failure was not an option.

Following the announcement of his name, Jules came sprinting out of the tunnel, throwing his hands up in the air. His enthusiasm was infectious, pumping up the roaring crowd. Finally, his time to shine had come.

"He might be enjoying the spotlight a little too much," Lily giggled.

Minisc nodded, but he knew otherwise. When he looked at his friend, he could see a far different sight than a jubilant student excited to battle. Minisc could see a look of confidence, a swagger that Jules carried with him into the ring. The boy was 100-percent focused and ready.

"Someone is quite the showman," the girl standing across from Jules chirped. His opponent, Reese, had the look of a natural athlete. She had long silver hair flowing down the back of her magenta sleeveless dress, and she did not look all too pleased with the hoopla surrounding her opponent.

As soon as Jules's feet hit the tiles, his attention turned to his opponent.

"Yeah, I guess I got a little excited. I couldn't help it, I've always dreamed about running out of the tunnel to a roaring crowd." He scratched the back of his neck, grinning uncontrollably.

"Well Jules, I hope you're ready. This isn't going to be like sparring in class—I won't be holding back." Reese gave a small bow before bracing for battle. She had an air about her, a quiet confidence that could be felt through one look. It was a fact that did not go unnoticed by Jules, either. One look into her emerald eyes told him all he needed to know about how tough his opponent would be. Even if they had sparred before, it had been months ago, and he knew all the students had grown since then. Still, Reese was not the only one with confidence. Jules refused to be intimidated by anyone. Yuri would never be, so how could he?

The stadium selected for the match was a field of glistening ice that looked more like a hockey rink. Not only would it be hard to keep one's balance, but sliding out of bounds would likely be the biggest threat to either competitor.

Even with that, Jules gave a fearless grin. In part thanks to his wind, he knew he would hold an advantage. Reese's mobility would be severely lacking, and even as an earth Elementalist, she would not be able to gain traction on ice.

Jules readied himself, and with the referee's flag thrust into the air, the battle began.

Jules unleashed a flurry of wind, hoping for a quick win. Unfortunately, he had not expected Reese's opening defense. As the swirls from Jules's body began to churn in the stadium, he found it almost impossible to keep himself balanced. The reverse force of his attack continued to push him along the ice. Reese, on the other hand, lifted her feet one at a time, then lowered them in a thunderous stomp, sending cracks through the ice.

Except that was only step one in her plan. Step two was a counter to Jules's original strategy of blowing her out of the ring. Her feet were dug deep in the ice, up to her shins, giving her the stability that she needed to keep from being pushed around. Although her mobility was lacking, she believed it to be her best move.

Jules ceased his attack, so Reese stepped out of the holes she created.

"I have to admit, that was pretty clever. Using your element to create cracks in the ground so you wouldn't lose balance. But you forgot one thing—that means you can't move either!" Jules leaped forward, ready to land a flurry of blows on Reese, but when he hit the ice his feet went out from under him, and he slid his way into Reese's clutches.

"Either you are supremely overconfident, or just careless. If the ice wasn't slippery enough, you should have known I could create tremors when my feet are planted." Reese kicked her foot up, slicing right through the ice like a hot knife through butter. She connected cleanly, sending Jules flying back with chunks of ice. He crashed along the slick surface, sliding to a stop just inches from the out-of-bounds line.

"Jules needs to do something. Why isn't he using his wind? He's going to lose," Lily shouted incoherently.

Minisc gave her a funny look. He could not believe it; the girl was like a crazed parent cheering her kid on. She could not sit still and instead overreacted to every movement. At least for Minisc, the theatrics were rather entertaining. He felt far more composed while watching his friend. Jules would not be beaten so easily, he wholeheartedly believed that. Calmly watching on, Minisc did his best to explain Jules's thought process to Lily.

"He can't use his wind, thanks to the ice. The force he generates would push him back as much as it would push Reese back, and with Reese firmly planted in the ice, she's more or less rendered Jules element useless."

"Oh…"

Jules could feel the roar of the crowd at his back as he managed to halt himself from slipping out of the ring. If he planned to last more than a minute in what could be his only match, he would need a better strategy, and quick.

Reese stepped out of her footholds, moving on the ice with ease. Each powerful step left shattered ice in her wake as she used her element to keep balanced. Jules scrambled to his feet before blocking the furious blows coming his way. He did all he could to stay closer to the middle of the ring, but dangerous potholes stunted his movement.

Reese continued her relentless assault on the boy. She lacked knockout power, luckily for Jules, but the hits were adding up. He had no time to react, and despite his best efforts, Jules felt his defenses penetrated with a pivotal strike to his ribs. He let out an audible gasp as he stumbled toward the edge of the ring.

"I guess it's time to finish this off; better luck next year, Jules!"

Reese stomped her foot, creating another tremor, causing Jules to stumble back.

"Oh no, he's going to fall out of the ring," Lily screamed.

Jules felt his foot graze off the edge as the crowd erupted.

"No!" Lily gasped.

"He lost..." Minisc whispered in shock.

"You should watch your overconfidence next time — it makes you an easy target," Reese uttered as she turned her back to Jules. She started to walk away, head held high in her victory.

"Easy, huh?" a voice called from the side of the ring. Reese spun around to see Jules rising above the edge like an angel, his toothy grin intact. The boy was levitating above the grass.

Lily, Minisc, and the rest of the building were perplexed.

"No way — is Jules flying? Is that possible?" Lily asked.

"Look underneath him; he's using his wind to propel himself up." Minisc gestured to the boy's feet. "I guess he wasn't kidding when he said he had a plan. Still, that must take a huge toll on his energy. Jules needs to act quickly if he wants to win this."

Reese smirked. "Guess I shouldn't be surprised. You always did have something up your sleeve when it counted."

"I should have just done this from the beginning — would have made things a lot easier than sliding on ice... but I was hoping to save it for the finals! Oh well, now it's my turn to counter-attack. Prepare yourself, Reese!"

"Still as cocky as ever if you think you're going to the finals!"

Jules launched his merciless assault upon the girl. She remained nimble, blows grazing off her, but Jules refused to let up. As long as he remained airborne, Reese had no way of countering. It was her turn to be forced into a corner, with nowhere left to run.

I can't keep this up much longer. I need to finish this! Jules thought to himself, feeling the tension in his body multiplying by the second.

With one final kick, Jules soared through the air. Reese braced her arms across her chest, absorbing the full force of the blow. As they collided, mossy green waves exploded and Jules's wind burst from underneath him. He sprawled backward, landing on the ice and sliding to the edge. However, the impact of the kick, mixed with Jules's release of wind energy, sent Reese sailing out of the ring, plopping down on the soft grass. He had won.

Cheers rang out all around the stadium. A chant of "Jules" broke out, making the boy smile uncontrollably. Even in his wildest imaginations, he could not have predicted the excitement that filled him at winning his first match.

"He won, he won, he won," Lily exclaimed, jumping up and down.

Minisc let out a sigh of relief before slinking back into his chair.

I don't know what's more painful – watching Jules, or Lily's violent reactions.

The final match of the first-year division was set up to be the biggest mismatch of the day, and likely of the entire tournament. Lily sat on the couch in her changing room, alone. At any moment, Minisc and Jules would walk through the door with a plan that would help give her the advantage against Coro... but something continued to weigh on her mind. Something she struggled to admit but knew to be true.

Right on cue, the door swung open, and her friends walked through, trying to hide their looks of concern.

"Hey Lil, how you feeling?" Minisc asked, taking a seat beside his friend. He could see the wheels in her head spinning. She showed just as much worry as her friends about facing Coro.

"Nervous," she said, "Coro is so strong, and we've all seen his ice barrages in class. Nobody has managed to last more than a few seconds against him."

"It's true, but I'm sure if we try, we can come up with a plan that can beat him, right? You can't just give up," Jules said, hoping to reassure her.

"Jules is right—we can come up with something, I know it."

"Thank you guys, but actually, I think I want to handle this on my own."

"What do you mean?" Minisc asked.

Lily looked to the floor for a moment before looking back at Minisc. "I think I finally understand why Ms. Wright chose me for the tournament. Ever since I met both of you, I've been depending on you two for everything. In all of our training, you two have always been my partners and did the heavy lifting, and I guess, soon, I became okay with that. I started to believe that I needed to rely on you two, when I actually came to EA to learn how to use my element better. But all I've been so far is a burden. You two have been hurt numerous times protecting me, and that's not the person I want to be. Don't get me wrong, I'm so grateful for all that you two have done for me—I never would have made it past the first day without you. But now it's my turn to take the lead. I want to do this on my own. I want to prove to myself that I can do this." Lily could see the looks of fear and concern from her friends. Granted, they were more than justified, but she had made up her mind. Even if she faced utter humiliation from Coro, she would do it while depending on herself. "Don't worry, guys, it's going to be okay. I won't go down without a fight."

Minisc remained unconvinced. If he let Lily fight, the result could be a disaster, a sight he could not bear to see. Yet he knew that talking Lily out of her convictions would be a selfish act. She had made her decision, and despite his fears, he had to accept them for what they were.

Minisc nodded in agreement. He looked at Jules and said, "Come on, let's go."

Minisc walked to the door, before turning back to look at Lily. He smiled sweetly. "Remember, just do your best. We believe in you."

Lily smiled back, giving him a thumbs-up. Even though she trusted her decision, doubt still swirled all around. Was this the right choice? Regardless, there was only one way to find out.

While Lily did her best to remain calm before her match, Coro found himself being chastised in the tunnel, waiting to hear his name.

"Leave me alone," he groaned.

"Why do you continue to refuse the power that I've granted you? You should be displaying both of your elements to the world. Allow them to see my work at its peak."

"I'm not going to be your guinea pig anymore. I don't need your stupid experiments. I'm going to do this myself, without you."

"You ungrateful child. If it weren't for me, you would have no life. My experiments saved you. You should idolize me, jumping at every chance I have given you to help serve me. But once again, this is how you repay my efforts."

A cold stare filled the momentary silence before the man stormed off in a fit of anger.

Coro stood with his back against the concrete walls of the stadium tunnels.

His father's goal was simple. He wanted to show the world that his genetic augmentation of one's element was the way of the future — the way to fame and fortune, while bringing glory back to the scientist's disgraced name.

Coro was to win the tournament at all costs. After winning and displaying his full power on the world stage, he would launch his father's research into the limelight once again. Coro, however, wanted to win for another reason. He resented his father for his treatment of others. Specifically, his mother and himself. If he were to win the tournament, he would do it using his own blessed abilities, not his father's genetic enhancements. Achieving victory without giving his father the chance to display his research would be the ultimate payback.

In the opposite tunnel, Lily slouched along the wall. Anxiety gripped her body and refused to let go. She had grown somewhat comfortable with her element; however, her match would be far more stringent than anything she had faced in her life. She took another deep breath. "Just do your best," she whispered to herself. She wanted to win. Of course she did. But she also wanted to prove to others, and more importantly to herself, that she was capable. Capable of fending for herself and her friends. Ever since she'd arrived at school, she had been seen as a liability. Her aversion to offensive powers meant she always had to be protected in battle. Watching Minisc sacrifice himself to protect her in their first fight had opened up the girl's eyes. Now she would have a one-on-one match with a prodigy — the perfect stage to show how much she had grown. Even though the odds were stacked against her, Lily had no intention of going down without a fight.

Meanwhile, Minisc and Jules were on their way to the stands when they ran into Don, who appeared to be waiting for them in the hall.

"Hello, you two, and congrats on winning in the first round."

"Thanks," Jules gleamed.

"What are you doing here, Father?"

"I had a little bit of free time so I wanted to watch the final match for the day. Your friend Lily is up next, is she not?"

"Yeah, we were just heading up to our seats actually."

"Surely you don't want to watch her match from all the way up there, do you?"

"Not really, but we don't have a choice; where else are we going to watch it from?"

"What about watching from the tunnel, then?"

"That would be so cool." Jules grinned.

"Security would toss us out in a heartbeat." The subtle hint sailed right over Minisc's head.

"Leave that to me," Don smirked before leading them down the other hall.

Lily stood across from her most frightful opponent since the cloaked man. She portrayed outward confidence, but inside, she shook from head to toe. She locked eyes with Coro. The boy's listless face was discomforting to stare at. It looked as if he had other things on his mind. She knew better, though. Once the battle began, those eyes would turn merciless. She had to be prepared.

The jumbotron started beeping as the lights circled round and round. The fate of the battle could come down to the terrain selection.

"Good, it hasn't started yet," Minisc said as he reached the opening of the tunnel. He spotted Lily in her aqua-blue battle dress before looking across at Coro. His cold gray hair sparkled in the sun. The boy was wearing a white-and-black shirt with dark blue shorts.

Minisc noticed the same disinterested look that Lily had seen. To him, Coro looked almost sad. Like he was hiding something that continued to eat away at him.

The match had not started, but Minisc looked on with clenched teeth. It was not his fight, but he remained fearful. He did not want Lily to get hurt.

Don walked behind him, placing his hand on his son's shoulder. Minisc jumped at the touch.

"Nervous?"

"Yeah… a little bit. Coro is just so much more powerful than all of us. Nobody has even been able to touch him in class."

"You have to believe, son. With the right strategy, anyone can be beaten. Even someone as strong as Coro."

The beeping of the roulette board came to a stop. Minisc looked over to see where it had landed.

"For this match, we'll be taking the combatants to the fire pits, a rocky charcoal bedrock—competitors need to watch out for the fire geysers that spout from the ground."

The floor lifted up, filling the void between. Dirt covered the ground with jagged, rocky barriers scattered about. Small parts of the surface were boiling red, waves of heat emanating off them. From one, a stream of fire burst up to the sky before dying down again.

"A fire stage; that's an advantage for Lily." Minisc and Jules cheered. Their first prayer had been granted. Lily could withstand fire much easier with her water element, while Coro's ice would not be able to freeze the entire arena. At least they hoped.

Seconds away from starting, Lily steeled the nerves running through her body. She tried to focus only on the task at hand: Coro's opening attack. Without getting around that, she would not last more than five seconds.

With the wave of the flag, the battle started as expected. Coro's body was enveloped in a cold blue hue, followed by a tsunami of ice. A predictable attack, but one that was near impossible to dodge. Lily knew she could not hope to match Coro's strength, but she had luck on her side, and a plan. With the ice baring down, she dove behind a spurting fire geyser. It was risky, but her only hope was to use the stage to her advantage. Lily squeezed her eyes shut, saying a silent prayer. The ice enveloped the stadium surface and beyond with shattered spears of shrapnel flying off in all directions.

Minisc and Jules both gritted their teeth as Coro's ice collided with the fire spout.

Before Minisc could recognize what was about to happen, the shrapnel raced toward the opening of the tunnel. He covered himself in preparation for the hit. But before it landed, Don flashed in front, holding his left hand out; it shined like the sun as the man's hand repelled all glacial blasts into different directions. Minisc and Jules looked up from their arms. The surroundings in the tunnel had icy residue on the walls and floor, but they remained unharmed.

"That boy is incredibly strong," Don acknowledged as he lowered his hand.

"Unbelievable; you shattered that ice like it was nothing," Jules praised. Still mesmerized, he momentarily forgot who was out on the battlefield. Then, remembering why he was there, he drew his attention to the action. Except he noticed one person missing.

"Wait, where's Lily?"

The surrounding surface had frozen over.

Lily opened her eyes to a beautiful, crystal-like wonderland. The geyser she had been stationed behind froze like a giant popsicle. However, the most important thing in her quest to win had happened. She survived. Taking a second to examine her body, she could not find a scratch on her, only feeling the warm heat barely penetrating the layer of ice that covered the geyser. Through smarts, a miracle, or both, Lily had taken Coro's best shot and remained standing.

"She survived the ice barrage," Minisc cheered.

Back in the arena, the ice thawed due to the overwhelming heat, bringing the field back to its original terrain. Lily had to think fast; she had been granted one lucky break in surviving Coro's opening attack, but she could not hedge her bets on a second. To start, Coro's ice blast had been far stronger than anything she had seen in class. She realized just how in over her head she was.

During classes and training, Lily had always taken a defensive role, allowing others like Minisc and Jules to do the front-line fighting. With that no longer an option, she had to think fast to win. Although it would push her far out of her comfort zone, she assumed that had been Ms. Wright's goal all along.

Springing into action, Lily leaped high into the air. She needed to show a mix of skill and smarts if she was going to prove she was good enough to compete. Thrusting her hand out, Lily directed a blast of water toward Coro. The boy grunted, slightly picking up his right hand and giving it a frosty wave. With a flash of cold air, Lily's stream of water froze in place. A bright gleam shone off the sculpture.

"That's exactly what I wanted," Lily smirked as she pirouetted in the air, landing gracefully on the makeshift grind rail. She knew her speed alone could not keep up with Coro's, but sliding down the rail, picking up the pace, she gave her opponent no time to react. In a flash, she had gone on the offensive. Much like everyone who had been entered in the tournament, Lily had done her fair share of extra training. With the help of Ms. Wright, Lily had put in many after-school hours working on her fighting skills just as much as the use of her element. She may have had the look of a frail girl, but that would be the last thing to stop her.

Lily led with a kick, striking true into Coro's chest. The boy soared through the air toward the boundary, on his way to a ring-out. Either out of shock or openly mocking Lily's meager hit, Coro made almost no effort to stop himself, a task he could have easily achieved.

"He's heading out of bounds," Minisc yelled, thinking Lily had survived. Coro would prove not to be that easy of a victory, though. As he neared the edge, a small barrier of ice shot up from the ground like a wall, stopping his momentum with a vicious thud. He picked himself up, looking less than amused.

No time to waste, let's go. Lily rushed toward Coro with blazing speed. Neither she, nor any of her class, had seen Coro's hand-to-hand combat at full speed. They had practiced in groups many times, but that was a far cry from real battle. That meant in Lily's mind, her best bet would be to not match him element for element, but instead stay in close and fight with her fists. Since Coro was so close to the edge already, it was not a matter of brute strength, but continuing her attack to overwhelm him till she scored a ring-out.

Lily started shooting bubbling water at Coro from every angle. If she kept moving, the boy would not be able to get a clean shot on her. She blitzed in, throwing all her might behind her punches, mixing things up between element and brute force. Coro held up his arms across his chest, blocking the blows. Lily hopped back, causing a brief pause in the battle.

I'm slowing down; I shouldn't be this tired already. I've barely used any energy. She gasped, trying to catch her breath.

She began her assault again. A blast of water, then an attempted punch, but it was no use. She lacked the energy to make any impact. Coro brushed off her blows like he was being hit with a pillow.

"Oh no, she's slowing down," Jules said.

"She's getting tired, but how? The battle just started."

"It's the heat of the arena. It's draining her energy faster than normal. Even doing usual movements will drain energy twice as fast. She must be physically exhausted and not even realize it. Her resolve is strong. She wants to win at all cost, it's quite admirable, but her strategy might prove costly," Don said.

Steam rose through the sky as Lily attempted to catch her breath. She jumped forward into a spin kick. But try as she might, Coro raised his arm, blocking it effortlessly. Lily landed, trying to brace herself for the inevitable. She shut her eyes, waiting for Coro to finish her off with one climactic blow. Yet what happened instead caught her by surprise.

"Give up," Coro bargained in a low voice. Lily's eyes snapped open. "What?"

"You're pushing yourself way too far, all for a silly tournament. You're going to end up getting hurt," Coro explained, his voice showing the most emotion Lily had ever heard from him. Thinking about it, she knew Coro was right. Physically, her body cried out for her to stop—she had no experience fighting in such heat or with so much vigor. The tolls were beginning to add up. Even knowing that, giving up never crossed her mind. Minisc would not give up, nor would Jules. They would put their bodies on the line and never give up if it meant helping someone. If she quit, it would only serve to show everyone she lacked the capability to be like them. Ms. Wright had not selected her just for her to quit at the first sign of trouble.

"For some of us, it's not a silly tournament, Coro. I came out here to prove something to myself, and win or lose, giving up will not prove anything. So I'm going to do my best no matter what! If you won't take this seriously, then fine, but I am, and I will find a way to win, no matter how much better you are than me," Lily responded with a new resolve.

Coro paused for a second. From his vantage point, Minisc could see a flicker of emotion in the boy's eyes.

"I'm not giving up, Coro, so you're going to have to beat me fair and square. Got it?"

Lily charged Coro with whatever remained in her tank, just like her teacher had taught. Flailing with fists enveloped in water, she remained determined to give her best and nothing less. Unfortunately, Coro remained infinitely more skilled, turning her blows away as spots of fire continued to raise the temperature higher. Lily glistened in sweat as she felt her body growing ever weaker. Still refusing to back down, Lily went for a punch with all her might. That, however, would spell her end.

"I'm sorry," Coro whispered as he caught the dainty girl's wrist in his tight grip. The crowd gasped as the battle came to a halt. Lily struggled to free herself, but lacked any remaining strength. She knew her fate had been decided.

"This is over," Coro murmured. He stuck his free hand inches away from Lily's chest. They both watched along with the roaring audience as a blinding blue light engulfed the arena.

The next thing Lily knew, her body was sailing through the air before smashing violently into the back wall outside of the ring.

The crowd was overtaken by shock, but nothing compared to Minisc, who had a look of absolute horror painted on his face. He remained fixated on his friend, who lay only a few feet away from him, motionless on the grass. Taking a shaky step forward, he reached out to Lily. The world around them came to a stop as Minisc felt his heart leap into his throat.

Jules put his hand on Minisc's shoulder. "She's breathing, she's okay," he assured his friend, pointing to the girl's rising and falling chest.

After a moment, Lily gradually got up to her feet. She had cuts on her body, and she looked sickly exhausted.

Minisc, seeing his friend in such distress, could not stop himself from running out of the tunnel to meet her. As he did, he grabbed and hugged her tight before taking a step back to look at her.

"I guess I lost…" Lily mumbled weakly.

"You did your best," Minisc whispered back to her.

Taking one step forward, Lily collapsed into his arms. Shocked, he caught her limp body in a warm embrace, doing everything he could to hold her up. For a brief moment, time stood still. The roaring fans, the announcer's voice, none of it played in Minisc's ears. All he could focus on was the girl in his arms. Refusing to let go, Minisc heard a small whimper before feeling a teardrop fall onto his shoulder. He squeezed Lily a little tighter.

CHAPTER 11
THE BONDS THAT TIE US

WITH THE LAST MATCH OF THE DAY WRAPPED UP, FANS and participants alike left for the night. Everyone except Minisc, who sat curled up in an uncomfortable bedside chair. His feet were hanging over the side, and a small pillow was jammed under his head. It was far from an ideal situation, but one that he was willing to accept. The room remained silent, with only the light chirping of crickets and soft howls of wind blowing through the cracked window.

Scotia Coliseum had a small infirmary used for overnight stays and minor injuries from the tournament. Unfortunately, Lily had been one of the overnight patients after her match with Coro.

Minisc gazed over at the poor girl tucked away in the narrow bed. She looked oddly at peace considering where she found herself. She certainly looked more pleasant than Minisc at the moment.

Lily had only sustained minor injuries from Coro's final strike. A small band-aid on her cheek and a few bruises, but no worse for wear. Coro had held back considerably, knowing the state she was in. He wanted no harm to come to his classmate, a sentiment Minisc was eternally grateful for. The doctor's diagnosis found that the poor girl had simply worn herself ragged, expending more energy in far higher temperatures than she was accustomed to. After the adrenaline had died off, she had nothing left. Minisc and company decided she would be held in the infirmary to rest as a precaution.

There, she would make a full recovery in short order. Minisc and Jules still struggled to believe the doctors based on what the two had witnessed, but they had no other options.

Even so, Minisc had opted to stay the night next to Lily, not wanting her to wake up alone in the middle of the night. Besides, she had waited for him when he found himself in the school infirmary. It only made sense for him to return the favor.

Half-asleep awkwardly in the chair beside her bed, he struggled to find comfort. Enough time had passed for him to calm down, and after the doctor had given Lily a clean bill of health, Minisc had eased up considerably, but his mind continued to relive the traumatic event like a horror movie on replay. He could not forget the fear that gripped him so tightly. The fact that Lily had not woken up nearly eight hours later certainly did nothing to help.

Jules had tried to convince his shell-shocked friend to go home and rest, but he refused. Much to Jules's dismay, he could see the concern on Minisc's face, and arguing was out of the question. He carried an equal amount of concern but understood they were both powerless to do anything.

The tournament had only just begun but it seemed to be taking its toll on those remaining, and even on those who weren't. As the intensity grew, so too did the dangers, a sobering thought for Minisc.

His semi-final match would start the next morning, and his opponent would be none other than his best friend, Jules. The two had known it was a possibility that they could face-off, and Jules had even fantasized about it, but now that reality started to set in, Minisc could feel a new sense of dread rising.

Jules had dreamed about winning the Tournament of Elements ever since his brother had been crowned champion many years ago. Minisc wanted to see his friend win as well, achieving his dreams. It would make Minisc as happy as Jules, if not more so, to see his friend succeed. But now he found himself standing in Jules's path. Somehow, it didn't feel right. Minisc wanted to win the tournament—of course he did. He had his own goals and dreams, but one continual thought from his childhood haunted him: Ignis.

Minisc and Ignis had once been inseparable, and Ignis had lofty dreams, the same as Jules. He'd planned to one day fight alongside his mother and father as part of the EC. Then his hopes were shattered with the untimely death of his parents. And so the blame for those lost dreams fell onto Minisc's shoulders, justified or otherwise.

Now, Minisc found himself in the same position once again. With a win, he would break the dream that Jules had worked so tirelessly toward, a dream that he'd probably had before the two were even friends. What if, like Ignis before him, Jules began to resent him, or even left him? Only three people were truly important to Minisc: his father, Lily, and Jules. He'd just had a momentary scare seeing Lily hurt; he could not risk losing Jules as well.

Stuck with doubtful thoughts racing around his mind, Minisc heard a soft, weak voice call out to him.

"Minisc…"

Wistfully, he opened his eyes, recognizing the sweetness of Lily's voice. He looked over at her bed, seeing the girl sitting upright. A beautiful moonlight glow bathed her skin in a soft blue, making her look like an angel from the heavens. Minisc could feel the emotions welling up inside him as he tried to find the words to speak.

"You're awake…" he whispered.

"Where are we?"

"Your hospital bed."

"Oh… I guess things didn't go as planned, did they?" She seemed rather unconcerned about being in an infirmary.

"I'm just glad you're okay," Minisc whispered again, leaning in for a soft hug. For the moment, he could breathe. One scare had been rectified.

"I'm a little sore, I guess, but I'm okay… What time is it?" Lily yawned.

"Midnight."

"Midnight, what are you doing here? You should be getting a good night's rest before you face off against Jules tomorrow," Lily said, rubbing the crust out of her sea-blue eyes.

"That ship sailed the second you landed in this place."

"That's sweet of you."

"How do you feel?"

"Tired."

They both showed a small grin.

"My parents are probably worried sick…"

"Don't worry, Jules and I took care of that."

"Huh?"

"Let's just call it returning the favor for you calling my father that first week of school." The two giggled softly.

"I'm sorry, Minisc, I guess I should have let you guys help me… maybe I could've won then. It's just, I wanted to prove to myself that I could do this on my own. I wanted to show I was strong and reliable, like you and Jules.

"You don't need to apologize, I understand. Besides, the effort you gave against Coro proved far more than your strength. You should be proud of what you accomplished, even if you did lose. You gave it your best shot, and that's all you can do."

Lily fought back a second yawn, her eyelids beginning to droop.

"Thanks, Minisc. I'm so glad I met you."

"So am I… now you should try to get some more sleep," Minisc pleaded with the girl. One look and he could tell she still lacked any energy to stay awake.

Minisc took the blanket off his chair and placed it on top of Lily. Before she could dispute the notion, her heavy eyes slammed shut. Like the silent night, she passed out cold once again.

"I need to get some sleep as well…" Minisc whispered, snuggling back into the tiny chair.

"Guess what, I took the day off work, so I'm coming to watch your match today," said Yuri.

"No way. That's so cool," Jules exclaimed. Yuri could feel the boy's excitement through the phone.

Jules sat in the changing room with just over an hour left until his match with Minisc. His excitement had bubbled to the point he had arrived early, making sure he would not run into his friend. Jules made no qualms about hoping to face his friend in a high stakes match. For as long as they'd known each other, the two had never gone head-to-head in a meaningful competition. Part of that was because Minisc had never wanted to work on his element or train, unlike Jules, but the other part had been that they liked to team up in class when they got the chance. In hopes of embracing his role as the *Hero* and Minisc as the *villain,* Jules had even decided to treat Minisc as such, which meant cutting off all communication before the match. For the day, Minisc represented the bad guy standing in his way. Not in reality, but Jules thought it was sort of fun to think of his friend as the enemy he must defeat and letting him act like his brother, saving the day.

Unlike Jules, Minisc did not share the same level of enthusiasm. Rising from his stiff slumber Minisc attempted to hold his rushing doubts at bay. That, however, proved more challenging than he expected, with negative thoughts and fears attached to him like his own shadow. At this rate, he would exhaust himself mentally before the battle had even begun.

He looked at the clock. Less than an hour. The tension in his body continued rising. A quick thought of withdrawing popped into his mind but left just as fast. Jules would never forgive him if he quit the match. Fighting appeared to be the only option, even if it was the one Minisc feared most.

He peered over at Lily. She lay rolled on her side, her hands snuggling the fluffy pillow that supported her head. She looked so at ease. Minisc hesitated to wake her up. He needed to talk, to spew out all the emotions he had inside. Normally Jules would have been someone else he could have turned to, but not about this — Minisc did not know how to talk to Jules about not wanting to face him. He even ruled out talking to his father, as the man would never accept quitting. Lily was the only person he felt would understand. He wanted to tell her of his trepidation, of his fear of losing Jules, but waking her up would not be right. She had been through enough. This was a burden Minisc had to bear on his own.

With the match about to start, Jules stood on the arena floor, stretching down to touch his toes. He followed that up with some high jumps as he loosened up for what in his mind would no doubt be a momentous battle. He looked at the other tunnel, waiting patiently for Minisc to walk onto their grand stage.

Minisc, however, lazily made his way up the steps and into the ring, looking far less enthusiastic. He had yet to make up his mind about what route to take, but time was running out.

"Finally. For a second, I thought you were going to chicken out on me," Jules laughed.

Minisc remained quiet, his body hunched together in a lot of discomfort. He avoided meeting Jules's eyes, opting to gaze at the ground.

"Hey, are you okay?" Jules asked.

"Yeah, I'm fine," Minisc lied through clenched teeth. He could feel his stomach churning. He wanted nothing to do with this fight. His decision was slowly being made for him.

The two watched as the roulette wheel spun, fans roaring as each panel flashed to a steady stop.

"Electricity."

A field armed to the teeth with electrical tripwires. Large ceramic tiles akin to the open round surface rose into place. Once they set, an electric field phased in and out around the stadium barriers. For Jules, it meant he would not be able to pull off his first-round flying strategy to save himself in a pinch, which handed the first advantage to Minisc. That would not damper Jules's excitement, though.

"This is going to be so much fun," Jules chimed.

"Yeah…" Minisc trailed off.

Not willing to waste a second as the battle started, Jules kicked off the show with a bang. A flash of green surrounded him while a flurry of gusts began to swirl. In an electric stadium where each step could potentially lead to added damage, Jules wanted to make sure he could move Minisc off his spot as much as possible.

Minisc cried out as a jolt of electricity shot up his left leg. He had been pushed onto one of the many electric panels placed under the stadium floor. Seeing Minisc lift his leg from the shock, Jules pounced on his opportunity to strike. He rushed in, swerving in and out of the shock pads with ease. Throwing a few quick jabs at his friend, he watched as Minisc blocked them using his forearms.

Even though Minisc was still debating if he intended to fight, his instincts were tough to go against. Considering throwing a fight was one thing, but it was another to willingly let himself get punched.

With Jules in close, Minisc used his free arm to jam a ball of light into his friend's chest. The blast sent Jules sprawling back, but it lacked conviction, and Minisc and Jules both knew it. A clean hit from Minisc at full power would have been at least enough to stun any opponent, but for Jules, it sent no more than a warm tingle into his chest. As Jules readied for another strike, Minisc instinctually saw his opening. He fired a series of blasts at Jules, but again they were nothing more than pillow hits. Jules trapped the blasts in a vortex of wind, lifting both attacks high into the sky before watching them fade into nothing.

"You're going to have to do a lot better than that if you want to beat me, Minisc," Jules laughed. He appeared to be having the time of his life, not paying any attention to Minisc's lack of effort.

Don stood in the tunnel; he liked being close up to the action compared to being up in the press boxes. It also allowed a much better view to see his son's technique and movements. Having watched Minisc fight many times, he hardly recognized his son's style against Jules. Sloppy, predictable, lacking confidence. It mirrored his first day of training more than the budding warrior his son was growing into. Don crossed his arms.

"What's going on, Minisc? You look unsure of yourself out there."

Entrenched in the fight, he felt a light tap on his back, causing a chill to run up his spine. Much to his surprise, he found himself staring at a cheerful young teen. Her brunette hair was held back by a pale blue ribbon, except for one long strand that lay to the right, shaping her round face. She had an infectious smile.

"Hi," the girl chimed.

"Uh, hello...?" Don stared blankly at the girl. It took him a moment thanks to the new hairstyle and plain clothing but then he recognized her. "Oh, you're Minisc's friend... Lily, correct?" She showed high spirits for someone fresh out of the infirmary.

Lily nodded. "Yep, we talked on the phone that one time."

"Yes, I remember. Minisc talks about you a lot. He's lucky to have a friend like you."

"I'd say I'm lucky to have him. Not many people would stay bedside with me the night before their biggest match," She giggled, "Minisc said that I could come and watch from here with you instead of the stands. If that's okay with you?"

"Of course, you're more than welcome."

Taking a few steps forward, Lily wanted to see how her friends were faring, but only a few seconds in she could see how lopsided the match appeared to be. She rubbed her eyes to make sure what she saw was correct before turning to look at Don.

"What's wrong with Minisc? He looks nothing like himself," she asked in confusion.

"I don't know," the man answered truthfully.

"This must be my fault. He was so worried about me that he exhausted himself before facing Jules."

"I don't think so." Don put his hand to his chin. "He doesn't look tired, or at least in the usual sense; it's something else."

The two continued to watch as Jules relentlessly dominated the match, keeping Minisc on the edge of defeat at every turn.

Knowing he had the upper hand, Jules refused to let up. He channeled his energy into a vicious windstorm. The entire stadium felt like it could be picked up and tossed around.

Minisc covered his eyes for a second, trying to cut down on the force of the wind as debris swirled around.

I knew Jules was improving every day, but I didn't realize he had gotten so strong; this is insane.

With Minisc doing his best to see through his arm, Jules pinpointed his opening, pouncing without hesitation. He dashed in front of Minisc with a burst of speed, swinging up with all his might—a critical punch into his opponent's midsection. Unlike Minisc, Jules held nothing back. With his fist lodged in his friend's stomach, Minisc let out an audible gasp. Pain ripped through him from head to toe as his body screamed violently. He stumbled back from the force before accidentally making his way onto one of the electrical shock traps in the middle of the arena. With the surge of electricity zipping through his body, Minisc dropped to his knees. His vision began to blur and the arena grew darker with each passing second. The roars of the crowd became distant.

Lily held her hands up to her mouth as she gasped. She refused to cheer for any outcome. She knew how much winning meant to both her friends, and although one had to lose, she just hoped neither of them would push themselves too hard and end up like her. But the sight of Minisc crumpled on the ground in such pain made her sick to her stomach.

Minisc negotiated his defeat, graciously accepting the results. *I guess this is a good thing. Jules will go on to the finals, and I can cheer for him instead. I'm sure I'll be crucified by the papers tomorrow for losing, but oh well. I can live with that. It's not like Jules isn't worthy of being in the finals. Even if I used all my strength, he might have still won. Though I guess there's no need to worry about that now. Jules and I will remain friends, and who knows, maybe I can win next year? Assuming I get out of the hospital, that is. I know he's going all out, but man that hit stings.* A silly win was nothing compared to the thought of losing his best friend.

A hush fell over the stadium as Minisc sat on his knees, doubled over. They wanted to react but were not sure if they should. The fight had been so one-sided that it left the audience unsatisfied.

"It can't be over already," Lily said, sharing the reaction of the crowd.

Jules walked up to his crumpled-over friend, a look of frustration on his usually cheerful face.

"Get up," he demanded.

Minisc flinched as the words entered his ears. Did he hear that right? Surely, he must have misunderstood what Jules said.

Jules yelled it this time: "I said, get up." Now he stood above his friend turned opponent, arms crossed and brow furrowed. He could have easily finished off the vulnerable Minisc, but chose not to. Not like this. He could tell his victory had come far too easily, nothing close to the climactic battle between friends at the top of their class. Instead, all he'd received was a façade.

Minisc's eyes snapped open. He continued staring at the ground, a small puddle of water forming in front of him. It was not sweat dripping, but the tears he tried to fight back. Putting his hand on the ground, he pushed himself up weakly until he found himself face to face with an infuriated Jules.

"You're not taking this seriously. Me, you, and Lily promised to try our best, no matter what. Why are you not giving it your all?"

Minisc looked broken. The display of raw emotion caught Jules by surprise.

"Minisc... what is going on?" Jules's tone softened considerably. He had not seen his friend so emotional since he'd lost his mother.

Don watched from the tunnel. "Minisc doesn't want to win," he realized as he saw the broken look of his son. The pieces were starting to fit together.

"What? Why would Minisc not want to win?"

Minisc stood rigid for a second, trying to open his mouth. He searched for the words but remained at a loss.

"I didn't... want... I didn't want you to lose..." Minisc sputtered, lifting his head to look into Jules's eyes. "You wanted to win this tournament so badly. Making your brother proud, hoisting that trophy at the end. I didn't want to stand in your way; I couldn't take something so important away from you. This tournament means so much more to you than it does me. I didn't want you to resent me for standing in the way of your dream. I was afraid we wouldn't be friends anymore. I couldn't deal with that thought. It was just easier to lose. I don't want to fight you, Jules."

Lily turned to the burly man who knew Minisc best.

"Minisc was willing to throw the match so he wouldn't lose Jules as a friend? But Minisc must want to win as well. He wouldn't have worked as hard as he did otherwise."

Don looked somber as he explained.

"Although Minisc doesn't like to talk about it, growing up, he had a rather lonely childhood. I tried to keep him sheltered as best I could from my spotlight, but as a result, he didn't have many friends. Most kids his age wanted to get close to him to meet me. He became reserved, spending most of his time either playing in his room or with his mother. With Minisc at his lowest, Jules showed up and wanted to be his friend without wanting anything from him in return. That meant more to Minisc than anything in this world. He would never want to jeopardize that. Even if it meant throwing the match."

A sad smile came over Lily. She knew that Minisc was often reserved and wary about getting close to people, but she had not realized how lonely her friend must have been all those years.

Back in the fight, Jules chastised his friend for such wrong-minded thoughts. "You dummy; why would you think we wouldn't be friends?"

Minisc lifted his head, his eyes still covered from the blond locks falling in front of his face. "I thought... Ignis..." Minisc sputtered out the incoherent sentence, but for Jules, it made all the sense in the world.

"Minisc, how many times have you told people not to compare

you to your father, because you're not him? You're you. We've talked about this. You're Minisc, and you're my best friend. So I'm not Ignis, and I'd never leave you; whether you like it or not, you're stuck with me till the end. You should know that." Jules smiled. "Besides, I'd hate you more if you just handed me this fight. I want to beat you fair and square. At your best."

Hearing the words, Minisc let a weak smile appear on his face. He wiped the pools of water from his eyes.

The weight of the world rose off Minisc's shoulders. "Thank you, Jules. I'm sorry, I should have had more faith in you than that."

"It's okay, I understand, but frankly, I'm insulted you assumed I couldn't beat you at your peak." The two shared a laugh as they cemented their friendship. "Now… we promised we were going to give it our best no matter what, and I'm going to hold you to that. This time, you better come at me with everything you've got," Jules exclaimed as he readied himself for round two of the fight.

"Alright, I'm ready, but this time I won't make it so easy."

"Good, let's start from the beginning then," Jules laughed, stepping back a few paces.

"Yeah, minus the excruciating pain I went through with the beatdown you handed me," Minisc smirked, rubbing his ribcage.

"That one's your problem. You should've blocked."

Minisc shrugged; the boy had a point.

"Countdown from three?" he asked.

"Sounds good."

Jules held his hand up in the air like a conductor. The fans caught on to what he was looking for. Following his lead, they erupted with a boisterous countdown.

"Three… Two… One… Battle!" the shaking stadium roared in unison.

Minisc, given a fresh start, felt rejuvenated, the pain that had been ripping him apart now ceasing to exist. He looked looser and at ease, ready to show his friend just what his best really entailed.

Leading the charge with enthusiasm, Minisc bore down on Jules, opening with a small flurry of punches, followed by a vicious haymaker. Jules found himself off-balance for the first time all match. Minisc was flying around, his movements hard to keep up with. A weight had been lifted, and although imaginary, with his newfound freedom, Minisc's speed seemed two-fold ahead of Jules. Left with no other option, Jules jumped into a defensive position, shielding his body from the overwhelming blows. He looked for an opening but could barely keep up enough to find one. Minisc pounced back, a light illuminating from each hand. A quick flick of the wrist sent both glowing orbs speeding at Jules.

"You're going to have to be better than that." In an attempt to counter, Jules caught the spheres in a vortex of wind.

"So predictable."

With Jules tied up, Minisc raised his right hand to the sky, gathering an exorbitant amount of energy. The ball shined as bright as a second sun, blinding the audience. Even if the two had not fought at full power before, they still were best friends, and they knew each other like brothers. Minisc knew all of Jules's moves and tendencies, while the same could be said in favor of Jules. The winner would have to display some unpredictable skills.

"Let's see if you can hold this one off." Minisc laughed as he snapped his wrist forward. The humongous blast ripped through the horizontal vortex, quickly overtaking the two smaller orbs in its path of destruction. Sparks flew all over the arena's surface, matching the growing intensity of the battle and the crowd.

Jules tried to think; he found himself in a sticky situation. He had no hope of blocking an attack of that magnitude, but with a lack of other options in his arsenal, he would need to overpower the blast at all costs through sheer willpower. He squeezed his eyes shut, summoning as much energy as his body could produce. The vortex increased in speed and power as Jules radiated a shimmering lime green. He'd just begun to push the attack back when he heard a voice begin yelling from the tunnel behind him.

"Come on Jules. You can win this. Give it everything you've got."

Although the yelling sounded faint from behind, Jules instantly recognized who was giving him the words of encouragement.

"Yuri."

He's right, I've come too far to lose this now. I'll make you proud, brother.

The encouragement from his brother rejuvenated and reinvigorated Jules. He intensified his attack, pouring all he had into it.

"I'm going to win this, Minisc, whatever it takes."

Jules threw his hands into the sky, directing the tornado and everything in it toward the rooftop opening, followed by a deafening boom. The sky lit up again, the crowd applauding at the incredible display from the two first-year students. Sparkles from the explosion rained down over the building, evaporating as they sprinkled to the ground. Minisc and Jules both looked up at the spectacle, reveling in every moment of their battle. The two looked at each other, wearing goofy grins.

"Thought you had me with that one, didn't you?" Jules chirped.

"Yeah, not going to lie, I didn't think you'd be able to stop that."

From the tunnel, Lily began looking more relaxed herself. "Minisc looks so much more at ease now." The joy and enthusiasm of her friends had started to infect everyone watching.

Don nodded in agreement. Even with a birth in the championship on the line, at their core, it was two friends trying to one-up each other.

"Yes, it seems a weight has been lifted off of Minisc's shoulders. He now feels confident nothing will come between him and Jules, and that is allowing him to fight freely and with his full strength."

Minisc and Jules panted heavily as they tried to catch their breaths.

"So how much you figure you got left in the tank?" Minisc coaxed.

"More than you, I bet."

Minisc smirked at his friend's overconfidence. Not that it was unwarranted. Win or lose, Jules had proven that he was not only a worthy choice for the tournament, but also that he had the strength to go up against any opponent. However, none of that scared Minisc, as his confidence was just as high.

"Why don't we test that theory then, shall we?"

"Alright. No holding back, winner takes all," Jules agreed, with an updraft of wind building underneath him. His hair started to blow all over the place as the gusts increased. He remained oblivious to the soreness of his body, only focusing on the moment at hand.

Minisc followed suit, his entire body exploding into a golden aura. The two were ready for a final standoff.

"This is it," Don realized aloud, watching the boys releasing all their energy.

"Huh? What do you mean?"

"They're about to lay it all out on the line. This last attack will decide the winner of the match."

The tension in the stadium grew with each passing second. Minisc and Jules stood meters apart, sparks flying all around them. The laughing, smiling opponents had been overtaken by a concentrated intensity. With both boys running on fumes, the winner would come down to whoever could hold on the longest. It no longer was a battle of strength, but a battle of will.

"Remember Minisc, no holding back. Evolution Storm," Jules roared. Swirls of tornado-like wind rushed toward Minisc.

"Here's all I've got. Solar Blast!" Minisc shouted, sending a beam of light back in return.

The two attacks streaked toward each other, erupting in the middle of the stadium. Light filled the building from the collision, sending ripples in all directions. Minisc gritted his teeth, his body taking the full force of the backlash. Luckily, he had narrowly missed another electric square.

Jules could feel his muscles constricting, his body being pushed far past its limits, but none of that mattered. They both refused to give an inch. Only he with the greater will would come out victorious.

Guess he does still have some energy left. But so do I. Minisc started to push the attack forward, an attempt to take over the battle.

Jules's knees were furiously clattering, hanging on for dear life. *Oh no, I'm slipping, I need to dig deeper.* He knew he would have to push even further and pull out all the stops. He had come too far, worked too hard to give up with a championship birth so close. Jules refused to concede, sending a surge of energy into his Evolution Storm.

Minisc began to slide back from the force. The two were once again even, but Jules could see his demise on the horizon. To pull even, he used every last drop of strength he had. Minisc, on the other hand, remained refreshed. He had only begun to draw out his remaining energy.

"Thank you, Jules, for everything. I could never begin to repay the memories you've given me. All the times you've helped me see the light through my own darkness. I wouldn't be here without you. I really didn't want to be the one to shatter your dreams, but we both said we would give it our all... so this ends here. I'm sorry." Minisc shut his eyes for a second, his breathing gradually slowed to a steady pace. Despite the overwhelming pain coursing through his body, and the amount of energy he had expended, he felt good. He had not realized it at the time, but his extra training was beginning to pay off. The hard work he'd put in during his summer with his father, the additional work at school, all of it served to deepen his energy reservoir to depths unknown. With all that power stored away, now, in a time of need, he could call on his inner strength to finish the match.

Minisc opened his eyes again, a small grin forming. The battle had all but been decided, and he and Jules both knew it. As hard as Jules tried, shaking amid the clash of elements, he could see the inevitable around the corner.

Step by step, Minisc started to push the stalemate forward, Jules inching backward. Minisc's overwhelming energy began to take over the battle, leaving the other boy helpless.

"I guess you win this one Minisc... but don't think I won't get you next year." Exhausted and defeated, Jules was devoured by the stream of light. With a dazzling flash, the battle was over.

An explosion of cheers rippled through the crowd as Minisc stood in the middle of the ring. Jules lay crumpled on the ground near the edge of the ring, just outside on the grass. Forgetting the results of the battle, Minisc ran over to check on his friend. He could celebrate later, but he needed to check that his friend had not been hurt too badly first. He looked down at Jules, who was battered and bruised, the veins in his arms swelling to twice their regular size from the over-exhaustion of his element.

Jules opened his eyes to look up at Minisc, who stood holding his hand out.

"I guess I lost that bet, huh?" Jules laughed weakly. All Minisc could do was chuckle at the reaction. It was so typically Jules. Even in defeat, he had a big grin on his face.

"You can pay me back after the tournament. Now let me help you up." Jules looked at Minisc's hand as if it were a foreign object.

"I don't think I can move a muscle."

The two laughed again before hearing a voice call out from the tunnel. Lily rushed out, beaming at her friends.

"Guys, that was amazing."

While she went to join the celebration, Don remained in the tunnel, arms crossed and a genuine smile playing across his lips. Seeing the three friends cheer, smile, and celebrate together warmed his heart. It was the happiest he had seen his son in years.

With the battle over and friendships intact, Minisc had locked his place in the championship match.

CHAPTER 12
COMBUSTIBLE

THE TOURNAMENT GROUNDS WERE FULL OF LIFE BETWEEN semi-final matches. Each booth had long line-ups, while each patio had filled up with hungry customers. However, none of that appealed to Coro, who coasted by without a second thought. All of the excitement that came with the games was of no interest to him. Especially not the fanfare that he had picked up after his win against Lily. Every competitor had picked up some fans along the way, but for Coro, it was just another pointless distraction. Making his way through the hordes of people, he overheard some small murmurs in the crowd.

"Is that Coro?"

"He looks so angry…"

"Five bucks says you won't ask for his autograph…"

Coro paid little attention to the voices. He had no desire to take part in their social squabbles; he had other problems plaguing his mind.

Eventually, he came to a small secluded alley behind the stadium. He stepped in to avoid the gazes of others, before he held out his hands. In the left, a small snowflake formed, and in the right, a flickering blue flame danced. As he slammed his right fist shut, the fire extinguished with a puff of smoke. Coro gritted his teeth, tightening his palm. Just thinking of his flames made him want to punch something. He tightened his grip until a small drop of blood flowed down his arm, falling to the cement.

****

Mechanical rumbles and beeps filled the quaint room, while the walls were a lovely pastel blue, the color one would see in a newborn baby's room. But instead of teddy bears and dinosaurs, the place had been decorated with posters of the human body. In the center of the room was a lone crib, and inside that crib lay a malnourished infant, on his back, trapped behind the bars. Nothing but a small white diaper kept the baby from being scant naked.

Running along the edges of the crib was metal tubing that plugged into the high-tech machines, which pulsated in precise intervals. On the other end, the tubes wrapped around the back of the baby's neck, tunneling into separate nostrils. Each tube had a distinct bag, one a warm orange liquid and the other an icy blue. They alternated drops into the boy's nasal passage.

The baby squirmed, swinging his barely formed arm in the air. Along with looking dangerously famished, his limbs were tinier than a parent would hope for their newborn.

Positioned at the front end of the room was a large glass window, and on the other side stood a young couple who refused to take their eyes off the child. The man towered over the woman, with buzzed black hair and small streaks of gray melding in. He wore a large white lab coat with a solid black shirt underneath, and looked through his oval glasses toward his son. The woman, his wife, had long curling bluish-silver hair, like a beautiful maiden. A simple checkered dress hugged her figure, with a small brown belt wrapped around her slender waist. She gave the baby a somber smile, fighting back the tears, her voice timid and shaky.

"Hey Coro," she whispered, pressing her fingers on the glass pane.

As if recognizing the voice, Coro reached toward the window. He let out an ear-curdling cry, ripping his mother's heart apart. She felt powerless to do anything. There her son lay, tethered to wires and machines. She was merely a dozen feet from her baby, and yet she was unable to tend to him. She could not hold him or hug him. All she could do was depend on machines to keep the light in her life alive. She fought back the tears once again, this time unsuccessfully.

"It's okay, my baby boy; everything is going to be okay. I promise. We're going to take you home soon." Her voice cracked.

Taking notice of his wife on the verge of breaking down, the man wrapped his arm around her.

"We should go. We've done all we can. The medicine needs to begin circulating through his blood and take effect. He will be healthy soon enough." The man was steady and firm in his speech, keeping his emotions in check. He had no right to be so confident, though. He was using his old research and praying. It had never worked before, so why would he believe it to work now? Simply because he had no other choice.

"Okay."

She waved to her son before being ushered out the door by her husband.

****

Coro gradually unclenched his fist, memories of the past still haunting him. He reached deep into his pocket, feeling a soft, scrunched piece of cloth. He held it in his hand, carefully unfolding the green wrapping to reveal two small blue pills. He glared at the items as if they were his mortal enemy. More substances given to him by his no-good father. Coro debated if taking the pills was worth it, and decided against it, as he often did. He did not need his father's help, and he most certainly did not want his father to get any credit for his achievements. He folded the wrapping up and slid the items back in his pocket, never to be seen again.

His match was starting soon, and he decided to head to the dressing room. On his way, he came across the large video board on the outside of the stadium. It was showing highlights of the last match, Minisc propping Jules up. Coro stared at the board for a moment.

"Hmph."

Jules had taken over Lily's resident spot in the infirmary, but only for a few short moments. He and Minisc had both been checked in as a precaution after the match. Even with that, they still had bandages that outdid Lily's by a mile. Jules had white cloth wrapped up to the elbow of his right arm, and Minisc had bandages around his ribs.

"You guys really did a number on each other — how do you feel?" Lily asked, examining the injuries.

"I feel fine. Back is a little sore, but it's all good," Jules assured the girl while rubbing his lower back.

"Actually, I feel pretty good too." Minisc laughed. The boy raised his arms up and down, showing off his still-intact mobility.

"Hope so; you still have another match to go," Jules said before hopping off the bed.

"That reminds me, we should get going soon. We don't want to miss Coro and Ignis's bout," Lily suggested.

"I definitely don't want to miss that; it's going to be intense."

While they were being tended to, Lily walked over to a small TV in the corner of the room. It displayed the daily news report, although this time it had breaking news crawling along the bottom of it. On-screen was a news anchor. She had a light chocolate complexion, and her hair was midnight black with blonde streaks running through her neatly pulled-back ponytail. A name bar took up the lower third of the screen above the news crawl: *Vinuja, Scarborough Reporter.*

Scarborough was a small section of Toronto, known for being a rather peaceful place filled with mostly humans. Elementalists liked to remain in the heart of the city for the most part, flocking to where they could use their element to make more money. With the EC also being in the heart of the city and a sizable percentage of Elementalists working there, it made logical sense for them to live closer.

The reporter's backdrop was a plain-looking, rundown church next to an empty parking lot. The area had been sealed off by police, who were walking in and out of the location with focused looks. Lily clicked the remote, increasing the volume.

"We are coming to you live with a breaking report. Earlier today, there was an attack on the Eastside Scarborough Church. No injuries have been reported yet, but it is believed that an Elementalist was involved. The motive has not yet been determined, but police are wary that it is connected with the string of attacks over the last few months. The EC has denied all reports that they believe the group known as Luminosa is back and rallying followers, but the public concern is growing with each attack. If you have any information, please contact the police. We'll keep you up to date at the eleven-o'clock news. Back to you, Lana."

Minisc and Jules walked over to the TV just as Lily muted it. That was when she saw something they had not discussed much since the event took place. The footage showed a hooded figure running into the church, but the person seemed much smaller in size.

"Guys, look," Lily said. Minisc and Jules followed her eyes.

"You don't think…"

"I don't know. He looks a lot shorter this time around, but it's the same coat and style, so it could be."

"Looks like the EC is having trouble keeping it under wraps as they'd hoped."

"But she said it was related to Luminosa… does that mean —" Lily looked at Minisc.

"I don't know. Every time I've ever tried to ask my father about what happened, he'll duck the question and say we have nothing to worry about. I don't think we can write it off, though. The only problem is nobody in the EC will tell us what's going on, and those are the only people who know, so now what?"

"I can't say I know much about Luminosa other than the stories, but Yuri might. He's too young to have fought them, but he knows a lot about the history of Elementalists."

"It's worth a try," Lily said, her eyes filled with more worry than her friends'.

Jules led the group to the third floor of the stadium, where the luxury suites were. The infirmary had been on the second floor, right below Yuri's suite, which had been bought through his agency. Although the entire building was elegant and luxurious, the third floor took it to another level. With a sea of red carpeting and pillars that carried elegant vases filled with blooming flowers, it barely even looked like an arena. It more resembled walking through a mansion, so much so that Minisc feared if he looked the wrong way something would break. Once they arrived at the suite—room 316—Jules pulled down on the stainless steel handle, granting him access to a mansion within a mansion. Inside was the highest-quality furniture they had ever seen, a wall of glass that stretched across the room as a viewing area, and even a bar with drinks and food at the ready. Yuri had been standing at the window, looking down to the battlefield as Coro and Ignis were about to start their bout. He was dressed up in a blue-and-red checkered shirt and white khaki pants, hair neatly brushed. When he heard the door open and saw his brother, he could not contain his excitement.

"That was absolutely amazing, you two," Yuri boasted ruffling his brother's hair. "Minisc, that final attack, the amount of energy you released was incredible, and Jules, your desire and willpower when you had nothing left. You both should be extremely proud of yourselves. You put on a show for the ages."

Jules and Minisc both smiled sheepishly at the compliment.

"Thanks, Yuri."

Below the suites, in the stadium, Coro and Ignis stood in a swirling wind tunnel. For the match, the wind terrain had been selected, and neither competitor looked all too pleased. Ignis had a disgruntled scowl. Competing in all black with the sleeves torn off to show his muscular arms, Ignis had cruised through the first round using his tenacious fighting skills and blazing fire element to land a decisive victory. In fact, he had been so ruthless that his opponent, Talia—a classmate—had been left in critical condition. That did not come as a surprise to Minisc, but in a way, it still disappointed him.

Coro had also dispatched Lily with ease, but stopped well short of injuring his opponent.

Minisc looked down from the suite trying to get a good view of Coro. The usually disgruntled boy looked even more spaced out than normal. Minisc appeared to be the only one of the three to care, though.

"This food is not for you, Jules," Lily scolded as she watched him make a mess on the lunch bar. Condiment bottles, sandwich meats, and slices of bread were scattered like a war zone.

"But I'm hungry. I used so much energy against Minisc; I can't help it," Jules argued as he picked up a plastic knife. With high precision, he started spreading butter onto the piece of bread before slapping it onto the top of the tower of meats. He picked up the triple-stacked meal and took a massive bite out of it. Lily looked on, shaking her head in repulsion.

Ignoring his friends' bickering. Minisc stood pressed up against the glass, looking down on the battle. He wanted to pay close attention, knowing the winner of the match would be his next opponent. That one would be for all the marbles.

Minisc had grown up with Ignis, so he was relatively familiar with the boy's aggressive fighting style. He'd also had the luxury of already facing the hate-filled boy back in the first week of school. Though the two had grown leaps and bounds in power since then, it was better than nothing. In no way did he want to fight Ignis, though. He dreaded facing his former friend. That battle would be testier, and Ignis would want it to the death. Coro, on the other hand, was an enigma. An insanely powerful ice Elementalist, but outside of that, Minisc knew nothing about him.

In the ring, Ignis and Coro were locked in a stare-down, neither competitor blinking.

"I'm so sick of hearing how great this prodigy boy is. I'm going to make sure your defeat is extra painful," Ignis snarled as the wind died down around him.

Coro said nothing.

"Oh, right, I forgot, you don't talk." A cocky smirk slipped onto Ignis's angry exterior. "I guess I'll have to rip the screams out of you with my bare hands then."

Ignis darted ahead, unaffected by the insane wind speeds. His fists burst into raging flames, flickering back and forth.

Coro's lower body began to glow blue as he opened with his predictable ice barrage attack, watching as Ignis charged ahead. Except, Ignis remained unfazed by the daunting move, jumping high into the sky. Unlike Lily, he would not need to rely on luck or the stage to help defend himself. He would use nothing but raw power. With a violent punch, Ignis's fiery fist smashed into the thick tidal wave of ice. Everyone watched in awe as it shattered like glass.

The wind picked up, whipping shards of ice back at Coro, who braced himself for the shrapnel. His arms were sliced open from his own attack, handing Ignis his opportunity to inflict real punishment. The fire Elementalist landed in stride, opening up with a flurry of fierce punches. The action happened fast, fans standing and applauding non-stop.

While they watched from above, Yuri took notice of Minisc, who had his eyes locked on the match.

"These two are quite incredible, aren't they?"

"They really are," Minisc replied, not breaking concentration. "It's easy to see how much they have learned and how hard they have worked to make it this far."

Jules and Lily strolled over to where the other two resided and began commenting on the match.

"Ignis looks like he's taking over the match," Jules noted as they watched the boy continued to push back his opponent.

"Yeah, I thought Coro would be putting up more of a fight; it's strange," Lily pointed out.

"Coro's holding back."

Lily and Jules looked at Minisc with shock, but Yuri confirmed the thought.

"You're right. Something about his style is off; he's not as crisp and as precise as he was with Lily. He looks unfocused. Something is bothering him."

"Like when you and I fought?" Jules asked Minisc.

"Maybe…"

Coro continued to absorb each blow. He was looking for an opening to counter, but nothing would present itself. A defensive battle played little to his advantage; Coro's strength focused on an overwhelming assault, but Ignis gave the boy no time to assert that power. Seeing Coro break down, Ignis went for the knockout. He had no interest in dragging things out either. He sent his fist sailing toward Coro, but before the finishing blow could land, a flash of white light lit up the stadium. An ear-piercing clash rang out as Ignis's vicious punch plunked off his target. Coro had frozen his arm in thick ice to protect it.

Ignis jumped back, shaking his beet-red hand, the knuckle dripping in blood.

A smug look graced Ignis's hard face before he leaped back into the fray with a screaming right jab. Coro resorted to the same defense, shielding himself with his ice armor, a move Ignis fully anticipated and had a counter for. His fist exploded with an inferno-like flame, smashing into the icy defenses. A deafening ring split the air again, only this time Ignis held the punch, watching as it began to melt the ice. Coro did his best to hold his ground as the heat started to make him sweat.

"Didn't you learn anything in science class? Fire melts ice."

Just as the last inch of ice faded away, another roaring wind swept through the battlefield. Ignis's flames quickly extinguished as he was wisped away from the finishing blow once again. Thanks to that, Coro was granted his opening, and he wasted no time turning the tides. With a fire element, Ignis was at a clear disadvantage as long as the gusts remained.

Dashing forward with unparalleled speed, Coro began taking control of the match. Punch after punch. Blow after blow. His speed had increased twofold from the start of the battle. It was an overwhelming blur to watch.

"How did Coro suddenly get so much faster?" Jules questioned.

"I don't know. But whatever was bothering him, it's clearly stopped," Minisc answered in awe. He could not believe what he was witnessing. No one had ever landed such a barrage of blows on Ignis, but Coro was making him look like an amateur all of a sudden.

Ignis continued to wear down, while Coro kept pushing the pace of battle faster. Ignis attempted a counter, swinging wildly, but was quickly trapped by his opponent's palm. A devastating punch lodged itself into Ignis's midsection, slowly sinking in like quicksand. Sprawling back, Coro saw his moment to seize victory, and a brilliant cold blue light trailed behind a ferocious ice wall. The swirling wind turned into a hailstorm from the drop in temperature. Before Ignis could react, he found himself buried underneath an avalanche of tiny ice rocks.

"Is that it? Is it over?" Jules wondered as silence filled the arena. The storm died down, leaving only a pile of ice cubes in an icy tundra. Coro stood breathing heavily, the puffs of air visible from the cold.

"I—I think so. Nobody could survive an attack that ferocious," Lily fretted quietly. She too was stunned. They were all stunned. That was the first time they had ever seen Coro exert himself in battle, and seeing the power only cemented that he was on a far superior level to anyone in their class. A frightening proposition.

The ref did a full count, making it to nine, but before he could announce Coro as the victor, an intense red light gleamed through the icy avalanche that had imprisoned Ignis. Pillars of flames began to burst out of the ice, followed by a deafening explosion. A shadowy silhouette stood hunched over in the middle of the volcanic eruption. He screamed at the top of his lungs as the fire continued to explode from his body. His entire half of the arena, which had once been covered in ice, evaporated instantaneously, and the flaming tornado enveloping Ignis gradually dissipated around him.

Small flickers of fire flew through the air as the boy tried to catch his breath. Everyone in the stadium burst into cheers.

"I told you. Fire... always.... melts... ice," Ignis seethed in white-hot anger. He picked up his head, shooting daggers at his opponent. Coro stood frozen. He could not imagine how someone had managed to break free from such an assault. That was his best shot at winning. He had used an unfathomable amount of energy to create that hail storm.

Ignis looked infuriated. He took a step forward, his hand sparking into a roaring flame. The boy was red hot and ready to dish out some punishment. But as Ignis took a second step, the raging fire inside went extinct. He fell forward, collapsing onto the floor, motionless.

"Ignis is unable to finish the battle. Coro wins!" the ref announced, pointing to Coro's side of the arena.

From above, Yuri admired the boy's determination. "Ignis used every ounce of energy he had, and even after all that, he still wanted to fight. He has a fire burning in him the likes of which I have never seen."

"I just wish he wasn't such a jerk," Lily lamented.

The stadium watched as a stretcher came out, and paramedics carried Ignis away.

The group of four walked over to the couch in the center of the room. Lily and Jules took a seat down on the fresh black leather couch while Yuri pulled up a chair from the bar. That left Minisc to take refuge on the glass coffee table in the middle.

"So with that over, Jules, you said you had something you guys wanted to talk to me about?"

Jules looked over at Minisc first before speaking. "Yeah, actually, we were hoping that you could shed some light on Luminosa for us." The room fell silent. Yuri looked at his brother before glancing at Minisc and Lily, then back to his brother.

Raising an eyebrow, he said, "Why are you asking me about Luminosa?"

"Well, we saw a report that a church in Scarborough was attacked by a man in a black cloak. The picture they had of him looked eerily similar to the guy who attacked us a few months back. Which also looked like the guy who attacked you last summer... It seems like a lot of the attacks on the city are somehow connected. The EC silenced us from talking about the incident with anyone outside of their ranks, but technically you are part of the EC, so we figured we would ask you."

"My father won't talk about anything EC-related with me, but clearly something is going on. Do you know anything?"

"I understand why your father wouldn't want to talk about it; I'm sure it's not easy for someone who lived through the heart of the confrontation." Yuri paused, thinking through his next words. The topic of Luminosa was not one easily discussed. Still, he opted to continue. "I can't say that I know much, but I do know that the EC has been tracking someone matching the description of your guy. I looked into the EC's records as well after the three of you were attacked, and even I couldn't get answers on who they were. Nobody wants to willingly admit that Luminosa could be reforming, or that Dusk may have somehow survived the battle with your father, but at this point we can't rule it out."

Although they had expected as much, the acknowledgment that Luminosa may have reformed still haunted Minisc, much like it haunted society.

"We have to stop them then," Jules argued, "We need to find that monster and take him down before he causes any more pain."

"I wish it were that easy, Jules. I really do. Although I wasn't around for the initial rise of Luminosa, I've worked with enough people who were. The way Luminosa rose was through fear and deception. With each crime they committed, right up until trying to purge the human race, they were strategic and calculated. Dusk and his followers were always on the move, attacking humans and disappearing into the night without a trace. That style kept us from being able to connect the crimes, eventually causing fear among all humans. But more importantly, it stoked anger toward all Elementalists, something that was already prevalent at the time. So that turned humans on Elementalists, which turned Elementalists against Humans, reinforcing Dusk's belief of a divided world that could never be shared. I think that is why the Elemental Council has done its best to not pin the situation on Luminosa. They are hoping to avoid panic for the time being until they can find a solution. All three of you need to stay vigilant while the city remains under these attacks, but as your father said, we will stop them just like we did before."

"I'm so sick of waiting for Brooklyn to return. I signed up so I could use my powers freely, not wait around playing cards," Bex groaned as she stuffed her face with what looked like a rotten apple.

"Just be patient for once in your life," Bronx retorted, throwing a few poker chips into the center of the table. "Three of a kind," he called, spreading the cards along the table. Three nines, a seven, and a jack.

A razor-thin smile graced Bex's cut lips. She started giggling before plopping her cards down over Bronx's.

"Flush," she howled, much to the dismay of Bronx. Claiming victory, she reached in and hugged the modestly sized pile of chips on the table.

"I swear you cheat."

"I don't cheat; you just suck."

"Brooklyn needs to hurry up and get back with that serum."

While Bronx angrily dealt a new round of cards, their not-so-friendly game was interrupted by the jiggling of the doorknob.

"Finally," Bex exclaimed. She threw her cards down and turned to look at Brooklyn, who walked in wearing a raggedy T-shirt and ripped jeans. He popped a small metallic case on the table.

"Well? Did it work?" Bronx asked as he leaned back in his chair.

"This is just a prototype, but I have no doubt it'll work." Brooklyn held a small vial in his hands with a clear thick liquid in it. "If this serum is injected into one's bloodstream, it will devour all the elemental cells that manipulate the powers within an Elementalist."

"In English?"

"Stab someone, and they'll lose the ability to use their element."

"So how do we know if it works?" Bronx asked.

"We need to inject someone with it." Brooklyn pulled a syringe out of his pocket, using it to absorb the liquid. He flicked the top with his finger. A single drop of fluid splashed off the tip onto the table, causing smoke to rise from the wood.

"I say we try it on Bronx," Bex voted, throwing her hand up with childlike enthusiasm.

"Why you—"

"Will you two shut up for a minute? I already know who we're testing it on. We need to make sure that damn Premier child wins the tournament; once that happens, we will be able to enact the next stage of our plan. That means your target is the other participant, Coro Normanday. Lure him away and drain his power, he could prove to be a pain in my ass if he gets any stronger. Better to dispose of him now. While you two do that, I will be making a little stop with the Adenji gang…"

"Ohhhhh, this will be exciting. Hurry up, Bronx, let's go." The girl flew off the chair, running out the doorway with glee.

"She's way too enthusiastic about this," Bronx said before following her out of the underground lair.

Later that night, Minisc, Lily, and Jules had gone their separate ways. Lily took the train home for the night, while Jules and Yuri headed out as well, leaving Minisc to his own devices. He was to head home with his father in under an hour, but the man still had some last-minute errands to attend in association with the finals. That left Minisc to kick around the tournament grounds for a bit.

The festivities had all but died down for the day, and the grounds were no more than a deserted carnival without the rides. It was hard to believe that the area had housed thousands of people only a few hours ago. Minisc took a stroll to the back of the arena, where the patios were. Since he had some time to kill, at least he could sit around and enjoy the warm fresh air on such a nice night. However, as he continued his leisurely walk, he heard a crashing bang, followed by what sounded like shattering ice.

What the heck was that? It sounded like an attack. Minisc halted his step for a moment, trying to tell where the violent sounds were coming from. Another sound of shattered ice followed, this time from just outside the back entrance of Scotia Coliseum. Although he had not explored it much, the back of the building connected to a long, underground tunnel that led to Union, the hub of all train stations.

What if it's Luminosa again? Minisc hesitated, knowing he needed to find his father if the cries of battle were caused by the group. But he had no time, and his father was somewhere in a building far bigger than he had time to explore. Knowing he was running headlong into danger, Minisc made his way to the tunnel, running down the stairs and passing through the side entrance.

It's empty... Minisc swiveled his head, looking back and forth. The tunnel had been illuminated by lights lining the walls, but they still cast a few shadows for him to try and remain hidden. He knew it was late, but not late enough for the tunnel to be as empty as it was. As Minisc looked down the black corridor, an ice-like dagger soared past him missing by a narrow margin. That was followed up by a bright blue light dancing like flames in the distance. Against his better judgment, Minisc ran down the tunnel, praying that he would not be too late. Seeing two black-cloaked figures, Minisc came to a skidding halt. They were not alone. Another boy had been the target of the attacks this time. Although Minisc prepared to jump in to even the numbers, he soon realized the boy was having far fewer issues fighting them than Minisc had before. Then he recognized the target.

Is that Coro? Why would Luminosa go after him? Minisc stayed back in the shadows, but remained on his guard, although he had nothing to worry about. Coro showed his impressive skills by dodging a series of Shadow Balls and Ice Knives, landing hit after hit with his fist encased in ice. What truly caught Minisc off guard was what happened next. Coro, needing to thaw out his hands, began to glow a shade of reddish-blue. Minisc could feel the temperature rise just as he had felt it drop whenever Coro used his ice element. That was when Coro's fists exploded into a torch-like flame, much like Ms. Wright's and Ignis's could.

What? No way. Coro can use fire and ice… but how is that even possible? I thought dual-element experiments were banned.

"Who is this kid?" Bronx whined as he fought to catch his breath. He glanced over at Bex, who looked ready to pounce despite being outmatched. "Hey Bex, you can use that serum anytime now, would ya? It's the only reason we're even here."

"I know," Bex snarled. Just as she sprung toward Coro, he burst into flames, again making Bex leap back. As she did, Coro sent a barrage of ice at the girl, hitting her clean in the wrist. *Crack.* Liquid started to pour out of her sleeve as she started to freak.

"You bastard, that serum was the whole reason we showed up," she yelled. She ripped off her sleeve to show small shards of glass stuck in her wrist, quickly becoming blood-soaked. "Brooklyn is going to kill me."

"Damn it Bex, you had one job." Bronx began to tiptoe backward. "Come on, this fight is over," he ordered.

"No way, I am going to make this snot-nosed kid pay," she barked back, readying a strike.

"Bex," Bronx demanded this time. "I said fall back. Without the needle, this whole thing is pointless — we are only drawing attention to ourselves." He looked back at Coro, who appeared to be content with the stalemate they were in. One glimpse of the dancing flames around their target and Bronx knew they had made a mistake. He raised his hand into the air, making a fog of black smoke. Falling into the fog, he and Bex evaporated, leaving Coro free from danger.

However, he was not completely alone like he thought. Sensing someone, Coro turned around, catching a glimpse of Minisc from the shadows. He fired a warning shot, the ice hitting against the wall, leaving a cold sleek abstract painting next to Minisc's head.

"Whoa, easy Coro, it's only me," Minisc freaked as he hurried his way out of the shadows.

"Minisc? What are you doing here?" Coro spat, followed by a

chilling glare. He seemed more disgruntled than usual, but not because he had just been attacked. More so because his secret had finally been found out.

"Who were those guys?" Minisc asked, finally seeing Coro face-to-face. "And why were they attacking you?"

Coro grunted and started walking past him, clearly not interested in talking.

"Hey, wait, you're not even going to tell me why some strangers were trying to fight you?"

"I don't know, and I don't care," Coro said in a deadpan voice. He started walking down the tunnel, leaving Minisc befuddled and confused. Before he could say another word, the boy who would be his opponent in the finals disappeared.

Minisc didn't know what to do—nobody had been hurt and that was a good thing, but it brought up a few other questions only perplexing him more. Was that Luminosa? Why were they after Coro, or had he caught them by a stroke of misfortune as Minisc had? And most importantly, Coro had displayed dual elements, a trait all but lost to time, or so he had been told. Something seemed fishy, but Minisc felt so tired after the day's events that he decided he would deal with it after some rest. He had the night to recoup, and boy did he need it. That would give him time to ask his father about Coro's dual elements as well. He wanted to mention Luminosa, but knowing his father's aversion to the topic, he figured it would be better left alone. After all, he had no proof it was not just a random group of criminals Coro had stopped.

Later that night, Minisc found himself once again on the front porch of his cozy home. He watched as the grass swayed to the quiet howls of the midnight wind. There was a certain calming effect when staring up at the beautiful shine of moonlight.

Minisc put his hands on the porch, which was cold to touch, but he did not mind. He was staring at the stars that gleamed bright amidst the black sky. The world fell quiet, but the boy's mind only grew louder. He struggled to take his mind off of his opponent. Coro. Just thinking about him gave Minisc a knot-like feeling in his stomach. Not the same as when he faced Jules, though. This was a feeling of sadness. Something Minisc had not been expecting to feel. The evening's events had played on his mind more than he would have thought. Coro was hiding something, and Minisc figured it was the reason the boy acted so distant all the time.

A slight breeze took hold of his hair, blowing it out of his face. Minisc knew he needed to focus on beating his opponent; nothing else was supposed to matter. Yet that could not be further from the case. Minisc thought about his mother in the silence. Often, he would sit outside at night and talk to her through the void of his yard. It provided a way for him to think ideas through out loud.

"Hi Mom," he started, "I have great news. I made the finals in the Tournament of Elements. But now I'm facing an opponent, and it's strange; he looks so sad, and alone, like he's lost. He talks to nobody, and everybody avoids him. I wish I knew how to help him. If you were here, I know you'd know what to do." Minisc spoke into the vast opening of his front yard. The wind howled back as if it were Minisc's mother acknowledging her son's thoughts. While he was still debating scenarios in his head, he paused his mind when he heard the front door creak open. The muscular shadow of Don peered through before the man took a seat next to his son.

"How're the ribs?" Don asked. The boy rubbed his stomach. Jules had hit him hard, and no doubt it remained sore, but nothing he could not handle.

"They feel good; it shouldn't be much of a problem for the finals." Minisc gave a half-hearted smile. Even after all their time together, the boy struggled to open up to his father. Don always thought with a clear and logical mind. Minisc often thought with his gut and his heart. He was more like his mother in that respect. Besides, he did not care to talk much about the finals — what he wanted to talk about was Coro, but he was unsure if he should even bring it up.

He assumed his father would say something like *quiet your mind* or *focus on winning,* and he already knew all that.

Don did not pick up on his son's conflict right away, instead continuing to ask about the tournament.

"So... are you excited for tomorrow?"

"Yeah, I guess," Minisc mumbled.

It was not a lie. He was excited in one sense. He had been granted an excellent opportunity; he could make his father proud. Minisc could make Jules and Lily proud as well. If he won, he would be known as a champion, even getting a guaranteed job at the EC, which would be a massive step in his goals. He also knew how many people were rooting for him, and wanted to live up to those expectations. To make them proud. Did that really matter now though? Minisc was not so sure.

Finally, after his second lackadaisical answer, Don clued in that his son had other conflicts on his mind.

"I guess? That doesn't sound very excited to me." The man recognized how when his son started to get into deep thoughts, it often got him in trouble. "What's going on, Minisc? I know that look. Something's on your mind."

He knew as well as Minisc did that he was not always good at giving advice, unlike his late wife, but that would never stop him from trying.

"It's nothing, really." Minisc dismissed the question, averting his gaze from his father up to the stars.

"Minisc, you are the absolute worst liar. Come on, you know you can talk to me."

Minisc hesitated for a moment. His father was right, of course— he could talk to the man. They had grown closer over the past year, but still, it felt like Don only had his mind set on winning the tournament. Despite all that, Minisc decided to open up.

"Okay... You know my opponent is Coro," Minisc spoke, his voice a bit timid.

Don nodded his head in understanding.

"Yes, he's quite powerful. I must admit I've never seen someone so young show the ability he has. But you are every bit as strong as him. I've seen it over and over again," the man encouraged, thinking that his son lacked faith in his abilities.

"It's not like that. I saw him this afternoon chasing some criminals off, but he used two elements to do so."

"Oh?" Don looked genuinely surprised by the nugget of knowledge. He knew of the experiments that had once taken place before the creation of the EC, but he was not aware that anyone so young could have been experimented on. The EC was believed to have shut down such tests years before Minisc or any of his classmates would have been born.

"I don't think anyone in our class knows about his secret either; he hasn't practiced it once since the start of EA, and he hasn't used it in the tournament thus far either. It's strange. I think he wants it to be a secret, but I don't know why. Ever since I saw it, it's bothered me. He's always looked so cold to people, but lately, he looks sadder and more alone than stoic or aloof."

"I can't say for sure this is the case... but you know how humans used to view Elementalists as subhuman?" Minisc nodded, signaling for his father to go on. "Well, when word started to spread about the experiments to create dual elementalism, the backlash was fierce, not only from humans but from Elementalists ourselves. Dual elementalism was viewed as unnatural experiments, and those tested were known as mutants or worse. Many people on both sides wanted all those experimented on to be killed, as they were seen as far too great a threat to society. I could see why Coro would not want to bring that sort of power to the limelight."

Hearing his father's words made Minisc sick; the thought of children who were forced into experiments being labeled monsters by society seemed cruel and disgusting. Was it possible Coro thought he would be seen that way? The boy was impossible to read under his crusty exterior, but it would have been a good enough reason to hide such great strength.

"But someone your age having two elements, that's impossible."

"I know what I saw."

"I believe you, it's just... that leaves a lot of questions unanswered. Regardless, that's for after the tournament; for now, you should go to bed — you have a big day ahead of you tomorrow."

"Yeah, you're probably right." Minisc yawned, standing up. "You coming in?" he asked as he put his hand on the silver door handle to the house.

"I'll be in shortly."

Minisc disappeared inside, leaving Don by himself.

Is someone conducting experiments on Elementalists? Is that the secret behind Coro's overwhelming strength, especially for one of such a young age? Something is amiss. Don had many questions, but they were to be figured out later. Tomorrow he was hoping to hand the trophy to his son and show him off to the world.

CHAPTER 13
A BOY'S DREAM

BIRDS SANG PLEASANT MELODIES AS THE SUN CRANED into the morning sky to start the day. Scotia Coliseum was bathed in a beautiful orange hue that spilled all along the ground. Today, of course, was no ordinary day on the calendar, but what most would consider the biggest day of the EA school year. The Tournament of Elements finals. One of Minisc or Coro would be crowned champion; the other, nothing. An event with that much pressure could weigh down even the most seasoned Elementalist at EA, but Minisc felt unusually calm about the fight. So much so that he had woke early, an anomaly in itself, and arrived at the stadium well before his match was slated to start.

It was hard to believe after such a bustling place over the past week, things could be so calm. Yet, Minisc walked in peaceful bliss. He did have a reason for arriving early. Today, he wanted to see the grounds at their purest—no entertainment, no noise, no cloaked attackers, just quiet delight. It gave him a relaxing way to ease his mind with a long day awaiting him. Long, quiet walks were an activity that he used to do with his mother. The two would find a silent place to stroll and relax Minisc's overactive mind by taking in the scenery.

He stepped onto a large, grassy field, and to his right stood a large tent. Hanging just underneath the roof was an extensive, colorful menu filled with food choices to the nines, and scattered nearby were several empty wooden picnic tables. Beside the tent, a humongous video board had also been set up. The board continued cycling through the previous matches in the tournament.

This must be for people who couldn't get tickets inside, Minisc thought as he walked over and took a seat on the bench. The structure made an uneasy creaking sound, causing Minisc to look down skeptically at his chosen spot. Seeing no better option, he decided to take his chances and remained. He turned his attention back to the video board and recognized the girl letting out a powerful stream of water. It was Lily's valiant effort against Coro. Next up was Minisc overpowering Jules for his latest victory. That started to make the boy think about the events that had taken place.

It's hard to believe how far we've all come since starting EA... It really is incredible the amount of work everyone has put in just to try and achieve their goals.

The board flipped to Ignis, dominating his opponent in the first round.

We've all grown so much...

A clip of Minisc being struck with a lightning bolt from Trotz showed. The boy grimaced at the sight. Not a great memory, but it was a memory nonetheless.

The final clip showed Minisc and Coro in split-screen form. Minisc waved to the crowd, while at first glance, Coro had a hardened mask on. Minisc, though, could see differently. Through the cover of a scowl, he could see the sadness in his soon-to-be opponent's eyes, the frustration, the loneliness. It hurt Minisc to see anyone feel that way, but he knew he could not let emotions get in the way of his match. Nothing but his best would cut it against Coro, and though he knew the challenge ahead of him, he felt ready. Far more at ease than his fight with Jules. He had built up the deserved confidence and was beginning to believe he had a real shot at winning.

Yet something continued to weigh on the back of his mind. If he won, it would be with Coro at a distinct disadvantage. If Coro refused to use his full strength, how would Minisc be able to prove he deserved to be champion? Winning the finals because of a thrown match would feel tainted — a bit of an ironic thought. Even so, with everyone giving it their all to win, Minisc wanted to see Coro do the same for both their sakes.

With people sparsely beginning to arrive for the day, Minisc decided it was a good time to head inside. He had killed more time than he intended, but it had let him clear his head.

On the walk back, he heard distant shouts. Concerned, he followed the argument to an alleyway just off the side of the building.

"You're a disgrace to this family; I've given you a great opportunity in life. I've given you power, I've given you intellect, and I even gave you life. Yet time and time again, you refuse to repay me like a spoiled rotten child! We could be richer than you could possibly imagine. Glory... success... I could be known as the greatest scientist to ever live. But you refuse to pull your weight." The man continued his tirade, his voice growing hoarse. "You will go out there. You will use your full power. And you will obliterate the Hero of Light's son. Do I make myself clear?"

Minisc followed the voice, peeking into the mucky alcove for a second. He saw a tall, red-faced man with a finger jammed up against a teenage boy. Minisc ducked behind a dumpster, trying to remain silent. The last thing he wanted to do was to end up in the middle of whatever argument was taking place.

After a few seconds of listening, Minisc peeked up, recognizing who the lucky recipient of the verbal assault had been.

That's Coro... but who is the man yelling at him?

"Did you forget that without my experiments, you'd be dead? You're nothing more than a monster, a creation from my hard work. Now, as my creation, you'll do as I order," the man growled.

Coro stood still, not reacting to his father's words. When he was younger, he would have fought back, lashed out even, but as the years went on, he'd become numb to the man's hateful rhetoric. As far as the world was concerned, Coro fit the bill of a monster created by science. He knew that, and because of that, he would have to stand and take the tongue lashing, no different than so many times prior.

"If you know what's good for you, then you'll take these pills. It will increase the potency of your fire and reduce the strain as well. With it, we will have all but guaranteed you the win," the man argued, forcibly shoving a small bottle of white pills into his son's hand.

"Don't you dare lose to that Premier child," the man warned, storming off into the opening.

Minisc quickly darted back behind the dumpster again, plastering himself up against the cold metal.

He would often feel intimidated by his own father, although it was usually unwarranted, but he knew his father would never speak to him like that. It was disgusting. No child deserved to absorb the vitriol that Coro had.

The man blew past Minisc, not taking a second to look if anyone had overheard his shouting. With him disappearing into the crowd, Minisc let out a sigh.

Meanwhile, Coro remained frozen, holding the tiny tablets. In disgust, he tossed the pills on the ground before giving them a vicious stomp. "I don't care what you say, I'm not taking these stupid pills. Not now. Not ever again. I'll win on my own, I don't need you, I don't need anyone."

He promised himself he would no longer be a slave to his father's experiments, and more importantly, he pledged to his mother the same.

Stuck behind the dumpster with nowhere to go, Minisc debated what his next move would be. He wanted to say something to his classmate, but was it his place? He knew the reaction he would likely receive: *It's none of your business*, or something to that effect. On the other hand, he also knew his mother would have encouraged him to help people as much as he could. In this case, his mother was right.

He peeked back around the dumpster and saw Coro stomp the pills once more. It did not matter if the other boy refused to admit it. Minisc could see him drowning in his own resentment.

Finally Coro snapped, "Who's there?"

Minisc jumped back, caught off guard.

How does he do that?

Minisc stepped out from behind the dumpster to reveal himself.

Guess there's no going back now, he thought before giving a sheepish smile to Coro.

"Hey Coro."

"How much did you hear?" Coro eyed him sharply.

"Cutting right to the point, I guess." For a second, Minisc debated if he should lie or not. Despite his fears, he saw an opportunity to help Coro, and passing up such a chance would not feel right. "Something about being a monster and a creation," he replied quietly. He was trying to be calm about it. He did not want to make light of the comments, but at the same time, he wanted to ease the tension.

"Forget you heard anything," Coro demanded, with a stare that matched his icy powers.

Minisc could hear the anger in Coro's voice, but he remained undeterred. He was fixated on the boy's drooping eyes. It was a tactic his mother had taught him about reading others' emotions.

"Your face can tell a lot of lies, but your eyes… your eyes will always be honest. Look into someone's eyes, and you'll always find the truth."

Minisc could hear the woman's voice in his mind clear as day. One look at Coro's eyes told him everything he needed to know. The resentment, the rage, the sadness — Minisc could see it all. Coro was trying to hide the scars inflicted on him. That much seemed apparent.

"Coro… was that your father?"

"That's none of your business. Now I said butt out."

The boy's tone matched the malice in his eyes. His fists were clenched, and his body tensed up. But unlike the night before, Coro had not started to walk away, a signal that maybe Minisc could talk to him.

"Come on, Coro. I heard what he said. No one should have to listen to that sort of abuse. Especially from their own father. Why would you put up with that?"

"It doesn't matter what he says," Coro spat as he finally started to walk past Minisc.

"I beg to differ, or you'd be using your full power," Minisc goaded with his tone sharpening. Coro paused, turning around slowly. For a second, Minisc thought he might have gone too far. But much to his surprise, Coro began talking.

"Fine, you want to know why I don't use my damn fire element? Listen up, because I'm not saying this twice."

Not sure if it was a moment of weakness or the boy was calling out for help, Minisc figured the best thing to do was heed Coro's advice.

"I was born with my ice element, but there were complications with my birth. I had an overwhelming amount of element in my veins, to the point that it was freezing my body from the inside. Elementalists evolved to have their bodies be less affected by such elements, unlike humans, but mine remained so strong that I couldn't handle it. Being a newborn, I couldn't control my element, so there was no way to stop the damage being done. My father was one of the leading scientists in the field of elements, and his defining study had always been dual elements. Once doctors declared I would die, my father took his tests and miraculously infused me with a fire element to help balance out the ice. But since that day, my fire element has caused me nothing but trouble. I burned our house down, injured my mother, and have been seen and called a monster by everyone around me."

Coro paused for a moment thinking about that faithful night.

****

"Where is the boy?" Coro's father growled, standing in the wide hallway of his family home. His voice was cold, almost menacing. It was late at night, with the main hall dimly lit, but a few lights were on in the adjacent rooms.

"He's in the bathroom, throwing up," the woman scolded. His mother. She wore a pink shirt and form-fitting blue jeans down to her calves. "Whatever you gave him, it made him deathly sick!" The boy's mother narrowed her eyes in frustration. She had seen enough. Day after day, experiment after experiment, she bore witness to her son undergoing strange and mostly painful reactions from each of her husband's experiments. This time, she planned to stand her ground and protect her son.

While his parents argued, Coro sat on his knees around the corner of the hallway, his little head planted inside a dirty white toilet bowl. He continued dry heaving every few seconds, his body sweating profusely. Listening between heaves, he could hear his parents fighting through the cracked door. He had never heard his mother so distraught before.

The incident started when Coro had been forced to take one of his father's experimental pills, a common occurrence for the young boy. He often filled the role of the subject due to his father not having any budget to hire willing test subjects. Unfortunately, the pills would often cause severe pain or horrendous sickness in the boy. Throwing up could be seen as a blessing in some cases.

"He needs to take these; they should decrease the strain from his fire element," the man argued, holding two more pills, these ones red.

"No. No more of this. I know things have been tough, but you can't keep treating your only son like this." The woman pushed the pills back into her husband's chest. "You can't keep making him take these harmful things anymore, he's only four years old. He's a baby," the woman cried, sticking up for her son. She hated seeing her little boy ill from such vile tests.

"He's taking the pills, and that's final."

The man tried to skirt by his distraught wife, but she refused to move.

Coro finally stopped vomiting and popped his head out around the corner, looking to where his parents stood. His face was pale, and his eyelids were drooping as if sleep-deprived. He had never heard his mother speak in such a furious tone. It scared him, but more so it made his chest hurt with the pain of seeing her so upset.

"He's not some experiment you can test on as you please; he's a young boy, and your son. This has to stop," the woman exclaimed as she blocked her husband from going any farther.

Without hesitation, the man struck his wife with a smack that sent her flailing to the ground.

"Out of my way, woman."

Drunk on power, he showed no remorse for his actions, only looking to seek out his son.

Coro stood at the end of the hall, mortified at what he had witnessed. Horror quickly turned to anger, tears filling his eyes as Coro's hands exploded with a scarlet-blue fire. A product of his father's experiments. Coro ran in front of his mother, his fists scrunched up, tears now streaming down his round cheeks.

"Stay away from Mommy. I won't let you hurt her!" Coro screamed as his body shook. Although he had been trained on how to use his power and it exceeded that of most, if not all young Elementalists, his fit of rage blinded his acts. Before the boy's father could say anything, Coro shot an uncontrolled fireball, which brushed past the man before hitting the wall.

"Coro..." his mother said as she opened her eyes enough to see her son standing in front of her. Her cheek was beginning to swell. Coro's father turned to look at where the flame had hit. He was met with a blaze of fire springing from the drapes.

"Stupid boy," the man yelled as he pulled out a cell phone from his pocket. The blaze grew, engulfing the house in minutes.

Smells of smoke and ash bled not only onto the street but also through the neighboring homes as flashing red and blue strobe lights filled the night sky. Emergency personnel and even a few members of the EC were taking their time investigating the situation that had unfolded. With that going on, Coro stood staring up at his once-beautiful childhood home. No less than half the house had been left in a charred state, looking like a light breeze could send it tumbling down. He shook vigorously from the events, even jumping when a cop came to wrap a warm blanket around him. The char from where most of his home had been was still smoking, with a thick ashy smell even after the fires had been put out. While Coro remained in shock, his father, a few feet away, began talking to another police officer. A few firefighters and another water Elementalist were also spraying down the rest of the house, making sure the blaze had been extinguished for good.

Coro's mother had not been as lucky as the other two, lying on a stretcher. She had severe burn marks on her body, along with a welt from where she had been hit.

Coro watched the scene unfold as two men in blue and white uniforms pushed the stretcher into the back of an ambulance. Tears started to stream down his cheeks again as the doors to the vehicle slammed shut. The poor boy had no idea what was going on around him. However, he could hear the words of neighbors gathering to see the commotion.

"That little boy is a monster, one of those elemental freaks."

"I can't live beside a child who could burn down our house from a temper tantrum."

Coro's family lived in an entirely human neighborhood. And his neighbors had been less than welcoming to the child who bore not only one element, but two. For the most part, he stayed indoors with his mother, but that did little to keep vandals from tagging his house. With him still too young to understand the hatred toward him, and since his father could have cared less about outside opinions, the brunt of the responsibility was left to Coro's mother, who not only had to convince her son he was no monster but that the world did not see him as such. It was a task that seemed almost impossible.

Coro overheard his father talking to the police, a conversation that only served to unravel the child's self-belief in his mother's words once again.

"The boy became angry. He hadn't got his way and set the house ablaze; the boy is a monster."

Coro would spend the night in the hospital room next to his mother, who was recovering in a bed. She sat upright, holding her son tight against her chest as he sobbed uncontrollably.

"I don't wanna be a monster anymore. I don't want to hurt people anymore. I want to help people," Coro cried, his words muffled by the woman's chest as she held her son tight. She ran her slender fingers through her son's messy silver hair.

"Coro, this is not your fault. It doesn't matter what people call you—you're not a monster, and you're not an experiment, you're my son. My incredible son, with an incredible gift. A gift you should not hide from the world. I know you will grow up to be the most helpful Elementalist this world has ever seen. Don't forget that."

****

Coro paused upon finishing the story. "After that night, the EC ended up investigating my father for his experiments and put a stop to his work. He let it slip that I could use fire and that didn't match my birth registry as an Elementalist. Then, after the EC shut down those experiments, what was left of my father's career died. The man lost what little sanity he had left, and in some respects, he has resented the EC ever since. In response, he began trying to rebuild his career, looking for the next great breakthrough. But with no funds and no subjects, that only put me more in the spotlight. He planned to use me, the monster he created, to bring his name back into prominence. But I grew tired of being treated like a test subject, and when I refused, he lashed out. He's dying for me to use my dual elements to show that his research is still relevant. He doesn't even care about the consequences. So to spite him, I never use it unless in an emergency. But as long as I refuse, he will continue to lash out."

Minisc did his best to keep his jaw from dropping to the ground. He had no words for such an awful story. To think Coro had been deemed a monster by the man that raised him, let alone by those around him. No wonder he buried his emotions through a stoic demeanor. He had been shunned by all those around him for simply being himself.

"I—I don't know what to say…"

"Say nothing, and forget I said anything while you're at it."

"Fine, but regardless of your feelings, you better not hold back against me. Monster or not, I won't accept anything less than your best, got it?"

Coro brushed by Minisc, exiting the alleyway into the crowd without a word.

"Well, that was awkward."

The sun had arched high into the sky as the morning sped along. It was almost time for the match, so Minisc decided it was time to get a move on. The finals awaited him.

Meanwhile, Lily and Jules were pacing back and forth in the dressing room. They looked frantic as they wore the soles off their shoes.

"Where could he be?" Lily worried as she paused in her pacing for a second.

"You don't think we missed him, do you?"

"No, his backpack isn't even here." The two grew more worried with each passing second. Minisc's match would start in minutes, and he still had not arrived.

Before they were completely panicked, a beep signaled that the door had been unlocked. The two turned to look at what made the sound. Seconds after the door popped open, Minisc casually strolled through it.

"Hey, what are you two doing in here?" Minisc asked as he walked by, throwing his bag into a stall. He took off his white-and-red jacket and threw it into the booth beside his bag. Grabbing his uniform and throwing it over his messy hair, he turned around to see his two friends staring daggers at him.

"What?"

"Where have you been?" the pair yelled, startling him.

"Huh? I was walking around outside." He saw no reason to mention his run-in with Coro, and besides, he had other ways to handle that situation.

"Where's your phone?" Lily grumbled, pulling out her device, which was covered in a deep purple case. She waved it inches from Minisc's face.

"My phone?" Minisc laughed, reaching into his backpack and pulling out the little black device. "It's right here."

In the middle of the screen were more than a dozen messages from Lily and Jules.

"Wow, what emergency did I miss?"

"Emergency? You fight in ten minutes, and we showed up early to make a strategy," Jules argued.

"You need to find a way to deal with Coro's ice barrages. Unless you're planning on hitting the lottery with a fire stage like I did," Lily pointed out.

"Don't worry, guys, I have a plan." Minisc laughed with a sly smile. Lily and Jules took notice of their friend's confidence, each finally sighing a breath of relief.

"Of course you have a plan. I shouldn't even be surprised," Jules chuckled.

"You seem way too... relaxed." Lily eyed her friend.

"I've got to go. Don't want to be late for the finals." Minisc grinned, putting his phone away in his backpack.

"Okay then, good luck." Lily smiled before wrapping him in a tight embrace. Jules followed suit, joining in the hug.

"Remember Minisc, we're right there with you, no matter what," Lily cooed.

"At least in spirit. Cause, you know, we're sort of going to be in the stands."

"Thanks, guys."

"Now go out there and end this thing with a bang," Jules encouraged as the three separated.

With the match about to start, Lily and Jules quickly scrambled to their seats. Yuri had a bit of morning work, so he would miss the start of the match, and because of Don being back up in his box with Zale, that relegated Lily and Jules back to the competitor seating for the finals.

"I'm so nervous," Lily fretted. "Coro's so strong, but Minisc seemed so calm. Do you have any clue what his plan might be?"

"Nope, but whatever it is, I hope it works... for his sake." The two were with their friend in thought, but that did little to console the helpless feeling they both had. For the foreseeable future, they were no different than the thousands of spectators filling out the audience.

Minisc and Coro stood meters apart from each other, but to

Minisc, it might as well have been nose to nose. The crowd continued raging in anticipation, but he only heard silence. All that played on his mind was his opponent. He stared toward Coro. Something looked different. The other boy didn't show his patented hollow scowl, instead he looked entranced in thought. Minisc was familiar with the look, and it seemed obvious what thoughts plagued Coro. His father's hate-filled words were still lingering. Minisc knew if he found himself in Coro's position, it would eat away at his psyche forever. The fact that Coro had dealt with such hate in silence for so long showed the willpower he had developed of his own accord. Minisc could only dream of that lone-wolf strength. As someone who had spent most of his childhood alone, he knew how much stronger he had grown only thanks to Lily and Jules being by his side.

They watched the roulette wheel rotate over and over again until it selected the terrain. Coming to a halt, it displayed a mountain range, and before they knew it, the fighters were surrounded by staggering rocks and bumpy, mountain-like surfaces. Such a landscape would be neutral for both fighters, meaning the winner would be decided by skill and willpower, nothing else.

With the competitors set, and the arena selected, the finals were finally ready to start.

Let's see how focused Coro is. If I can get him off balance early, then just maybe, I don't have to use my strategy for his ice barrage.

At the flap of the flag, Minisc bolted forward like he was shot out of a cannon. Much to his surprise, Coro responded in kind. Meeting in the middle, Coro and Minisc connected fists. Ripples rang out, rocking the stadium and the crowd. The two wasted no time pouncing back simultaneously. The breakneck pace kept up as a familiar icy aura outlined Coro. Minisc knew what the next move would be, a full-fledged tsunami of ice. This might have been the biggest hurdle for Minisc. He had no chance of melting the attack the way Lily or Ignis had, meaning if he could not block the blast, the fight would end before it even began.

Still, secretly he grinned with confidence at the task. In his battle with Jules, he'd discovered something important dwelling within him. A dormant power that had been lying deep down inside, waiting for the moment it was called upon. If he could unload that hidden strength the way he had to win against his best friend, he was confident he could match the ice blow for blow. On top of that, watching Coro's fight with Ignis had brought him a bit of insight. Ignis had managed to smash right through the ice wall with ease. Even though he used fire to help melt the interior, it let Minisc know that the wall might not be as strong as it looked. Of course, it was entirely speculation. If his hunch backfired, he would lose in no time flat, but it remained the only chance he had.

Minisc put his hands together like he was saying a prayer. A surge of energy built up through his muscles. He looked at Coro, watching as a flash of crystal ice tore through the air, screeching toward him.

"Oh no, the ice barrage is going right for him," Lily cried in fear.

"Come on Minisc, you have to have something up your sleeve," whispered Jules. The two were horrified to watch but could not convince themselves to look away.

Minisc chuckled. "Well, hope this works..." In the face of obliteration, he remained ready. Not a single doubt entered his mind as he stretched his shining golden hands out in front of his chest. *Pillar of light.* A brilliant explosion of gold rays shot out of the boy's palms like a thousand flashlights focusing on one single target.

The two attacks collided in the center of the stadium with a defining ring. More shockwaves cut through the thick smoke created from the blasts before a momentary pause gave the smoke time to disperse. Once it had, the damage could be seen in the form of a jagged crack through the middle of the rocky flooring.

"No way," Lily and Jules exclaimed in shock. They blinked twice as they saw the damage inflicted on the stadium. From only two attacks, the building felt like it might collapse.

Minisc grabbed at his left arm; the strain he'd put on his body from his Pillar of Light wasted no time sinking in. *I might've overdone it just a bit there,* Minisc thought as he tried to catch his breath. *But I was right to use that much energy so early. If that Pillar of Light didn't shatter the ice barrage, I was done for anyways. Who would have thought, Ignis actually proved helpful…*

He turned his sights on Coro, who stood in amazement that his strength had been met head-on so easily.

"Come on, Coro, that can't be the best you can do."

Oddly, Coro spoke up, not in an angry way, but certainly not joyous either.

"You might have been able to match my attack once, but that doesn't mean you can do it again. Let's see how long you can hold up for." In the blink of an eye, Minisc found a second raging ice wall labeled with his name on it. He went back to the well again, sending another Pillar of Light to counteract the ice. The forces collided with the same result as the last time. Minisc had demonstrated he could match Coro hit for hit, but how long could he keep it up for?

Interesting – he's willing to expend all of his energy to protect himself from my attacks, Coro thought as he deciphered his opponent's plan. Minisc, meanwhile, could feel the effects of using so much power. His body was not as comfortable with being pushed and expending the necessary energy, but his options were limited. The pain would heal over time – only winning mattered.

I need to save as much energy as I can for his ice attacks. Everything else I'll have to avoid on foot. Minisc watched Coro send a wave of smaller speedy icicles at him. Quickly tap-dancing around the attacks, mixed with using his rocky mountain surroundings, Minisc dodged the flurry with little effort. Hearing the last of the eight spears crash into the ground, he popped out, ready to go on the offensive. His over-eagerness would end up proving careless though, as his feet went out from under him. He looked down, feeling the cold sensation seep through his backside as he groaned in pain. A slick patch of ice covered the ground. In fact, around a quarter of the field in various spots was covered in the slippery white ice.

Oh, that's not good. Minisc gulped, staring up at Coro, who had a chilling look about him. An icicle in the shape of a rock flew at

Minisc. Thinking quick, he kicked off the boulders beside him, sliding across the ice to cover.

Finally given a second to breathe, something about Coro's last assault had caught his attention.

There's no way I should have been able to dodge that... are his attacks slowing down? He can't be reaching his limit already, can he? Wait... his body. With a closer look, Minisc saw an organic residue of ice coating Coro's arms. *It's the ice, that's what's slowing him down. He must be losing speed with every attack, so he does have a weakness. Now's my chance.*

Minisc hurried to his feet. He began pushing the tempo of the battle. Ignoring the tension ripping through his arms, Minisc continued to punch and kick with all he had. Much like Lily had tried in her match, he attempted to keep the distance close between himself and Coro. Taking the match to his opponent, Coro still defended each blow with simplicity. But Minisc remained relentless, not giving him an opening to counter. Finally, after an unforgiving assault, Coro's defenses broke down. Minisc slammed his left fist into the boy's abdomen, sending Coro flying through the air.

The crowd held their breath as Coro left his feet. He screamed toward the edge of the ring before a series of ice pillars shot out of the ground like poles in a fence. Coro smashed into the makeshift barrier, crashing to the ground. Despite the damage, he managed to stop his momentum from carrying him out of the stadium.

"Awww, I thought he won," Lily sighed.

"Coro really is incredible, but Minisc is taking it to him. Maybe he can win this after all."

Minisc chuckled to himself as he watched Coro push himself back up. "I should have known it wasn't going to be that easy."

Still, the punch had not been entirely ineffective. Minisc could see the growing frustration on Coro's face.

The other boy rushed forward, trying to counter Minisc's close combat with punches of his own, which itself was unusual for the boy, who had an overwhelming and seemingly limitless element in him. Even more unusual was what Coro failed to notice — with the growing ice on his body, his movements were clunky and easy to predict.

I need to wait for the right moment to strike.

Minisc delayed, patiently standing his ground as Coro charged toward him.

Once the boy got within a few feet ready to strike, Minisc saw his chance.

"Now!"

Minisc ducked under the punch, his hand glowing gold as he jammed a ball of light into Coro's ribs. It exploded, sending him flying back, skidding across the ground, but again he pushed himself up. He gripped his fists in anger, losing the composure that he typically fought with. He had never been pushed so hard in a battle since coming to EA. In the back of his mind, doubt was starting to form. If he lost to Minisc and did not use the full extent of his power, that would only serve to prove his father right—that he was weak and needed the experiments. Coro summoned a barrage of icicles from the ground.

With no way around it, Minisc prepared for another Pillar of Light. He stood firm as waves of ice bore down on him. Taking a deep breath, he countered with a third blinding ray of light, again shattering through the ice, this time with far more ease. Minisc let out a wincing cry. His body started cramping, and the veins in his arms looked like they were going to burst.

Watching from above, Don muttered to himself. "Minisc is prepared to deal with the consequences of using that much energy in one attack. It very well might have been the only way he could stop Coro's devastating ice, though." He was standing in a booth hanging over the edge of the last row of seating.

Behind him, the chairman sat on his phone, paying little attention to what transpired a few hundred feet below. Don would be presenting the trophy, and while he tried to avoid bias, he knew full well he was rooting for his son.

"You can't continue to strain your body and block my ice; it'll be your undoing," Coro said, seeing his opponent hunched over, wincing. Both of them were trying to catch their breath.

"You can't fool me, Coro. Those ice waves take just as much a toll on you as my light does on me. Look at your body; you're shaking as much as I am. This fight is going to come down to willpower, and with that, I won't lose!"

Both Coro's forearms were more than half covered in ice. He was gradually becoming immobile, and that would leave Minisc free to attack at will. Coro could quickly fix the problem. All he needed to do was use his fire and melt it. Even though he was more than capable of using his elements in tandem, he still refused. He would win on his own, whatever the cost.

Of course, that fact was not lost on Minisc, either. Coro had no intention of using his fire element to melt the ice off his body, and somehow knowing that frustrated Minisc. He remained adamant that winning with Coro at a clear disadvantage tainted it. Minisc wanted to win the tournament, but not by default.

"Why are you still not using your full power?"

"Who's to say I'm not?" Coro spat back.

"Look at me, Coro. You haven't landed one hit, and with the amount of ice on your body, you won't anytime soon. You and I both know if you used your fire element, you could melt that ice off your body in seconds."

"Shut up... I don't need your lectures."

Coro cast his hand forward, sending an icicle spear at Minisc. With no hesitation, he blocked it with a Lum Blast, using a minimal amount of energy. The two attacks collided, canceling each other out once again. Minisc stood still, his hair blown back fiercely by the recoil of the explosion. For the moment, he looked in total control of the match.

Ready to begin again, Coro started to charge at Minisc.

What is he doing? He knows he can't keep up with me at this point; he must have something planned. Minisc braced himself for the unexpected. He let Coro get in close and quickly blocked the blow before realizing Coro's true intentions.

"Got you," Coro smirked, his fist turning into an open palm. Before Minisc could register the boy's words, Coro released a blanket of ice.

Luckily for Minisc, he landed a counterpunch into Coro's midsection, but it had come with a heavy price. A frigid cold ran up his left arm. Then, just as quickly, the feeling turned to nothing. His left arm was encased in ice. He had no control over his ligament anymore.

Unbelievable – he attacked with reckless abandon, knowing he was going to get hit, just to freeze my arm. This guy's really determined not to use his fire at any cost.

"Let's see how good of a fighter you are with one arm." Coro glared as he picked himself up off the ground.

Ugh, no, I can't break it.

Minisc struggled to find the feeling in his arm but with no luck. The body part was nothing more than a nuisance for the time being.

Thankfully, Coro continued to grow slower, the ice on his body building up, with spots appearing on his clothing and skin. He was visibly shaking from the attacks, but he started to gain some fire in his eyes. He looked more determined to win than at any point previously.

Not wasting any time, Coro's foot began to glow with a chilly vapor swirling off it, and before Minisc knew it, a path of ice developed on the ground, heading in his direction. Coro slid along the ice, closing the gap faster than Minisc could react. *Thud, thud, thud.* Coro landed a series of punches to the boy's gut, sending him sprawling.

Minisc skidded, smashing into a large rock, his body quickly being covered in ice as well. He tried to get to his feet, but his body felt twice as heavy as normal. The weight of the ice was starting to overcome him. Coro had turned the tides of the fight as quickly as Minisc had started it.

I need to find a way to break this ice. If I don't, I'll be turned into a popsicle.

Coro showed no signs of stopping his assault, sending a barrage of icicles at Minisc. Left with no other options, he started to roll out of the way. Coro's attacks were slowing down considerably, but Minisc was equally immobile. Three icicles grazed him, gashing his cheek, his right arm, and his left leg.

Minisc dropped to a knee. His right arm throbbed, with blood flowing down it, a sharp contrast to his now-numb left arm.

The crowd gasped as the boy fought to get to his feet.

Don whispered, "Those wounds are serious; his entire body has reached its limits. He's running on pure adrenaline right now. I bet he has no clue how much pain he's really in. Even with that, Minisc is showing tremendous resolve to continue this fight. He has grown so quickly in such a short time. It's astounding." He watched his son take blow after blow and continue to rise.

"If you do not get up, I'll be forced to call this match," the ref informed Minisc, who remained on one knee.

"No, don't call it. I'm not done."

Not ready to concede defeat yet, Minisc slowly pushed himself back up. Hunched over, with both of his arms useless, he prepared to fight again.

"Why won't you give up? Those injuries are far past what any normal person can take," Coro snarled, looking at his opponent, who was covered in a mix of blood and ice. He had never seen anyone take the punishment Minisc had and continue to fight.

"Look, Coro, you're not the only one with pressure on you. You think people expect the Hero of Light's son to just give up? No. I came to this school so I could help people, and make my mother and father proud. Quitting would never do that. I understand why you refuse to use your full power, I really do. You don't want to be seen as a monster for your abilities. How you survived by yourself for this long is beyond me. I could never do it—without Lily and Jules to keep me from falling onto a path of resentment, I would never have made it where I am. I want to make them proud. They believe in me, and that's all I need to win. So, I'll continue to try my best, right up until the end." Minisc stumbled forward and swung his bleeding arm with all his might. Coro absorbed the impact, smashing into a jagged rock, which shattered to pieces.

"Listen to me, Coro. Whether you don't want to use your fire element because you think it makes you a monster, or because you resent your father and don't want to give him the satisfaction, frankly I don't care, but as long as you continue to hold back against me, you have no right to call yourself a champion!"

Coro stood frozen.

"But... if I use my fire, I'll be giving my father exactly what he wants. I'll be the monster I've tried to avoid for so long."

"You're not some monster, Coro. You're an Elementalist, with a special gift—now use it."

Coro's eyes opened wide. He thought back to his mother's words.

It doesn't matter what people call you, you're not a monster, and you're not an experiment, you're my son. My incredible son with an incredible gift. A gift you should not hide from the world.

Coro started to take in heavy breaths. He could feel his body heating up, the fire inside him building. The temperature in the stadium began to rise to sweltering highs, with the rocky ground giving off steam all around him.

Following an eruption of sparks, Coro's body exploded into a flaming blue aura, glistening all over. The ice around the battlefield melted away in an instance. Gusts of wind from Coro's power swirled through the arena.

"What the heck is going on?" Lily asked, bracing herself from the shocks.

"Coro has two elements?" Jules yelled.

"This is insane. How is he generating so much power?"

Minisc stood in awe, watching his opponent's power radiate out like a beam of light coming down from the sky.

"Finally..." Minisc grinned.

Don watched in awe. "Now I understand what you were alluding to last night, son. You've been trying to get Coro to use his full power this entire time. You were trying to save Coro from himself, weren't you? Even if it cost you the match, you still would rather help somebody in need," he said, watching the incredible light show. He was not surprised at what his son had done; he had seen it all the time. The boy tried to help everyone he could. It was in Minisc's nature. When he saw Coro and the struggles his opponent was going through, he could not stop himself from trying to free

Coro from his shackles. Minisc wanted to be the friend Coro never had.

Coro stood with pale blue flames dancing around him, looking at Minisc, who had a sly smile growing.

"You really are something, Minisc. You're in more pain than most people could imagine, yet you're still smiling. This is what you wanted, right? My full power. Well, here it is. Brace yourself, because I'm not holding back anymore."

Minisc could feel the sweltering heat radiating through the stadium as Coro raised his hand. Then he felt a tingle in his left arm. The ice began to melt off his body as well.

"No way. I can move again." Minisc needed to act quickly. Using every last drop of energy left, he prepared for his final Pillar of Light. Digging as deep as he could, the boy called upon all the power he had developed from training with his father, to his teachers, to his friends. All of it would be used to win the Tournament of Elements. His entire being started to shine bright, a powerful pillar shooting to the sky, releasing more shock waves. The whole building was beginning to crack from the damage.

Coro's fire became controlled around his body as the energy flowed into his hands. They became a bright bluish-red. With a vicious battle cry, Coro unleashed a swirling beam of fire and ice, which circled toward Minisc like intertwined ribbons.

Wasting no time, Minisc channeled all he had left into one final strike.

"Give me everything you've got, Coro." The blast exploded out of his hands like a shotgun's, the two beams heading directly for each other.

"Thank you, Minisc," Coro whispered as the two beams collided, creating a nuclear-sized explosion in the stadium.

"What's going on down there?" Jules yelled as he and Lily held on to their seats, trying not to be blown away by the recoil of the blast.

Eventually, the smoke cloud began to disperse in the arena opening. The rocky floor had all but been destroyed, and the walls of the stadium were just as cracked. Even the ref had to dig himself out of the rubble, trying to get a clear view through the thick fog cloud. As the air cleared, all eyes in the stadium were looking for the combatants.

"There's Coro." Jules pointed down to the boy.

He was lying flat on his stomach, a wall of ice blocking him from the edge of the ring. Despite heavy damage, it had been enough to stop Coro from going out of bounds.

"Where's Minisc, though?" Lily asked, looking for her friend frantically.

Out of the corner of her eye, she saw a boy lying in a heaping pile of rubble. A section of the stadium wall had been decimated, and Minisc found himself in the middle of the wreckage.

"No," Jules, Lily, and Don all cried simultaneously.

The ref looked at Coro and then at Minisc. Both lay motionless.

"Minisc has left the arena. Therefore, Coro wins," the ref announced to an eruption of cheers and applause. With a loud pop, confetti shot into the air, bursting into a rainbow of colors decorating the sky.

Coro was the first to regain consciousness, weakly getting to his feet. His knees were wobbly, every bone in his body aching.

A few seconds later, Minisc woke up dazed and confused, looking around, trying to gain his bearings. Some pebbles fell to the ground as Minisc shuffled his hands. He looked down to see the grass in front of him.

"Oh, that's not good…" Minisc groaned as it dawned on him where he sat. The match was over; he had been tossed out of the ring from the explosion. Realizing that he had lost, he attempted to rise to his feet, but his body refused the request. He looked like he had been through a war zone. His clothes had been ripped to shreds, and he had a large cut dripping down his left arm and leg, not to mention the injuries he had already sustained through the battle. Regardless, determined to see Coro, Minisc wiped the sweat and dirt off his forehead before feeling a small gash on his cheek.

Coro's full power is something else. I guess that's what I get…

A few men came sprinting out of the nearby tunnel and tried to scoop Minisc up, but he waved them off.

"No, I'm okay. I can walk," Minisc assured them as he pushed himself off the rubble. Even if that was not entirely true, he refused to be taken away. His feet hit the soft grass and almost buckled upon his first step. He looked at the rainbow of streamers and pieces of confetti lining his path.

"I think we overdid it this time," he laughed as he tried to find his balance.

Taking slow but steady steps, Minisc made it to the edge of the ring. The paramedics followed his every move, worried that he could collapse at any second.

"Congrats, Coro. You deserve to win." Minisc graciously smiled at his beaten and battered counterpart.

"Thank you Minisc, for opening my eyes—for helping me understand."

Coro almost cracked a smile. It was the happiest Minisc had seen the boy since they'd met. Even in defeat, the sight filled him with joy. In a time of need, he'd reached out and helped Coro see through the resentment he had been drowning in, and in the end, Minisc had done the right thing. Even at the expense of himself.

With the tournament over, Minisc found himself in the infirmary. The rest of the finals for each division had taken place in the meantime, but none were as dramatic as the first-years'. His entire body and part of his head were wrapped in white bandages. He tried to move his fingers, but the best he could do was a little twitch. From head to toe, the boy was confined to his bed.

I am so sick of this place.

Stuck alone and bored out of his mind, Minisc gazed around the hospital room. Now that the champions had been decided, everyone from fans to participants had been invited onto center stage in the stadium bowl for the trophy ceremony.

Not able to go home until his father finished his duties at the ceremony, Minisc turned to the familiar TV hanging on the wall.

The screen was showing coverage of the tournament's closing ceremonies.

Minisc could see his father standing on a podium in the arena, much like the setup before the games had started. He was torn, not knowing if he wanted to watch the ceremonies or simply sleep. Every one of the competitors stood out there, being cheered and congratulated, but Minisc was stuck in a hospital bed. Worst of all, he could see Coro standing beside his father. Even though there were three other champions on the stage with them, the one that mattered most was Coro. Minisc knew he had lost fair and square, but that did not ease the sting of defeat. He could have been up with his father, receiving the trophy. It would have been a proud moment for him, but an even prouder moment for the Hero. Regardless, in the grand scheme of things, none of that mattered. Minisc understood that better now than any time before. What mattered was he did his best and helped someone along the way.

Back in the stadium, Don stood towering above the audience, his imposing figure casting a shadow over Coro, who stood in between the man and President Osiris. Coro looked almost as rough as Minisc, but he was stable enough to accept his championship trophy. In front of the podium was a square silver table, and on it lay four large oval awards, sparkling gold and glittering in the afternoon sun. The fans were standing in masses, feet away from the stage, flowing back like waves in the ocean.

Zale walked up to the microphone that hung off the podium.

"Thank you, everyone, for coming out to this year's Tournament of Elements Championship. This week has been an incredible success, and I'd like to take the time to thank all of the wonderful fans who came out and supported the tournament all week. Second, I'd like to extend my congratulations to all of the fighters in this year's tournament; each and every one of you gave it your all and put on a show that the fans will not soon forget. You have no doubt made your teachers and your peers proud, and with such bright stars, the EC will be in good hands for years to come. Keep up the fantastic work. Thirdly, I'd like to congratulate our finalists for putting on a series of matches that exemplified dedication, perseverance, and sportsmanship. All of you are worthy champions. And last but certainly not least, I'd like to extend our congratulations to our four new champions for this year's tournament."

One after another, the victors claimed their spoils, with Coro being the last to go. He walked up gingerly; besides a few cut marks on his body and his clear exhaustion, he looked healthy enough. The boy made his way to the front of the podium, while Don walked behind him to the other side of the little table. The Hero of Light picked up the trophy by one of the rounded handles, while Coro held the opposite one.

"It is my honor and pleasure to crown you champion of the Tournament of Elements, first-year division. Congrats, Coro, you have truly earned it," Don boasted in that hero voice of his before shaking the boy's hand. Flashbulbs from cameras lit up the sea of people as they applauded.

Coro took the trophy, holding it in both hands. He was happy to win, but he still had that stoic look plastered on his face. He held the trophy in front of his chest as pictures snapped one after another.

Lily and Jules were in the front row of the crowd, and Yuri stood a row behind them. The three clapped somberly as the trophies were handed out. They were disappointed by the result, but they knew Minisc had done his best. They could not be disappointed by his effort.

Don stepped back, letting Coro and the other champions stand front and center. He was trying his best to put on an act of joy during the event, but on the inside, he felt more disappointed than anyone. He'd had all the confidence in the world that Minisc was going to win, that his son would burst onto the scene and make a name for himself. It was supposed to boost his confidence to no end.

Still, if none of that happened, the man remained proud of his boy, even in defeat. He recognized that Minisc had put himself through an extreme amount of pain and anguish just to make it to the finals. Also, he could not lose sight of how his son placed trying to help his classmate over taking an easy victory in the finals. That was admirable, and what made Minisc, Minisc. Always trying to help others even at the detriment of himself. He took after his mother in that way.

Minisc sat up in his bed. A sense of disappointment had rushed over him, watching his father hand the trophy over to his classmate. It could have been him up there accepting that trophy, his picture taken with his father. He tried so hard to make the man proud. To make Lily and Jules proud. They had been so helpful and supportive, and he had let them down. Especially after seeing the way Coro was treated, it made him appreciate the support he did have more than the struggles he'd endured.

"I know I did the right thing. If I had won with Coro holding back, it wouldn't have felt right," Minisc vented to no one as he watched the crowd's roar, heaping praise and glory onto Coro. The boy tried to push his frustration out of his mind. He knew beating himself up would not make him feel better in the long run.

He continued to replay the match over again in his head. In hopes of clearing his mind, he glanced back at the TV. Then his heart started pounding through his chest. His forehead began to sweat as the color drained from his face. He was gasping for air. In an instant, everything changed.

CHAPTER 14
THE HERO OF LIGHT

ALL THOSE WHO HAD RECEIVED THEIR TROPHIES MADE their way off the stage. Only Coro remained in the spotlight, with Don behind him. The trophy gleamed, its light reflecting brightly throughout the stadium. Following the shine, Don looked up to the sky. A cold shiver rippled down the man's spine.

"Look out!"

Don bolted toward Coro, tackling him hard to the ground.

Boom.

Flying through the stadium into the podium, a seismic Shadow Ball exploded where Coro and Don had just stood. Thick black smoke flooded the lower bowl, clouding the vision of everyone inside. The stage collapsed into a pile of rubble from the surprise attack, and somewhere underneath, Coro and Don lay buried.

Lily and Jules both covered their ears in an attempt to soften the deafening screams that rang out in fear. Reacting on instinct, Jules attempted to find his way through the smoke, but the thickness made such a task impossible. Even Lily, who had only been a foot away from him, fell out of sight.

"Lily, where are you? Are you okay?" Jules called out.

"Jules, I can't see anything," Lily cried, her voice trembling.

The masses stampeded for the north entrance, trampling over each other to escape. Hysteria took over as spectators scrambled for their lives. Nobody knew for sure what had happened, but waiting around to see if it would happen again was not an option.

What was that? Jules wondered, his thoughts barely discernible amidst the screams. He stumbled a few steps forward but could not see enough to gain his bearings.

A few feet away, Lily walked blindly, her slender figure trembling with each minimal step she took. She could not see her own hand, let alone find Jules. The girl paused for a second, trying to catch the breath caught in her throat. Before she could move again, a tight grip landed on her shoulder. She tried to let out a scream, but the cry failed to escape her lips. Lily disappeared farther into the fog.

Jules began to feel the wind swirl around his feet, but he paused. *Why is the smoke not fading? Something isn't right,* he thought. *Even if I wanted to clear the smoke with my wind, I can't see anything. I have no way of avoiding people while using my element; it's too risky.*

While he froze, unsure what his next move should be, a hand broke through the fog and grabbed Jules, forcefully ripping him back into the smoke.

"What the—" Jules yelled as he hit the ground. He scrambled to look behind him. Yuri had a grip on his collar.

"Thank goodness you're okay."

Yuri had supreme control of his element and managed to use his wind in such a confined space that he could see Jules and Lily through the shadowy mist.

A sigh of relief overcame the younger sibling as well. Seeing the calm, determined face of his brother instilled a grain of confidence in Jules. He let out another long exhale as he saw who else Yuri had a hold of. In the clutches of his brother's other hand was Lily's arm.

"You two need to get out of here now. It's too dangerous to be here."

"We're never going to make it through the crowds," Jules argued. He was trying to keep his composure mirroring his brother's but it was hard for him; he was as terrified by the surprise attack as anyone else in the building. He looked over at Lily; her face was ghostly pale and her voice non-existent. She took deep breaths, to the point of hyperventilating, and her heart pounded so hard Jules thought for sure it would pop out.

Yuri grabbed his brother's attention again.

"Listen to me, Jules. Take Lily, go straight from here down the tunnel, and follow the crowd into the building. Take this key. Go up to the suite and hide there for now. Do not leave until I give you permission, understand?"

He grabbed Jules's left hand and stuffed his suite key into it before pushing it back into his brother's chest. Yuri's priority was making sure that Jules and Lily were safe, but he knew going outside the building might be even more dangerous. It was better if he knew where they were and that they were likely safe.

"What about you? You have to come with us," Jules insisted. He did not want to leave his brother behind in such a mess. It was far too dangerous, even for someone as strong and seasoned as Yuri.

"No, I'm staying here; I have a feeling I know the cause of this…"

"We can't just leave you here, it's too dangerous. Let us help you," Jules cried out. He refused to leave his brother alone to try and take on someone who could cause so much damage in a single attack.

"No. Jules, look at Lily." Yuri turned his brother to look at the girl. She had a shell-shocked expression, with glazed-over eyes staring off into the abyss. Lily had not said a word, nor heard a word of the plan, frozen on her knees like a statue.

Yuri dropped his voice to a much softer tone. "You need to get her out of here now."

"Okay, I understand." Jules nodded. "Come on Lily, we're getting out of here."

Jules grabbed Lily's arm, lifting her to her feet. She followed like a lifeless puppet as they took off into the shadows. After a few steps, the two disappeared into the darkness.

Back at the impact site, Don burst out of the rubble. On the left side of his shirt was a thick red blotch soaking into his deep blue dress shirt. He grabbed at it, wincing. In his haste to protect Coro, he had thrown himself in front of the deadly blast, taking the brunt of the force. Even so, he had no time to examine the extent of his injuries, remaining focused on the task at hand. The fog made visuals impossible to see, but the distant cries told him that most of the audience had escaped to the interior of the building. He held his hand up to the sun.

"Flare," he shouted.

A large, glimmering sun rose into the sky. Within seconds the flare rained pillars of light down, loosening up the thick smoke. It failed to eradicate the fog, but if nothing else, it allowed the man to see shadowy figures moving around. With his newfound light source, he noticed a hand sticking out from the rubble.

"Coro." Don rapidly removed the rocks around the arm. Lifting the final stone, he found himself face-to-face with an unconscious Coro. Already weak after his match with Minisc, his body had taken even more of a toll from the avalanche. Don had to get the boy to safety, but he couldn't do that until he found the perpetrator of the attack.

Coro's eyes fluttered open to meet Don's.

"Coro, are you okay? Are you able to walk?" Don asked, attempting to help the boy to his feet. Coro stumbled a step forward.

"Yeah... what's going on?" he asked in a daze.

"We're under attack," Don answered, keeping aware of his surroundings. He waited patiently, the looming sense of danger still abundant. Turning, Don wrapped his arm around Coro and leaped towards what he believed was a path to the inside of the building. As he did, a second energy ball soared down and exploded just behind them.

"Coro, you need to leave now. It's far too dangerous to be here. Do your best to get out of the building and seek help."

Coro nodded without a word. Mustering what strength he had left, he escaped toward the tunnel and out of sight, while Don was left trying to figure out where the attacker was hiding. He suspected it to be an aerial assault based on the surprise factor, but he had little to no confirmation.

Back in the infirmary, Minisc gasped for air. His heart shot into his throat as he gawked at the TV. Nothing but static; the feed had been cut as soon as the blast hit. Thoughts of the worst raced through his already-cluttered mind. Everyone that he cared about had been in that audience. Lily, Jules, Yuri. On top of that, his father had been the target of the cowardly attack.

What if they're hurt? What if Lily and Jules need my help? Maybe they're okay – they have to be okay, Minisc argued internally, trying to keep his mind from running wild with rampant speculation. He had no clue what was happening but recognized it could not be good. The rumble of a second blast shook his bed; although faint, it had to be a massive explosion for him to feel it from the other side of the building. Running on pure adrenaline, Minisc forced himself out of bed.

He stopped as the building shook once again; this time fainter than the last, but he knew it had been another attack. Slipping his shoes on, Minisc readied to head toward the door. Thinking quickly, he reached for his phone.

"No service, damn it! What is going on?"

He placed the device back in his pocket and took off down the ghostly hallway. The power had been cut off throughout the building, but the fog only seemed to extend to the inner bowl of the arena. That at least gave Minisc a clear path to follow.

This place is a ghost town; everyone in the building must have been at the ceremony. Jules, Lily... Father... please be okay.

Minisc's pace quickened with each strenuous step.

Jules and Lily found their way to a small side door in one of the adjacent hallways. They bolted up the shallow stairwell, trying to get to safety as fast as they could. The looming threat that they could run into the attacker at any moment danced around in Jules's mind.

As they ran, Lily finally snapped out of her daze.

"Jules — what happened... where are we going?" she asked frantically.

"Oh good, you finally came to. I don't know what's going on, but we're under attack. Yuri told us to go to his suite and lay low for the time being. We'll be safe there," Jules explained, panting as he reached the top of the stairs.

Lily nodded, understanding the plan. She still had not grasped the scope of danger, but she trusted Jules enough to lead them to safety. However, when she hit the top step, she came to a screeching halt. A horrifying realization dawned on her.

"Wait! Minisc is still in the infirmary. He has no idea that the whole building is in danger."

Lily pulled out her cell phone and began dialing frantically, but it wouldn't connect.

"I don't have any service," she cried as the rejecting beep of her phone echoed off the concrete walls. Jules pulled his phone out as well only to be met with the same deflating sound.

"I'm going to get him," Jules declared, eyes narrowing as he made his decision.

"Here, take the key and get to safety. Wait for us there. Minisc would kill me if anything happened to you."

Jules handed the key over to Lily, but she refused, pushing it back into his chest.

"No, I'm going with you."

"Lily —"

"Don't 'Lily' me. I'm going with you. Minisc wouldn't stand by if I was the one needing to be saved. Well, it's my turn to save him," Lily ordered, suddenly taking the lead in their new rescue mission. She shot Jules a confident look that he had never before seen from his friend.

"Figures; the second Minisc is involved, she snaps out of her haze," Jules muttered as he sprinted down the hall, trailing his new commander and chief.

Don observed the stands, scanning for anything that stood out.

"The attacks must have come from above, so whoever is doing this has to be in the stands," he concluded before his attention was drawn back to the shadowy figure in the center of the ring. A large gust of wind exploded from the middle of the cloud, dispelling the veil of smoke with ease. Standing in the middle with a beautiful green aura shining around him was Yuri. His hair slowly fell back past his ears as the wind died down. The fog had finally been cleared out.

"Yuri," Don called. He knew that Lily and Jules had been with the man. "Where are the kids?" he asked as he approached.

"I sent Jules and Lily to my suite to lay low. I think everyone else got through the tunnels to the entrance."

"Good. But Minisc is still in the infirmary. He's in danger," Don said, fear evident in his voice.

"We need to alert the EC and get backup right away — we don't know what we're up against," Yuri advised.

It had been a minute or so since any blasts rained down on them, but they both knew it would be foolish to let their guard down. Standing back to back, they made sure to cover their bases. The arena might have been empty, but they were certainly not alone.

"I sent Coro to alert the authorities."

"You mean this kid?" said an almost childish voice. The two men spun around to face the tunnel that Coro had disappeared through. Stepping out of the shadows was a tall, slender man in a long black coat. Steel chains fell around his neck, and a silver line ran all along the seams of the cloak. He had a teenage face, pale skin, and looked incredibly scrawny. Nobody would have suspected any such power from him.

In his hand, he held by the scruff of his collar an unconscious Coro. The boy dangled in the air, his body limp. His eyes fluttered open for a brief second.

"I'm sorry…" he mumbled before they shut again.

The cloaked man strutted confidently out of the tunnel. The entrance was in shambles. Walls were smashed, the grass trampled and dirt smeared everywhere.

"I have no more use for you."

The man effortlessly chucked Coro into a pile of rocks to his left before letting out a spine-chilling laugh.

Yuri ran to where Coro had landed. Bending down, he placed two fingers along the boy's neck. He felt the faintest sign of a pulse. It was slow and weak, but consistent.

"He's still alive; he's just unconscious," Yuri announced, standing back up and looking at his new enemy.

"And who are you?" Don demanded.

"Who am I? I'm just a guy who hates the way you have infected this world, bringing peace to people who don't deserve it. That's why I'm here. You see, unlike these worthless humans, when I don't like something, I don't complain about it, I fix it. And that starts by getting rid of you, Hero of Light."

"If I'm the one you wanted, then why attack innocent bystanders like a coward?"

"Who cares about bystanders? I have no use for them. I'd have killed them for fun after I killed the Hero of Light regardless," the man pronounced, extending his arms to the sky in showmanship.

"You think you're going to kill the Hero of Light? That's laughable. You people never learn, do you?" Yuri denounced as he got up from where Coro lay.

"Speaking of bystanders, let's start with you." The man pointed his palm at Yuri and a Shadow Ball formed. Sparks of electricity sprung off it from the potency. At the flick of the man's wrist, it screamed toward Yuri with blinding speed. Even so, without flinching, Yuri countered with his element. The burst of wind put a halt to his demise only inches away from his face.

"If that's the best you have, you should quit while you're ahead. You'll never even hurt the Hero of Light; let alone kill him," Yuri mocked, firing the blast back at the intruder with as much force as he could muster. Swiftly, the man sprung out a pair of shadow claws and sliced the attack clean in half.

"Oh don't worry, I always come prepared."

The man snapped his fingers, ready for his grand show to start.

Three hooded figures walked out of the tunnel behind him. The one on the left already had her hood off with a disgusting glee painted on her lips. She was a young woman, looking more like a child, with light blue hair pulled into curly pigtails falling just past her ears. Turquoise eyes and a tiny nose rounded out her soft face. She flashed a sly smile, showing sharp, vampire-like teeth. Evil intentions radiated off of her like a foul stench — like she was made of pure evil, and eager to kill.

Yuri recognized the man on the right as the one from over the summer — Bronx.

"Brooklyn... we need to speed this up. They'll have reinforcements coming soon, and I'm sure the Adenji gang on the outside are less than competent..."

"Yeah, you're probably right Bronx. Let's bring out the special guest star for this show."

Behind Brooklyn, a loud stomp from the tunnel shook the ground, and then a second and a third, until finally, a big burly man matching Don's physique came out of the tunnel. He looked like a world champion wrestler, only his mouth had what appeared to be dark element in the shape of X's stapling it shut. He was riling for a fight.

"See, I'm not the only one that wants you dead — this big guy agrees with me, right?" Brooklyn turned to the beast of a man and nodded.

"No way. Is that — " Don tried to wrap his head around the man's image until it finally hit him. "That's the leader of the Adenji gang... but why would they join the likes of you?" he wondered aloud.

"Simple really. He wants to kill you, I want to kill you." Brooklyn turned to Bex.

"Bex, do you have the injection?"

"Yep," Bex chirped, rolling her thick sleeve up. The slight shine of a sharp needlepoint ran along her thin arm.

"Alright, let's start with the stragglers and let this brute wear down the Hero of Light. We don't care if he dies anyway."

Minisc hurried down the dim corridor, adrenaline the only thing keeping him from collapsing. The faint sound of voices carried down the hall, causing the boy to halt and take cover along the wall. He could ill afford to be caught in his condition.

"This is boring. Why do we have to keep watch? I signed up to kill the Hero of Light," a tall man whined. He was wearing a baggy, navy-blue robe with silver trim. He pulled his hood off, releasing his long silver ponytail. He had the look of a common criminal more than a member of Luminosa.

"Just give it some time—those guys in black coats told us to keep watch, but once we find his stupid kid, we can take him for ourselves. Besides, this is what the boss ordered. I don't like it, but those are the laws of the Adenji gang. We just need the Hero of Light dead so we can move on with our lives," a shorter, older man countered. He was bald and looked far more menacing thanks to a scar that went all the way across his left eye, stretching too well underneath his mouth.

I don't think these guys are members of Luminosa, but still, they want to use me as bait to kill my father. I need to escape... Minisc tried to think of a plan. *I don't have the strength for a head-on attack. My only option is to find a different route.*

He turned to retrace his steps but heard footsteps starting up. With no time to run, he needed to hide, and quick. Looking around at the lack of options, he had no other choice but to dip behind a scantily clad potted tree. It did little to cover even close to half his body but nothing else would do. His plan, however, proved as bad as perceived, as the taller of the two men rounded the corner and wasted no time noticing Minisc.

"Now what do we have here, a kid trying to play hero? Hey Smudge, take a look at what I found," the man bellowed as he walked toward Minisc.

That's not good, Minisc thought as he stood up, realizing his plan had gone awry. *Do I try to run? I'm way too weak to fight right now.*

Minisc weighed his options, his time fading with each step the man took toward him. He began to back up slowly down the hall. With no plan in mind, the more distance between him and them, the better. He knew at any moment he might have to take off.

The older man, Smudge, turned the corner to join his partner in staring at a helpless Minisc. The first man raised his hand, sending sparks out—he was preparing to strike.

"Iris, you idiot, don't you know who that is?" Smudge scolded. The sparks stopped as Iris lowered his hand.

Today just keeps getting worse. Minisc's concern level was growing out of control.

"That kid is the Hero of Light's son. This is perfect." He turned to address Minisc next. "Boy have we been looking for you, kid." He stepped forward. "Now if you are a good boy, and come with us peacefully, then maybe we will let you see your father before he's killed."

"Thanks for the invitation, but I'm not coming with you, scum," Minisc said, ignoring the threats levied against his father. Not that he didn't take them seriously—at this point, how could he not? Regardless, step one was escaping; if he did not do that, he would without a doubt be used in his father's demise. Seeing only one other option, Minisc called up whatever energy he had left and formed a small ball of light. It flashed with blinding sparkles like a star exploding... or at least that had been his plan. Instead, the light went off with a whimper, providing no more than a momentary inconvenience for his captors.

"Oh come on," Minisc whined. Now he had no options. Turning, he bolted down the hall in a lackluster escape attempt.

"Get him," Smudge ordered as Iris began chasing him down the hall. Luckily for Minisc, the man appeared to be less than competent in his skills, firing inaccurate sparks of lightning as Minisc rounded another corner in the hallway. However, just as he did, he crashed into an unnatural formation of rocks—one that had been created by an Elementalist.

"Damn it, the other guy must be an earth Elementalist." On his left was a long, rectangular window, presumably leading to the outside of the building's front entrance. For a split second, he debated the idea of jumping, but then vetoed such a horrible plan. He was going to have to fight his way out — not with his element, but with his fists.

Iris and Smudge turned the corner, seeing Minisc bracing for a fight.

"You foolish kid, you think you can actually beat the two of us without even having the use of your element? Time to show you the strength of the Adenji gang!"

Minisc, knowing he was done for, muttered a small prayer. A prayer that would be answered by words that he had never loved so much.

"Aqua Shot!"

"Hyper Tornado!"

A large jet stream of water mixed with a blistering horizontal tornado ripped through the hallway. The two attacks impacted both men standing at the intersection, launching them through the window and out of the building with a crashing bang. Minisc stood in awe, counting his lucky stars at the sight he had just witnessed. He had been saved.

The owners of the tag team strike came running full-speed down the hall.

"Minisc," Lily shouted as she screeched to a halt. "Jules, I found him," she yelled back as the boy lagged slightly.

"Lily. Jules. You guys are okay," Minisc uttered in disbelief. His friends were standing mere feet in front of him. Overcome with emotion, Minisc could feel small pockets of water forming in his eyes. Not only that, but they'd managed to keep him safe as well. He ran up and hugged his friends tight, squeezing the breath out of them. The two wrapped their arms around Minisc for a few seconds, all of them exhaling a sigh of relief.

"I can't believe it, you guys are okay," Minisc whispered.

"Us? We were coming to rescue you. What are you doing out of the infirmary?" Lily asked.

The three separated with the realization that they were not out of danger just yet.

"I was watching the ceremony on TV before the feed cut out from that massive explosion. I got scared you guys were hurt. What is going on?" Minisc choked back his emotions, trying to get a grip.

"We don't know, but we need to get out of here," Jules said.

Lily took a second to look out the window that she in part had helped shatter.

"Whoa," she gasped. The window was on the front side of the building, and she could see the gated entrance that they had grown familiar with entering. Red and blue lights flickered back and forth as more and more police cars lined up all over the main road. Officers dressed in dark blue uniforms were jumping out of the cars with haste, circling the building. Behind them were a series of men and women in white EC uniforms following up the rear. A crowd of thousands occupied the front lawn, while police were trying to escort everyone to a safe place.

"Guys, the police are here."

"And the Elemental Council," Jules added.

"We're saved!" Lily cheered.

"It's only a matter of time then. Minisc, we need to go to Yuri's suite and lay low till it's safe to come out. Come on let's hurry." Jules grabbed the boy's arm.

"No, I'm going to find my father," Minisc objected, much to his friend's dismay.

"Minisc, it's too dangerous. You can't even fight. You'll be a sitting duck if you get attacked," Lily argued, though she knew it was pointless.

"Whoever's doing this wants to kill the Hero of Light. I won't stand by and watch that happen. You guys get to safety. I'm going to help my father." Minisc turned to head down the hall before feeling an arm reach out and grab hold.

"You can't stop me from going," Minisc warned as he turned around to see who had a grip on him.

"Fine then, we're going with you," Lily said as she released her grip. Jules nodded in agreement.

United, the three friends were prepared to face anything that came their way.

Don and Yuri were under siege — the pair were outnumbered, and it showed. Don took up the battle against the Adenji leader, clashing in a one-on-one duel the likes of which few had ever seen. He held his own with ease, but the monster man continued to put up a worthy fight. Both gasped for air, the seismic blows taking a toll. Don's initial injury from the surprise attack had greatly weakened him.

While that was going on, Yuri was using a flurry of his most potent wind attacks to fend off Bronx and Bex.

Bex cackled wildly as she fired off wave after wave of ice spears. The pale blue glow left a streak through the air as it shot toward its target.

Yuri released a Galaxy Tornado to stop the ice, then sent it back at Bex. She jumped out of the way as the blast crashed at her feet. With the two locked in battle, Bronx attempted to catch Yuri off guard, but he effortlessly avoided the man. A solid punch to Bronx's back sent him sprawling into Bex. Yuri's reputation was on full display as someone not to be trifled with.

"Can you two hurry up?" Brooklyn ordered, watching as his two lackeys faltered. Off in the distance, he noticed Coro, who was still out cold. He took note of Yuri trying to draw the attacks away from where he was lying.

"They are protecting the one who bears two elements. I didn't think he would be of much use, but maybe..." Brooklyn thought of a new plan, "Bex, stop worrying about the man. Eliminate the power of that boy — he is the one with two elements!" Brooklyn said, gesturing to Coro.

"Okey dokey, boss," Bex chimed back with a smile. She jumped onto a nearby pile of rubble. Bouncing step by step, she quickly appeared in front of Coro. She slid her sleeve up, unsheathing the syringe attached to her wrist and flicked the tip with her nail.

"Say goodbye to your element."

Bex grabbed Coro's arm and attempted to inject the needle, but before she managed to penetrate the skin, Yuri flew into action, smacking the syringe out of her hand. It flew through the air, the tip shattering as it hit the ground.

"Argh, not again," the girl screamed in frustration.

Finally, Minisc, Lily, and Jules ran through the opposite tunnel, the sounds of powerful blows leading them directly into the line of fire. They stepped out to see Don and Yuri fighting for their lives.

"Who are these guys?" Lily asked as the three paused to assess the situation. Don and the Adenji leader exchanged blows while Yuri continued his protection of Coro. The fights were far more ferocious than anything the Tournament of Elements could have offered. These were real-life battles, with real-life stakes the likes of which most children their age had never seen. Even with Lily, Minisc, and Jules being part of a life-and-death battle earlier, it had paled in comparison to what they were witnessing now.

Minisc looked away from his father's battle to see Yuri smack Bex's hand away from Coro. The needle flew through the air, shattering as it hit the ground. He then turned to see Brooklyn and his purple claws from before.

"It's him. The one with shadow claws," Minisc said.

Don and Yuri turned to see that the kids had arrived.

"Jules, I said to get out of here," Yuri yelled, grabbing Coro and jumping away from Bex. Jules flinched, but he knew it was too late now. They were here, and they were going to have to make themselves useful.

Bex turned her attention to Jules. "Ahh, more kids, ripe for the picking," she whispered, licking her lips. She bolted toward the group.

"Incoming," Minisc warned as he tried to fire a Lum Blast. A small puff of smoke came out before evaporating. "Crap, I still haven't recovered enough."

"It's my turn to protect you, Minisc." Lily smiled.

She stepped in front of her friend and launched her attack at Bex. Sadly, her efforts did little to slow Bex down, as with a wave of her hand, she sent a draft of freezing air at Lily. A chill ran up the girl's arm, freezing her forearm before the water launched. Lily let out a cry as the ice climbed up her sleeve to her shoulder blade. Next Jules jumped in front, but his wind proved just as ineffective. Bex was too quick for him to trap. She got up close and punched Jules in the ribs, dropping him to the ground.

"Jules," Yuri shouted as he jumped into the fight again. He dropped Coro in front of Minisc and Lily. Turning his attention to Bex, Yuri swung rapidly, but she moved with ease to avoid each hit. She continued to cackle, taking pleasure in the deathmatch.

"Jules, take Coro and get yourselves out of here. Do it now," the man argued, smashing an icicle from Bex.

Before they could move, Bex froze both boy's feet, dropping them to the dirt.

If Yuri had not been preoccupied with keeping the others safe, he could have dealt with Bex and Bronx as it were. But with Minisc and Jules tethered to the ground by ice his priorities were another obstacle.

On the other side, realizing his son was in trouble, Don landed a devastating blow on his opponent, sending him crashing into the wall. He turned around and fired a light grenade at Bex, causing her to jump away from the group. He bought Yuri just enough time to chase her down and attempt a counter-attack.

Yuri swung his fist at her head, continually striking the air. Left open, Bex ducked in close to the man's chest. Before Yuri knew what had happened, he felt something prick his skin.

She had a second needle.

Yuri looked down at the syringe sticking into his arm. Bex had concealed it under the other sleeve of her cloak.

"You got careless. That's what you get for protecting others."

Yuri smacked the needle away before he began to feel woozy. His vision started to blur and darken. He could feel his entire body go numb for a moment. Whatever had been injected into his body, appeared to be reaping quick results. With an open opportunity, Bex hopped back a few feet and created an icicle barrage, pelting Yuri relentlessly.

"Yuri," Jules yelled as he watched his brother fall motionless to the ground. "No!" He let out a rage of energy, shattering the ice trapping him. With his freedom back, Jules slid next to his brother, trying to cradle him in his arms.

He had tears filling his eyes as he realized the trouble he had caused.

"Yuri, wake up—you can't leave me," Jules cried out, water starting to stream down his cheeks.

The man slowly opened up his eyes. His face was heavily cut, his body dripping with blood.

"Jules ..." the man coughed out.

Noticing the commotion going on behind him, Don decided it was time to take on the burden for everyone. Brooklyn and Luminosa were back, and they wanted him. He would not watch others, most of all his son, hurt in an act of collateral damage.

"Jules, get Yuri to safety. Leave this to me. Minisc, Lily, get yourselves and Coro out of here now! That's an order," Don yelled as he turned his sights to Bex.

"Come on, you're going to be okay," Jules consoled his brother as he wrapped the man's broad shoulder around his neck.

While trying to do anything to escape his icy prison, Minisc felt a warm sensation on his feet. He looked over his shoulder, trying to twist his body to get a view of the source.

"Coro?" Minisc whispered in shock. He looked past the fire user and saw Lily moving her arms freely as well.

"That's for helping me," Coro said before collapsing back to the ground again.

"You used your fire... Thank you, Coro." Minisc smiled as he stood up, running over to Jules.

"Let me help, Jules."

Minisc grabbed Yuri from the other side.

"Minisc? How did you guys get free?" Jules asked as they helped his brother to the back of the stadium.

"Coro—he woke up and used his fire. It was the last bit of energy he had before he collapsed again."

The three regrouped, placing Yuri next to Coro, and then turned their attention back to the battlefield. It was still a long way from safety for them.

"Bex, that needle was for the Hero of Light," Brooklyn scolded.

"I saw my chance, and I took it—besides, that Adenji guy can handle this, right? That's why you brought him here," she huffed.

"Hmm, maybe she's right…"

"Bronx, Bex, fall back," Brooklyn demanded, "We'll let the brute settle his score with the Hero of Light."

The man with X's stitching his lips together peeled himself off the wall, growling in anger. He dashed at Don, and the two exchanged a flurry of fists. The leader of the group was an admirable opponent, pushing Don around with a series of heavy-impact hits. He was agile, and each attack had authority behind it.

The man's movements quickened. Then he vanished before Don's eyes.

"Where'd he go?" Minisc wondered, looking around frantically with Jules and Lily, but they couldn't place eyes on the man.

He's quick, Don thought as he tried to stay alert. Before he could react, the man appeared behind him, hitting him with a blistering Shadow Ball and tossing him through the air. Don quickly stopped his slide and got to his feet, but he was given no time to think before his enemy disappeared again.

"We need to help him," Minisc cried, watching his father take hit after hit.

"Minisc… trust your father. He—he has a plan." Yuri coughed weakly.

"Yuri, save your strength," Jules said.

"The Hero of Light… you're a false hero. You betrayed your own. You became an icon for these pathetic humans. An act of such betrayal can only be met with death. I'll make sure the world knows who they should fear most. Now watch as my pet rips you limb from limb." Brooklyn cackled. Obeying orders, the man placed his palm inches away from Don's back, a Shadow Ball forming in the gap between them.

"Kill him — kill the Hero of Light!" Brooklyn slithered emphatically as the ball exploded.

"Father!" Minisc shouted as the explosion's smoke filled the stadium for a few seconds. Ripples staggered through the ground, shaking violently. Everyone looked stunned at the defeat they had just witnessed.

"Hahaha, the Hero of Light is dead," Bex cackled loudly.

"No..." Minisc whispered as he dropped to his knees. His face drained of all color, with a sense of despair overcoming him. A rush of anger, fear and loneliness began to consume him. He had lost the only family he had left. Without his father, he had nothing. Tears slipped down his cheeks as he pounded the ground with his fist.

"Father!" he cried out.

"Wait Minisc, look."

Lily pointed to something in the mist. Minisc picked his head up, making the figure out. Don was standing tall, a massive hole in the back of his shirt, but his skin showed no visible marks.

"He's... okay," Minisc whispered.

"Is that the best you can do?" Don jested smugly before turning to face the man again. Realizing his attack had no impact, the Adenji leader hesitantly stepped back.

Behind him, Brooklyn looked ready to throw a temper tantrum.

"Grrr, he was supposed to die. I was promised he would be killed. Why do we not have another needle to use?" He looked past the fight and saw another bargaining chip.

"Bex, you screwed this all up... go capture me the boy, and I want him alive, you understand me?" Brooklyn ordered, eyes narrowing as he locked his gaze with Don's.

"Yes, sir," Bex chimed.

"Lily, we have to protect Minisc," Jules said as the three braced themselves for a fight. None of them had any energy left, but it was a matter of life and death.

However, Don had other plans.

"As long as I draw breath, I will not let you harm my son," Don roared as he exploded forward toward his opponent. He met the Adenji leader's fist, colliding together. The two began exchanging blows that the naked eye could not keep up with. Each punch sent shockwaves that cracked the stadium walls, while the aftershocks pushed everyone backward, almost knocking them to the ground. Minisc covered his eyes with his arm, trying to get a look at the action. He was doing whatever it took to not get blown completely away as Lily slid back beside him.

"What is he thinking, fighting that guy straight on?" Minisc questioned as he watched the two exchange blows.

"Incredible, he's so fast," Jules gawked.

Don's punches sped up, one after another. Jules was not the only one who could not keep up, though. The Adenji leader was doing all he could to match hit for hit, continuing to take glancing blows.

"I can't get close to them. The shock waves are too much," Bex whined as she and Bronx tried to hold their position.

"You want to see the true power of the Hero of Light? Fine then," Don growled as he started punching faster, his fists beginning to glow with golden light. Don took a punch in the ribs, stunning the man for half a second, but he continued his relentless assault.

"You monsters are all the same, trying to hurt innocent people to get to me. Now you want my only son. Well, I won't let you get away with this. You think you can handle me at one hundred percent of my power? I guess I'll just have to go even further!" Don roared, his entire body starting to glow.

His movements, his punches, his footwork – it's just like that night in the forest. They're so fast... yet each move is calculated, increasing in strength with each hit. Is this the power of Celestial Light? Minisc could not believe what he was witnessing. The power was staggering; his father was stronger than anyone could have possibly imagined. It was off the charts. He could not fathom someone being that strong. This was the Hero of Light at his peak.

"As long as I live, I won't let your reign of terror continue, Luminosa," Don boasted.

Brooklyn watched as his new pet attempted a weak punch that Don caught in his palm. He swung ferociously, throwing the man up into the sky. Then Don leaped into the air, effortlessly smashing his fists down on his opponent. He came crashing down, shattering the earth beneath him as he landed inches away. Then he lined up for one last finishing blow.

"Prepare to witness a power that evil like you can only dream of."

A ball of light appeared in front of Don's open hand. He clasped it in his palm, squeezing tight. A flash of light engulfed his hand into a bright golden fist.

"Solar Impact!" Don roared. Digging into the furthest depths of his power, he thrust his fist into the man's stomach, shooting him back fast enough to break the sound barrier. The leader blew past Brooklyn and crashed through the entire building, leaving a tunnel to the outside world.

Minisc fought through the shockwaves to see his father standing in all his glory. Everyone in the stadium stood in awe, speechless at the sheer display of brute force they had witnessed.

"That... that's the power of the Hero of Light? That can't be real," Jules gasped in shock.

"He really is a legend," Lily whispered, still trying to believe what she had witnessed.

"He did it—he actually did it," Minisc murmured under his breath. A smile grew on his face as he saw the remaining cloaked villains back down for a second. He felt safe, his father was unbeatable, and he was going to keep them all safe.

Don stood in a cloud of smoke, brilliant gold light radiating off his body. It slowly evaporated, showing the man injured but not defeated. His clothes were ripped and blood dripped from the corner of his mouth.

"Your move," Don warned, turning his attention to Brooklyn. He had pushed himself so far past his limits that he could feel his insides shaking. He could not possibly put that much strain on himself again. So his only option was to bluff his eagerness for a second fight. As long as the enemy remained unaware of that facade, everything would be fine.

"This isn't possible. We can't win without the serum... Bex, Bronx we're leaving," Brooklyn growled, his fist clenched in a fit of rage. They were defeated, and he knew it. They both knew it.

"What about—" she began.

"Leave him. He's no use to us anymore."

Bronx held his hand up to the sky. Darkness filled the air, everything going pitch black for a moment. In a cloud of smoke, the three disappeared without a trace.

"Get back here," Minisc yelled as he ran up beside his father. Don stuck his arm out, blocking his son.

"Let them go, Minisc. We have more important things to take care of." The man pointed to the wounded bodies of Yuri and Coro.

A short while after all the commotion died down, the police and EC managed to inspect and evacuate the building, making sure that any low-level thugs were taken into custody. A special unit had been tasked with retrieving the Adenji leader who had been left clinging to life from Don's Solar Impact. Coro and Yuri were also taken to the hospital with severe but non-life-threatening injuries.

Jules, Lily, and Minisc were treated for non-serious injuries as well. Thankfully for them, they had not had to participate in the battle.

Jules watched through tears as Yuri was loaded into the back of the ambulance. Seeing his brother clinging to life broke him. Jules felt responsible for the results. If he had listened to his brother in the first place, none of this would have happened. He road with Yuri to the hospital, leaving Lily and Minisc to patiently wait outside Scotia Coliseum.

Meanwhile, Don was being swarmed by the press and media who had arrived to cover the story. They continued to pepper him with question after question.

"This was a strategic attack, to set fear into the public and the people of this city. We will not stand for such vile acts. As long as I'm around, we won't allow these attacks to continue. Luminosa will be defeated, I promise you that." Don addressed the crowd through the flashing lights and microphones in his face. He was surrounded by thirty to forty people in the scrum.

Minisc sat off to the side on a rock formation lining the entrance to Scotia Coliseum. Next to him, Lily sat, looking exhausted. They both watched the mass hysteria that surrounded the Hero of Light.

"Your father is really amazing," Lily gushed as she turned to face Minisc.

"You know, I never really thought he was that strong. I always heard the rumors and stories, but they somehow felt too fabricated. I guess now I know," Minisc agreed with a small smile.

The sun was dipping just below the horizon. Minisc looked over at his father. He felt horrible about the events that had occurred today. He wished he could have been more of a help, but he had been so useless. After the day he'd just had, Minisc did not feel worthy of being his father's son. Nobody was worthy. The man had single-handedly defended so many, and Minisc was no more than a burden. That feeling stung.

A yellow taxi pulled up to the entrance, with two adults jumping out of the car before running toward Lily. The girl hopped up in surprise as she heard her name.

"Lily, are you okay? Are you hurt? You're safe now!" the woman cried as she hugged Lily tightly. The man next to them joined in the hug. They were wearing rather plain clothing. The woman had dark brown hair that flowed down to her long white skirt and eyes that matched Lily's perfectly. The man was wearing a brown, collared shirt and blue jeans, and his hair was midnight black and freshly cut. He looked quite a bit like Lily except for the oval-shaped glasses he had on.

"Mom, Dad, what are you doing here?"

"We were watching the tournament on TV when the feed disappeared. Reports that the stadium was under attack started appearing, and we got scared. So we came here as quickly as we could." A high level of panic filled the woman's voice even though the events had ended.

It started to dawn on Minisc how quickly all the events had happened.

It's strange; the whole catastrophe took no longer than half an hour. Yet the whole thing felt like forever. Minisc looked back at Lily, who finally freed herself from her parents' suffocating hug.

"It's okay Mom, I'm fine, I promise." Lily grimaced at the small amount of embarrassment. She understood it, though—the trials that had occurred would be traumatizing to anyone. She looked to Minisc, suddenly realizing he was just staring, watching awkwardly.

"Oh... Mom, Dad, this is my friend, Minisc."

"Yes, yes, you're the boy who was in the finals today," Lily's mother greeted as the attention shifted focus.

"Hi," Minisc said, and smiled politely.

"Thank you for helping keep our daughter safe." Lily's father bowed with a warm smile.

"You're welcome, but it was she who saved me. I was pretty powerless..." Minisc trailed off, hanging his head a little.

"Nonsense." The woman leaned in to give Minisc a big hug as well.

"Come on, Lily, we're going home." The man held his hand out to help his daughter up.

"Okay," Lily agreed taking the man's hand. She turned to face Minisc and gave him an enormous hug.

"Thank you, Minisc, for everything." He blushed, his face turning a scarlet red. She let him go and turned around, leaving with her family. Minisc watched as they piled into the running taxi and drove off. Lily waved goodbye from the backseat, flashing a grateful smile. Minisc waved back, slowly watching the car sputter off into the sunset.

"Looks like it's just me left."

A large shadow began looming over Minisc, catching his attention.

"How are you feeling?" Don asked his son. Minisc still looked to be in rough shape.

"I've seen better days," the boy quipped back, cracking a sly smile.

"What do you say we give these media guys the slip and head home?"

Minisc stood up, nodding his head. All he wanted was to see his bed. He could sleep for a week after today.

After they arrived home, Minisc struggled to sleep. Instead, he sat in the kitchen, looking at the wall of articles. He continued to think about his father's heroics. Even as he heard the man walk in behind, he continued staring at the wall. Don placed his hand on his son.

"Shouldn't you be out cold by now?"

Minisc remained quiet. He turned around and said, "Father?"

"Yes? What is it?" Don asked, caught off guard.

"I'm sorry..." Minisc trailed off again, his eyes watering up. He was fighting his emotions, but he couldn't hold things back anymore.

"Sorry about what?" Don asked, staring at his son, whose tears were now dripping off his cheeks onto the kitchen floor.

"I failed. All I wanted to do was help people, but I just ended up getting in the way, I put Lily and Jules in danger... I wanted to help, but in the end, I couldn't even protect the people I cared about most." Minisc's voice broke as the last word left his lips.

Don knew his son put a lot of pressure on himself because of who he was trying to live up to. He knew Minisc did not want to be a hero, but when it came to protecting his friends, that was something he wanted to be strong enough to do. After the day's events and the finals along with the tournament as a whole, Minisc felt powerless to do that simple task. He had learned what it meant to be part of the EC, to be a beacon of hope for people, and to protect them. It was not as easy as it sounded.

Don hugged his son against his broad chest.

"Minisc, you showed something far greater than brute strength today. You showed courage, heart, and determination. You helped save everyone. As much as I did, and I could not be prouder of you." Don spoke candidly. He turned his son back to the articles. "I'm sure you never thought about it, but if you read every article carefully, they all have one common thing in them. Do you know what that is?"

"You?"

"No, surprisingly. Each one makes mention of your mother's efforts as a hero. She never punched anyone, she was not physically strong, but she had the courage and heart that few had. You share that heart with her. And I know she would be so proud of you today, not only for what you did against Luminosa but more so how you helped Coro. If she were here, I promise she would hug you and tell you to never lose that heart."

Minisc wiped the tears from his eyes and wrapped his father in a hug.

"I won't. I promise I'll continue to make mother's dream a reality. I'll never stop helping those in need."

Don returned the hug, engulfing his son.

"Good."

ELEMENTS
VOLUME 2 (PREVIEW)

"And what if the EC is too busy with the hospital intruder? What if that's part of Luminosa's plan?" Minisc tried to take off down the stairs again before feeling Lily grab his arm. She had a look of total petrification on her beautiful face.

"Minisc, you're going to get yourself killed. What did you just say about running in to protect your father?" she cried out.

Minisc sighed; he knew Lily was right. He could be making another big mistake, but a voice in his head said it was no mistake. No, it was a necessity. He had to do it. Even if it meant disobeying his father and upsetting Lily.

He looked at his friend.

"Lily... please don't hate me for this."

"Huh?"

Before she could process what Minisc had meant, his hand began to glow brightly. Lily closed her eyes as a flash in the black sky blinded her. Then she felt a chop on her arm as she lost her grip on Minisc.

"I promise this will be the last time I ditch you — now head to the EC, and I will see you soon."

Lily could only hear Minisc's voice as it faded into the distance. By the time the light faded enough for Lily to gain her vision back, Minisc had long since disappeared.

Running underneath the street lights with his heart pounding and his mind racing, Minisc hurried to the Rec center. "I'm sorry Lily," he whispered to himself. "I know this is dangerous... but I promise I won't die, and I won't let Jules die either."

AFTERWORD

Hello, this is William Richards, author of *Elements Volume 1*. I wanted to take a moment at the end of the book to talk to the readers, not through the voice of a character but as myself.

Thank you for taking the time to read my work. I hope you enjoyed seeing Minisc, Lily and Jules grow their friendship and learn as they ventured through the modern-day world of Elements as much as I did writing it.

I started writing this series as an outlet for my mental health. If you go back and read the dedication page at the front of the book, that message was dedicated to myself as much as anyone. I wanted to help people who felt the same way I did—who felt lost, alone, or not worth anything in life. That's how Minisc came into being. He became my outlet so that I could speak to myself and actually listen. So I hope that you can relate to him as well, and see how through dedication, trust in your friends, and doing what you believe is right, you can achieve great things. I hope you will continue to follow Minisc on his journey, and continue to watch him learn and grow.

I'd also like to take a second to thank Stalking P for doing the artwork for this book. It turned out so much better than my wildest dreams, and I could not be happier to have found her! Along with that, thanks to my editor for helping bring my story to life and making sure I put out the best work possible. To my friends and family, giving me unconditional support on my insane dreams, continuing to push me forward and make sure that I never gave up no matter how many times I rewrote this story—thank you for the continual support, and I hope to see you all in the next volume.